George Bryan "Beau" Brummell **was an Oxford-educated gentleman without any aristocratic lineage or family fortune, but his friendship with the Prince of Wales helped elevate him. An independent man of independent means who desired the best of everything—and got it—he rose to become the leader of fashionable society by his wits and his irresistible personality. His exquisite manner of dressing, disdaining of anything vulgar and his great appreciation of beauty combined with an extraordinary cool composure and rare charm define him as one of the truly unique characters in English history.**

Praise for *The Bloodied Cravat:*

continued . . .

More praise for *The Bloodied Cravat:*

"In the midst of all the well-researched period detail, Stevens manages to maintain a crisp pace and provide a convincing windup."
—*Kirkus Reviews*

"[*The Bloodied Cravat*], the third in a truly delightful series, offers humor, mystery and a dash of romance . . . Beau's narration, laced with witty observations on the manners and dress of his peers, along with confidential asides to the reader, makes us feel as though we are right there beside him. I highly recommend the entire series."
—*Old Book Barn Gazette*

"This latest . . . shows Ms. Stevens in top form. Mystery fans will appreciate the complicated, well-devised plot and fans of the ton will also be in for their share of fun as the author has included a fine amount of gossip, scandal, and sparkling wit."
—*Romantic Times*

Praise for *The Tainted Snuff Box:*

"[Stevens's] mastery of the language and knowledge of the conventions and morals of the British aristocracy allow her story to ring true. With a cast of enjoyable characters, both real and fictional, and a string of red herrings, hidden motives and plot twists as intricate as a well-tied cravat, this story will delight both historical mystery and Regency fans."
—*Publishers Weekly*

"Rosemary Stevens brings the essence of the Regency era, as well as the personality of Beau Brummell, to sparkling life . . . This is a delightful story with a well-plotted puzzle. Readers will be charmed by this tale of mores and murder . . .
—*Romantic Times* (top pick)

Praise for *Death on a Silver Tray:*

Beau Brummell Mysteries
by Rosemary Stevens

DEATH ON A SILVER TRAY
THE TAINTED SNUFF BOX
THE BLOODIED CRAVAT

The
BLOODIED
CRAVAT

ROSEMARY STEVENS

BERKLEY PRIME CRIME, NEW YORK

THE BLOODIED CRAVAT

A Berkley Prime Crime Book / published by arrangement with the author

PRINTING HISTORY
Berkley Prime Crime hardcover edition / May 2002
Berkley Prime Crime mass-market edition / June 2003

Copyright © 2002 by Rosemary Stevens.
Cover art by Teresa Fasolino.
Cover design by Ann Marie Manca.

ISBN: 0-425-19076-5

Berkley Prime Crime Books are published
by The Berkley Publishing Group,
a division of Penguin Group (USA) Inc.,
375 Hudson Street, New York, New York 10014.
The name BERKLEY PRIME CRIME and the BERKLEY PRIME CRIME design are trademarks belonging to Penguin Group (USA) Inc.

PRINTED IN THE UNITED STATES OF AMERICA

10 9 8 7 6 5 4 3 2 1

For my son, Tommy, with love

ACKNOWLEDGMENTS

Many thanks are due Melissa Lynn Jones for the hours we spent together discussing Regency language, social customs and history. Not only is Melissa a colleague I hold in high esteem, her friendship is one I value.

I wish to thank Steven Lovegrove of Syon House for making it possible for me to have a personal tour of this magnificent building owned by the Duke of Northumberland. Shirley Guest was a charming and informative companion as we explored the wonder of Robert Adam's creation. Syon House is open to the public from March to October annually. Anyone visiting the London area should not miss this gem of a house.

I also appreciate the kindness of the Oatlands Park Hotel staff while I poked around what was formerly Oatlands, the country residence of the Duke and Duchess of York.

Thank you to my editor, Gail Fortune, for her guidance and patience.

Barbara Metzger and Cynthia Holt: What would I do without you?

Thanks also to Connie Koslow and Amy Campbell.

AUTHOR'S NOTE

Besides Beau Brummell, the following characters either appearing in, or mentioned in, this book were real people: King George III; George, Prince of Wales; Caroline, Princess of Wales; Maria Fitzherbert; Frederick, Duke of York; Frederica, Duchess of York; Hugh, Duke of Northumberland; Frances Julia, Duchess of Northumberland; Georgiana, Duchess of Devonshire; Prime Minister Pitt; Admiral Nelson; James, Marquess of Salisbury; Lady Salisbury; Lord Petersham; Mrs. Creevey; Jack Townsend; John Lavender; Scrope Davies; Lord Yarmouth; Mr. Dawe; Richard Sheridan; Mary Anne Clarke; Mr. Stultz; Mr. Weston; and, of course, Robinson.

Beau Brummell did indeed keep a blue-velvet-covered scrapbook, or album, if you will, as described in this story. The fate of this collection of letters, drawings, and poems remains a mystery today.

We do know that upon Beau Brummell's death, all of the letters written to him by Frederica, Duchess of York, were confiscated by British officials. What happened to the letters after that is a mystery as well.

The Duchess of York did have a special dogs' cemetery for her beloved pets. One can still see the graves at what is now the Oatlands Park Hotel outside London. Phanor, one of the dogs mentioned in this story, was actually one of her Royal Highness's dogs. For a picture of Phanor's grave, please go to my website at www.beaubrummell.com.

According to the *London Encyclopaedia* (edited by Ben Weinreb and Christopher Hibbert), the column that supported the clock with seven faces that defined the London area known as Seven Dials was re-erected in 1882 on the green in Weybridge, as a memorial to Frederica, Duchess of York.

Readers will note that the Grand Masquerade held at the King's Theatre takes place on a Monday night in this book. I have thus far only found sources for the Masquerades historically being held on Thursday nights during 1806 and hope to be forgiven for taking this small bit of artistic license.

Regarding the wonderful Syon House, readers will note it described in this story as being made of white Dunstable stone. Visitors today will see the house has been re-faced with Bath stone. This took place in the 1820s well after the time period of this book. Again, for photos, including one of the north-eastend turret room, please visit my website.

Finally, a somewhat eerie note: At the beginning of this story, Beau Brummell mourns the death of his friend Georgiana, Duchess of Devonshire, who died on March 30, 1806. Beau Brummell died exactly thirty-four years later on March 30, 1840.

❧ 1 ❧

"I shall kill Robinson."

A feminine laugh rippled across the drawing room. "George, dear, you will do no such thing."

My hand released the green velvet drapery I had pushed aside at the open window. I turned from the country view where I had spent the past quarter of an hour willing a coach carrying my vain valet and my valises to appear down the Oatlands drive.

Fixing my expression to one of stern disapproval, I looked upon my most cherished female friend and said, "I assure you, Freddie, I shall throttle the man the moment I clap eyes on him."

Her Royal Highness, Frederica, the Duchess of York, is the daughter of a Prussian king. I am privileged to call her "Freddie" in private. Which I wish we were more often.

She lifted her gaze from the overgrown puppy in her lap and favoured me with an amused tilt of her lips. "Dearest, you could not bear to lose Robinson's care of your person and clothing."

"Lose it? I do not have it!" I declared. "Where the devil can he be? We set out from London by coach at the same time this afternoon. At least I think Robinson was directly behind me. There was such a crush of carriages, I cannot be sure."

"There is your answer, then," Freddie said in a reasonable tone. "The Season has been in full swing for over four weeks now. I am certain the streets are crowded, and that is what has caused Robinson's delay." The furry black puppy looked up at her with adoring eyes as if approving the theory. She rubbed his head affectionately.

Lucky fellow.

Around the room, ample evidence of Freddie's passion for canines abounded. Dogs forever frozen in time romped across embroidered chairs, were rendered immortal by Stubbs's precise brush in several paintings, and had been meticulously cast and sculptured into bronze and marble statues and placed on pedestals.

Real dogs populated the room too. In all manner of shape and colour they lounged across chairs, sprawled on the Axminster carpet, and meandered in and out of the room at will.

Freddie is married to a dog as well—a deceitful dog— the unfaithful Duke of York.

Freddie's delicate hand reached for a short length of rope at her feet. She dangled it above the puppy's head. He took the end in his mouth and began a game of tug-of-war. Her Royal Highness's brown hair, held back by a lilac bandeau which matched the violets trimming her ivory muslin dress, swayed as she gently wrestled with the little scamp.

Watching her—I am one to appreciate beauty—I forgot what she had just said until she looked up at me in expectation.

I called myself to order. "Very well. We have established the difficulty of travel during the height of the Season. Still, I arrived some two hours ago and there is no sign of the vexing valet. Two hours is a long delay. Robinson is up to something. Although he has tried to hide it, I think he has formed an attachment to some female. He might have attempted to see her before leaving Town, since we are to be here in the Weybridge countryside for five days."

"Oh my, Robinson and a lady friend. I wonder who she is," Freddie mused. "But it may not be a woman after all who prevents Robinson from joining you. You must allow that the weather has been warm for the first week in May. Perhaps Robinson merely spied a place to stop for a drink along the road."

I raised my right eyebrow. "At a common hedge tavern? Not likely. When travelling, Robinson carries his own liquid refreshment, as do I. One cannot depend on innkeepers to have quality wine on hand."

Speaking of which, I paused in my complaining, suddenly thirsty. I wandered to a side table and poured myself a glass of the Chambertin burgundy Freddie keeps for me.

Not surprised, are you? If you have known me for any length of time at all, you know my motto: "When your spirits are low, get another bottle."

I drank the first glass at a rate that would bring the condemnation of wine connoisseurs down upon my head, then poured another measure.

The puppy jumped from Freddie's lap and bounded across the carpet with the rope in his mouth. He leapt upon one of the dogs who slept in the sunshine pouring in from another open window. The sad-eyed hound I know Freddie calls Humphrey declined the generous offer of a wet end of a rope, heaved a long-suffering sigh, and closed his eyes against the rude intrusion of his slumber.

Downing the second glass of wine impatiently, I put the crystal glass back on the table and returned to the window. Peering out, I saw nothing moving. At least, nothing that resembled a coach. Freddie keeps a menagerie of animals here at Oatlands. The kangaroos jumped about in their paddock alongside the ostriches; eagles and macaws flew about the aviary; and three dogs raced by barking with glee, their coats gleaming, ears flapping and tongues hanging out. But no coach appeared.

I began to pace. "I tell you, Freddie, this is the outside of enough. The moment Robinson sets foot in this house, I shall unwrap his cravat just enough to strangle him with his own dirty neckcloth."

"Now, George, you know Robinson's cravats are as clean as your own. The poor man would faint if he knew you had so abused his linen." Freddie's blue eyes twinkled.

"Corpses cannot faint," I pointed out.

"Pray, stop your pacing." She patted a place next to her on the sofa. "Come sit beside me, dear, and we can be comfortable."

Comfortable? Beside her? How I would like to be.

But there was yet another dog—this one an enormous curly haired thing with a face bigger than a dinner plate—and her marriage—between us. Not to mention Ulga, Freddie's Prussian maid, watching over her charge as if Freddie were still five and ten, instead of a lady over thirty years of age known for her personal integrity and unassailable dignity.

I groaned inwardly and reminded myself that these impediments to any intimacy with the Royal Duchess would only help me maintain my status of an honourable gentleman. Which is what I want, I keep telling myself. Dash it.

"I shall sit down, but only to preserve my strength for when Robinson graces us with his presence," I said, my voice thick with frustration.

Though I managed to dislodge the monstrous mutt, I did not stop to brush the dog hairs from the sofa before seating myself, knowing my leather breeches would soon be speckled with fur. That would keep Robinson busy once he arrived. Revenge on a small scale is not above me, I fear.

There now, that gave me an idea. Perhaps my fussy valet was late in protest. While he holds the Royal Duchess in affection and respect, he abhors the dogs and, more specifically, the dog *hair* at Oatlands that always manages to find its way onto our clothing.

Robinson cannot be considered someone who is fond of animals, you know, a fact which could only be making his journey to Oatlands more miserable. He carries my birthday gift for Freddie. A gift I had gone through a great deal of trouble to obtain.

Her Royal Highness stretched her arm across the back of the sofa toward my shoulder, an act that immediately caught my attention. She is a tiny lady, and her fingertips fell short of touching my sleeve. I slid closer.

"I am happy you agreed to this house party, George," she said solemnly, her sweet face inches from mine.

"How was I to refuse when tomorrow is your birthday?" I said in a low voice.

She smiled. "I did plan things rather well."

"Wretched girl."

"What was I to do with you moping about Town, refusing to participate in the round of social activities of the Season?"

I looked away. "The Duchess of Devonshire's death was not a shock, coming as it did after her illness. Yet I was honoured to call Georgiana my friend. She was a wonderful creature, and I mourn her. We are losing England's finest people, Freddie. First Nelson last October, Pitt in January, then Georgiana."

Freddie leaned forward and patted my hand. "I know, dear. Shutting yourself away from the Season will not bring them back, though, will it? Five weeks have passed

since Georgiana died. You must think of your position in
Society."

I looked at her, feeling the touch of her hand on the
back of mine, warm and soft. We were close enough on
the sofa now for me to smell the rose scent Freddie wears.
I breathed in the fragrance. As is always the case in Freddie's company, I could not remain despondent for long.
Her character, the very essence of her, fills me with a
desire to . . . to . . . er, a desire to be the best sort of gentleman I can be, of course. Yes, that is what I mean to
say. Some of her attributes also work *against* my maintaining my role of gentleman. Devil take the Duke of
York.

Ulga cleared her throat.

I moved back a hair's width and let out a short laugh.
"My position in Society, Freddie? Yes, I expect you have
the right of it. For who else is George Brummell but the
Beau, the Arbiter of Fashion?"

"You say that disparagingly, George, but think of the
elegance you have brought to the *Beau Monde*," Freddie
chided. "Because of your influence people are actually
bathing, keeping their clothing clean, and you know the
gentlemen follow your lead in dress. Why, if not for you,
men would still be powdering their hair, painting their
faces, covering themselves with perfume, and wearing
garish coats."

"Dressing is an art," I pronounced. "Men of culture
cannot ignore my creation of a pleasing, neat, unobtrusive
appearance. To do so marks them as dull and insensitive
and clashes with the idea of civilised living."

Freddie nodded encouragingly. "Do not forget, dear,
that your gracious manners and good taste in all things,
not just in clothing, serve as a fine example for others.
Besides which, though you have kept it a secret, I know
you have assisted in bringing two murderers to justice.
You are far from the useless dandy."

"My princess," I said, reaching out to touch one of her curls, "you are too good, teasing me out of the doldrums. But you had best cease your compliments lest I grow egotistical."

Freddie squeezed her lips together, her eyes lit with laughter. I did not have to be a reader of minds to know she was thinking me egotistical enough already.

"You minx!" I exclaimed. We both succumbed to a fit of laughter.

In the corner of the room, Ulga glanced up from her endless knitting to make certain we were not *too* happy.

"Just remember our bargain, Freddie," I cautioned. "I agreed to rejoin Society's amusements only after you agreed to come to London once the house party is over."

The smile faded a bit from her lips. Freddie avoids London because of her husband. He lives in Town, and she lives at Oatlands, a long-standing arrangement. "I shall keep my promise and remove to my apartment at St. James's Palace next Monday. I honour all my promises, as you know, George."

A quiet overcame us then. Blast! Again I silently cursed Freddie's husband. Husband? Hah! What kind of husband breaks his marital vows and flaunts his mistress in his wife's face? Last reports had Mary Anne Clarke, a bricklayer's daughter, no less, living in lavish style, overseeing at least twenty servants, three cooks, and piles of gold plate. She could frequently be seen tooling about Town in one of her innumerable carriages, comporting herself as if *she* were the Duke's Duchess instead of his decadent doxy. Meanwhile, Freddie occupies herself with country activities and charities year after year.

At least the Duke had taken an absence from his duties as Commander in Chief of all England's land forces to take his paramour on a trip to Geneva. Freddie could come to Town without fear of an embarrassing encounter.

Seeking to change the somber atmosphere, I said,

"Who has arrived here at Oatlands so far?"

Freddie rose and wandered to a marble sculpture of a dog with long, silky hair. The gold plaque identified the dog as *Diogenes*. "Not too many people. Most of the guests will arrive around midday tomorrow. Mr. Roger Cranworth and his sister, Cecily, are here. Do you know them?"

"No." I stood as well and traversed the room to where she had moved next to another statue, this of a dog with shaggy hair. The plate had the name *Sundial* written on it.

"They live in the neighbourhood and do not go to London frequently. Both their parents are dead." Freddie stopped and considered the matter. "That is to say, I think Roger Cranworth visits Town, but Cecily Cranworth, though twenty, has yet to have been presented at Court and enjoy a Season. I feel rather sorry for her. She is an anxious thing."

"Why is she not on the social scene?"

"The Cranworths are landed gentry. They have a pretty house in the neighbourhood south of here. Even though they live close by, I suggested they stay here so we could spend time together. I believe Roger Cranworth has hopes his sister will make a match with someone in the county."

Translation: Roger Cranworth could not—or would not—pay the enormous expense involved in bringing a young girl out into Society.

We strolled to the window, careful not to disturb the slumbering Humphrey.

"I invited another neighbourhood friend, the Marquess of Kendrick," Freddie said casually. "Actually, I do not know him well, but rather, I knew his father. Having recently come into the title, the new marquess is having alterations made at his county seat. He will stay here for the party so we get to know one another."

"Ah, playing matchmaker for Miss Cranworth?"

The Royal Duchess shot me a disapproving look. "Of course not. And Lord Wrayburn is to come as well, George."

"Has he returned from abroad, then?"

Freddie nodded. "I thought it best to ask him, especially after the dreadful way his mother, the Countess of Wrayburn, died unexpectedly last autumn."

"Er, yes, good idea." Lady Wrayburn had been a horrid old tartar.

"The house will be full of people, but I was sure to include several of your friends. And we are to be honoured with the presence of the Duke of Derehurst and his daughter."

I could not prevent my lips from twisting into a wry grin. " 'Stuffy' Derehurst? Freddie, I compliment you on the array of your guests. We are bound to be nothing if not entertained. What are the plans for your birthday tomorrow?"

"I thought a barge party down the Thames in the afternoon would be pleasant, considering the warm weather. Then, in the evening, we shall have a feast and dancing."

"Will you wear the lace dress I gave you last Christmas?"

Pink tinted Freddie's face. "That was a very extravagant gift, George."

"You did not answer the question," I said, reaching out and stroking her smooth cheek with my finger.

She looked directly into my eyes. "You are too good to me, my dearest friend. I shall wear the dress if it will please you."

"You always please me," I replied.

"It grows late," Freddie whispered. "I must see Cook about dinner."

As if by an unspoken signal, Ulga struggled against her girth to rise and gather her knitting.

Faced with reality, I could do no more than bow. "I

cannot join you for dinner unless Robinson arrives with my clothing. I refuse to appear at your table improperly dressed."

Freddie nodded, but her disappointment showed. "I shall miss your company, dear."

Damn Robinson! Where was he?

❦ 2 ❧

I may not have had any clothing other than what was on my back, but I did have my cat.

Chakkri, otherwise known as Master and Supreme Ruler of the Brummell Household, had travelled in the coach with me, snug in his luxurious lidded wicker basket, the new one that I had had lined in a dyed blue fleece that matches his eyes. Robinson cannot be trusted with the feline, wishing as he does for the cat and all his cat fur—so troublesome when attached to clothing—to be banished to his native land, Siam.

Entering the bedchamber Freddie always reserves for my use, I saw Chakkri standing upon his hind legs on a low side table underneath a window, his front paws resting on the window sill. He gazed outside, muttering to himself, or perhaps he was chattering to the birds. I have long given up trying to discern what goes on in his feline brain. For all I know, he might have been conversing in Siamese with the monkeys Freddie keeps outside.

At my entrance, Chakkri turned and jumped gracefully down to the floor. He sauntered halfway across the room, expecting me to cover the additional distance between us.

Because I have become a slave to his every feline wish since a Siamese emissary gifted me with the animal last autumn, I went along with his plan and strode to where he stood. "Good afternoon, old boy. You did not happen to spy Robinson coming up the drive, did you?"

"Reow," he replied by way of a greeting. His brown tail swayed in anticipation of a good scratching and, more importantly, his evening meal. He has the most incredible dark blue eyes, which I feel hold deep secrets known only to Eastern mystics. They also hold the secrets of how to best torment Robinson, how to demand the finest of food, and how to commandeer the exact centre of the bed.

I bent and stroked the cat's fawn-coloured body. Chakkri is the sole representative of the Siamese cat in England. His face, ears, tail, and paws are all of the deepest brown. He is smaller than most felines I have seen, his body lean and muscular, while his fur is incredibly soft.

Elegantly formed as he is, he still has a voice that could drown out an argument in Parliament, and an appetite he demands be sated by the talents of my French chef, André.

I settled myself in a comfortable chair by the empty fireplace, Chakkri close at hand. Stroking the cat from head to tail, an act which causes him to purr loudly, I reflected on how much I loved this room, done in dark, masculine woods with touches of burnt red. The chamber has been exclusively mine since I first started visiting Oatlands several years ago. A special anticipation comes over me when I am here, knowing that Freddie is near. I cannot imagine being unhappy within these four walls.

A short time later, Old Dawe, Freddie's ancient footman, house steward, butler, and major domo all in one, entered carrying a heavy tray. "Mr. Brummell, sir, may I say how nice it is to see you again. Oatlands hardly seems complete without your presence." He placed the tray on the desk and motioned for the maid behind him to deposit on the floor the smaller tray she carried.

"Good to see you as well, Old Dawe. You are looking fit enough to keep up with the dogs' antics. And they appear hideously spoiled as usual."

A small man past his sixtieth year and fiercely loyal to Freddie, Old Dawe smiled. "One must love dogs to serve at Oatlands." He turned to the maid, indicating she could leave.

"Tell me, has there been any word from Robinson?" I asked.

Old Dawe shook his head. "No, sir, but I shall send him to you immediately upon his arrival. Now that I have brought your dinner, is there anything else I can do for you?"

"Thank you, no."

Old Dawe bowed his head and left the room, closing the door quietly behind him.

Chakkri had already begun his meal. He has a great fondness for roasted chicken in wine sauce, and thus relished the serving given him. He turned his nose up at the artichokes, but licked the olives and nibbled at the potatoes, which had been boiled, beaten with cream, butter, and salt, and placed into scallop shells.

Savouring my own meal, I smiled when I noted that Freddie had ordered Chakkri's food served on floral-designed china rather than her regular service made by Flight and Barr. The latter is a deep yellow and white with gold trim, and sports panels of dogs painted in shades of brown by John Pennington, the artist famous for his canine figures. How like Freddie to be so considerate of Chakkri's sensibilities.

After Chakkri and I finished our meals, he began the long, meticulous process of cleaning himself. He licked his right paw well, then used it to wash around his whisker pad. I approve of his fastidiousness.

I alternately paced, tried to settle down and read a copy of *The Gentleman's Magazine,* and gazed out the window looking for Robinson until it grew too dark for me to see.

Feeling like a prisoner—my bars being the wrong set of clothing—I finally could not stand being away from Freddie any longer. Judging that dinner would be long over, I decided to see if the Royal Duchess had returned to her chamber. Well, actually, to her private sitting room. Not even I would dare hazarding Ulga's wrath by attempting to visit her mistress's bedchamber.

Leaving Chakkri, his belly full of chicken, comatose in the exact centre of my bed, I exited the room, closing the door firmly behind me. I did not want to risk the cat wandering the house and falling out of an open window, or embroiling himself in a skirmish with one of the dogs. He cannot abide dogs.

Standing outside my door, I peered down the long corridor. Not a soul was in sight. Freddie's private sitting room and chamber are at the very opposite end of mine. In between are several other guest chambers. I expect you can imagine why the Royal Duchess feels the need to put so much distance between the two of us.

At any rate, I began walking down the dimly lit hall and was almost halfway to my goal when suddenly I had to throw out my hands and grasp the corner of a narrow table placed against the wall to keep from falling. Peering down to see what had tripped me, I saw Humphrey, stretched across the carpet looking up at me with a woeful expression. Now that the sun had set, he had abandoned his position near the drawing room window in favour of the corridor. I had disturbed his sleep. One thing you can always count upon at Oatlands is tripping over dogs in the most unlikely of places.

Concerned the toe of my boot might have hurt the canine, I bent and petted him, receiving a thumping of his tail on the floor as reassurance that he had not been offended. I rose, about to continue on my way before Humphrey could favour me with a bit of dog drool, when my attention was caught by the sounds of a heated argument coming from within the nearest guest bedchamber.

". . . You will, Cecily, and that is my final word," a male voice pronounced.

"Roger, only listen to me," a quavering female voice pleaded. "There was an understanding between Connell and me once. I did think he would marry me, though there was never a formal betrothal. You know all that changed when the old Marquess of Kendrick suffered a fatal heart seizure after his elder son's tragic death, and Connell unexpectedly inherited the title. Connell has all but turned his back on me since then."

"Then you must find a way to engage his attention! Damnation, sister, what's the matter with you? You're pretty enough in your own way, I suppose. Have you no feminine wiles? Oh, for God's sake, stop twisting your hands that way. Put them to better use, on his lordship's person, for example."

This last was said in a scornful tone, especially the words *his lordship's*, that, along with the rest of his speech, made me take an instant dislike of the man I could not see. I knew I should not linger and listen to any more of what was clearly a private conversation, but, alas, I am only human.

All right then, I am someone who has an insatiable need to know about my fellow members of Society. I am no gossip, as Gossip is a known Liar, but rather I am a gatherer of secrets, scandals, and salacious bits of information. Satisfied? Beyond my bon vivant exterior, I do *care* about people, some more than others.

"Roger, my dear brother, if only you could see your way clear to giving me a Season, I shall try to find a proper husband. I know you frequent London yourself, so why cannot I—"

"Cecily, try not to be such a ninnyhammer! Crops have been bad. I've hardly had enough money to throw the dice with my friends. I've only been to the races at Newmarket twice so far this year. This coat I'm wearing was made last spring, for God's sake. I can't afford the cost of a Season in London for you. The rooms we would need to let, the gowns and fripperies you'd need. No, it's out of the question."

"If you are so anxious to align our families, why not marry Connell's cousin, Lady Ariana? She loves you."

"Marry that ghost of a girl? I most certainly won't," he said with contempt. "No, Cecily, it is up to you. We're lucky to be neighbours to the Royal Duchess and of good birth, else we wouldn't have been invited to this party. And, listen to me closely, this party is your last chance to make Connell—*his lordship,* I should say—pop the question."

"Wh-what do you mean my last chance?"

❧ 3 ❧

Roger's voice turned sly. "I have received an offer for your hand from Squire Oxberry."

Cecily gasped. "Squire Oxberry! Roger, you cannot be serious. That is like something out of a gothic novel!"

"The matter is in your hands, sister. I need the money marriage settlements would bring. The Squire has named a generous sum. Besides, when you marry, that bequest from Grandmama will finally be released. Face it, Cecily. You must wed, and you have two choices: Connell, Marquess of Kendrick, or Squire Oxberry."

"No, I don't believe you would do this to me, Roger! Squire Oxberry is as old as the Royal Duchess's elderly footman. His teeth are almost all blackened. Dear God, you are serious. Please, Roger. . . ." She dissolved into tears.

"Cease your crying," her brother said coldly. "And make your decision. Bring the new marquess to the point of proposing, or marry the Squire. I'm going out for a walk."

"Wait! Th-there might be someone else. A worthy gentleman. He has not declared himself, but I believe his affections are true. I find him most admirable."

A burst of sarcastic laughter met my ears. Roger said, "The county doctor? Is that of whom you are speaking? Try not to be so stupid, Cecily. The man is beneath your station in life. No one but a fool marries beneath themselves."

A fresh bout of tears followed this assertion.

Her brother paid no attention to the show of emotion though, as before I heard the slamming of a connecting door within the chamber, he said, "I'm warning you, Cecily. You must make the Marquess of Kendrick propose during this house party. No matter what. You know the consequences if you don't."

More weeping, muffled now as if the young lady was crying into a pillow, was the only sound coming from the room.

I hesitated outside the door, my hands busy adjusting a painting that needed straightening. Roger Cranworth's thinking needed straightening as well.

As I walked down the hall to Freddie's sitting room, I could not help but feel a strong sense of outrage at Roger's tyranny, followed by a rush of pity for Miss Cecily Cranworth. Gothic or not, her predicament echoed that of many a young lady in Society. Fathers, brothers, uncles, and guardians were in control of a female's fate. Many abused the power.

I made up my mind to closely observe the siblings during the house party, and if there was any way I could be of assistance to Miss Cranworth, it would give me pleasure to do so. Her bullying brother needed taking down a notch if what I had just heard was any indication.

I wondered too about the new Marquess of Kendrick. From what Miss Cecily Cranworth had said, it seemed that there had been an alliance between them before "Connell" became Lord Kendrick. Perhaps now that he had the title, his lordship wanted to cast his net out to see if he could land a titled wife rather than one of the *landed* gentry.

I heaved a sigh. Ah, the machinations of Society never fail to fascinate me. Freddie was right. I could not continue to sit in my house in Bruton Street grieving for lost friends. I needed to be amongst people again. Even if it meant meeting those of Roger Cranworth's ilk.

However, Beau Brummell could not be seen in anything less than his usual immaculate grooming and flawlessly appropriate attire lest he be toppled from his invisible throne at the head of fashionable Society and flung back to the outside of nowhere. Which meant I needed my valet and my clothes.

Frowning, I paused when I reached Freddie's sitting room door. I admitted to myself that it was not just Robinson's skills in taking care of my person and clothing, valued as they are, that I cared about.

As unfashionable as it might be to think of one's servants as anything other than invisible entities who looked after one's needs, the truth is that, well, I have grown accustomed to having Robinson round my house. His moral character is just what it should be, he has a sharp eye for the cut of a coat, he is intelligent, and by God, I like the man.

Oh, by the way, *never* tell him I said these things, I beg you. He would only use my words against me in his never-ending battle to send Chakkri back to Siam.

I raised my hand and knocked firmly on the sitting room door. Freddie would need to send men out to look for Robinson at once. My initial irritation with the valet's absence had progressed to apprehension, especially now that night had come, leaving the countryside shrouded in darkness.

What fate had befallen Robinson?

Ulga's scowling face met me at the door to Freddie's

private sitting room. She effectively blocked the portal. Her Prussian features reflected her usual feeling toward me: disapproval.

Which just goes to show you the woman has no taste.

I steeled myself. "Ulga, inquire of the Royal Duchess if she can spare a moment to speak with me."

"Her Royal Highness is occupied at the moment," Ulga informed me in a voice which still retained a Prussian accent.

"I shall wait."

"Her Royal Highness vill be retiring for the evening soon."

"I must speak with her before she does so. Kindly inform her I am here." This last I said with my normal cool composure, but I said it through gritted teeth.

Ulga and I locked gazes. I would have preferred to lock her in a remote cottage and throw away the key.

"Her Royal Highness should not have a second guest in her private sitting room at this hour."

Casually, I raised my pocket watch and looked at the time: ten of the clock. Replacing the timepiece, I said, "Who is with her now?"

"Mr. Fishe."

"Ah, well, we are safe then. Fishe is the jolly fellow who looks after the dogs' needs. I, on the other hand, am a gentleman, and therefore the only one to be considered a 'guest' to the Royal Duchess." Nothing she could say to that, the old dragon.

With a show of great aversion to doing so, Ulga turned from the doorway to apprise Freddie of my presence. To further annoy the Prussian behemoth, I followed her unbidden into the room.

"George," Freddie said. "How glad I am to see you. I was about to send Ulga with a message for you to join me."

I raised an eyebrow at the maid, who turned without

looking at me and sat in the corner, busying herself with her knitting.

"You remember Fishe, do you not, George?" Freddie asked.

"Of course; how are you, Fishe?" I said.

Fishe is a man past fifty who is the only contender for Freddie's dogs' affection. He brushes them, bathes them, keeps them free of pests, nurses them through minor illnesses, makes sure they have heaps of toys and plenty to eat and drink. They love him with slavish devotion.

Fishe himself is one of Freddie's "strays," having been rescued by her from the workhouse. Unlike the well-fed dogs he takes care of, Fishe is skinny and bald, and one of his eyes is considerably larger than the other.

Fishe touched a place on his head where a forelock would have been had he any hair. "Happy to see you, Mr. Brummell, sir. But unhappy I am about Phanor."

I racked my brain trying to remember which dog was Phanor, but failed. "What is wrong with Phanor?"

"I'm not rightly sure, sir. That's why I've sent for Doctor Wendell."

Freddie sat in a gold velvet chair, her hands clasped in her lap. "Doctor Curtis Wendell is our county physician, George. He is a good man who often looks after our animals as well as our people. We can rely on him to come to Phanor."

"If it pleases your Royal Highness, I'll just step along downstairs to the sickroom. I don't like to leave Phanor for long," Fishe said.

"Thank you, and please keep me advised of any developments. I shall visit Phanor before I retire for the evening."

"Yes, your Royal Highness."

Fishe bowed himself out of the room, and I seated myself in a chair near Freddie. I wondered if Doctor Wendell was the very same man that Miss Cecily Cranworth had been speaking about, the county doctor her brother deemed unsuitable for her.

But my thoughts quickly turned to Freddie's distress over Phanor. "My princess," I said, ignoring the exaggerated clunk as Ulga set down her bag of yarn on the table next to her, "forgive me for not remembering, but is Phanor very old?"

"Not so very old, George, just never in good health," Freddie said sadly. "I am worried about him, as he is one of my favourites. Well, that is not precisely true, because I cannot name a favourite amongst my darling dogs. Perhaps if you will excuse me, dear, I shall go see Phanor— but no, you have come to tell me news of Robinson. Has he arrived? What delayed him?"

"Freddie, I am afraid he has not come yet. I believe it would be wise to send someone out looking for him."

Her blue eyes rounded. "Of course we must! Goodness, what could have happened to him? We shall go at once and organise the stable hands to search down the London road."

She rose and made as if to leave the room, but I stood and detained her by placing my hand on her arm. "No. You see to Phanor, and I shall enlist Old Dawe's help in organising the men. I cannot like seeing you overset like this, and only came to ask permission for your men's aid."

She managed a weak smile. "You are so very kind to me, George. I daresay I do not know what I would do without you. The way you are able to anticipate my needs, to know my very thoughts, is always a source of wonder to me."

I reached for her hand, raised it to my lips and pressed a warm kiss against her knuckles. "Go to Phanor then, and I shall—"

A commotion from the hallway interrupted us. Ulga rose from her chair with surprising speed for someone of her size and flung open the sitting room door.

The sight that met us threw my emotions into confusion and sent my eyebrows soaring to my hairline. Next to me, Freddie let out a gasp. No doubt it was one born of a mixture of despair and delight.

"Robinson! For the love of heaven!" Freddie exclaimed.

"Good evening, your Royal Highness," Robinson said, entering the room with great dignity considering his shockingly disheveled appearance. He bowed low. Turning to me, he continued in a long-suffering tone, "Here is the item you asked I bring to Oatlands, sir. What shall I do with it?"

I hesitated, my gaze taking in the valet's demeanor, then I said, "Give it to me."

Robinson sighed heavily, but obeyed.

Freddie's eyes gleamed with excitement when she looked upon the contents of my arms, but her innate concern for a fellow human caused her to focus upon Robinson. "What has happened to you? Your clothes are torn and dusty, and—oh!—is that blood on your cuff?"

She left out the part about how Robinson's blond hair, which he carefully combs into the fashionable Brutus style, was pushed back from his forehead and standing up like wheat in a field. Dirt smudged his left cheek, there was a small cut on his right cheek, and indeed, dried blood on his right cuff and his hand.

"Good God, man, where have you been? A pugilistic contest?" I asked, balancing the article I held in the cradle of my arm.

Robinson stood with his Martyr Expression firmly fixed in place. He spoke in a deceptively calm voice, the tone he employs when he has been tried to the maximum, survived the ordeal, and now wishes to convey the news of his heroism.

"A pugilistic contest?" he answered, his lip curled. "Certainly not, sir. I have only been following your di-

rections to convey the Royal Duchess's birthday gift here,
along with our clothing for our stay at Oatlands. A few
miles short of my destination, the coach I rode in was set
upon by a highwayman."

Robinson paused to savour the effect this statement had
on us.

Indeed, Freddie's jaw dropped, Ulga clutched her knitting to her chest, and I know my face reflected my shock.
"A highwayman? In this part of the countryside?"

"Pray, forgive me. I had quite forgotten," Freddie said.
"There have indeed been similar incidents over the past
two or three years, though only a few in the last year.
The villains have never been apprehended. No one has
ever been hurt, but people have lost money and jewels. I
shall report this latest attack to Squire Oxberry, our local
magistrate, first thing in the morning."

"Fred—er, Duchess, why did you not inform me of
this?" I asked Freddie, fear for her safety rising in me.
"You may have been in danger."

"Nonsense," Freddie declared. "No one would dare try
to rob the Duchess of York. Now, Robinson, pray continue. Ulga, pour him a glass of sherry. I am sure he
would appreciate it."

"Thank you, your Royal Highness," Robinson said. "I
was riding with Mr. Brummell's and my valises and his
gift to you, when, over the course of an hour, my coach
fell a considerable distance behind Mr. Brummell's. The
number of coaches leaving London made it impossible for
us to remain together. Later, a man crossing the road with
a herd of cows was the cause of the first major detainment,
then a farm cart spilled crates of chickens across our path,
further impeding my progress."

Robinson paused in the telling of his tale to accept a
glass from Ulga. After taking a restorative sip, he resumed
his story. "Apart from those postponements, the coachman, more of a drunkard than a driver if my opinion were

to be solicited, stopped at a hedge tavern for a glass of gin. I admonished him upon his return, but by that time, his state of inebriation enabled him to disregard my words without a second thought. He carried a bottle with him, which I have not the slightest doubt he drank from as he drove. A despicable practice employed by far too many coachmen.

"Perhaps half an hour later, the words 'Stand and deliver' rang out. The coachman stopped the vehicle at once, and, if I may say with no small measure of scorn, attempted to get down from his seat, but instead proceeded to lose consciousness, ending up face-first in the dirt of the road."

Robinson looked at me. "You had given me the strictest of instructions to take care of the Royal Duchess's birthday gift above all things, sir, and that is what I endeavoured to do. Because my hands were busy"—here, Robinson shot a look of sheer loathing at the contents of my arms— "the villain made away with as many of our valises as he could carry. Fortunately, he did not discover your mahogany dressing case, sir, and two valises remain. I would have fought the highwayman, but—"

"You could not as you saved that dear, dear little doggie," Freddie cried out in admiration. She turned to me. "Oh, George, I am not being too presumptuous in asking if that precious, beautiful animal is to be mine, am I?"

I barely heard her words. My mind grappled with a single concern. And no, not the loss of my clothes.

The highwayman could not have taken the bag containing my blue velvet book, I told myself. He could not have. I would find the scrapbook safe within one of the valises that Robinson said had been spared, right where I myself had packed it.

"George?" Freddie said, looking at me inquiringly.

"Yes, Duchess," I managed with less than my usual aplomb. I transferred the dog to her waiting arms. "I do hope you will be pleased with the little fellow. Happy Birthday a day early."

Freddie's lips curved into a smile. "How could I not be happy with him? Is he, indeed, the kind I think he is?"

"He is a spaniel of the King Charles breed," I replied absently. "I purchased him from the Duke of Marlborough directly, travelling to Blenheim to pick him up only a few days ago."

Freddie glowed with pleasure. "How I have longed for one of the Duke's spaniels! Only look at these beautiful chestnut markings on such a pearly white background. Thank you so very much, dear. There could be no gift that would please me more." She gently rubbed one of the dog's reddish ears, looking into his trusting brown eyes lovingly.

For once, I could not experience the rush of satisfaction at pleasing Freddie. The need to get to the valises, to be certain the blue velvet book and its contents were safe, gripped me. I felt it difficult to breathe normally.

"George, what is wrong?" Freddie asked me, taking her gaze from the dog in her arms. "Are you upset over the loss of your belongings? They were only clothes, clothes that can be replaced. Indeed, think of the pleasure you will take in designing new ones. The important thing is that Robinson is safe and so is this adorable dog."

Robinson stood very straight. "If, sir, you feel I have somehow failed you—"

"Of course not, Robinson. You did just as you ought. Go now. I know you wish to make yourself presentable again. Er, did any of your clothes survive the attack?"

Pray God both remaining valises had *my* things in them. That way there was more of a chance that the blue velvet book—

"Yes, sir. One of the bags did contain my things, the other yours. I have placed that one in your room and shall unpack it after I have washed."

I held up a hand. "No need. I shall do so myself."

Robinson gazed at me in some reproach.

"Do not glare. I am only thinking of your welfare. I shall not require you tonight. Take care of yourself. Your hand looks as if it has been bleeding."

Robinson cut a look at the dog, who emitted a low growl. "The animal objected to being held back from the highwayman. The thing thought he would be able to fight the villain."

"What a brave little soldier!" Freddie exclaimed. "He wanted to help defend you, Robinson, and got carried away. He must be sorry he bit you."

"Yes, your Royal Highness," Robinson said in a wooden voice, looking like *he* would growl at the dog at any moment.

"Step along to the kitchen, Robinson, and get something to eat. Cook will likely have a salve for your hand. If not, then ask Fishe. That reminds me, in all the excitement, I have quite forgotten poor Phanor's illness."

I nodded at Robinson, and he bowed from the room. An unprecedented urgency spurred me to action. "Freddie, perhaps you could leave the new spaniel here with Ulga for a few minutes while you look in on Phanor. I shall go to my chamber and see what remains of my clothes."

Freddie smiled. "Very well. I can see you are in dire need to view the damage."

"A brand-new pair of breeches could be among the casualties," I lied. "I must know if they have been spared."

Stopping short on her way to hand the dog to Ulga, Freddie turned and eyed me curiously for a moment.

I cannot trick her by playing the foolish dandy. She must have been wondering what was wrong with me, though neither of us spoke.

Then she crossed the room and handed an admiring Ulga the dog, bending and kissing the white lozenge of fur between his eyes before letting him go. From the look in the dog's brown eyes, I could tell he was already in love with his new mistress. Who could blame him? Not I. Freddie has always been my Ideal of the perfect lady. None can compare to her.

She turned and looked at me again, a question in her eyes.

"I bid you good evening, Freddie," I said. I felt a strong urge to touch her before leaving the room. Walking swiftly to where she stood next to the disapproving Ulga, I reached for Freddie's hand and bowed over it, kissing it tenderly. God, if anything were to happen to her because of my stupidity . . .

Without looking at her again, I turned and walked with seeming calm from the room. Once in the corridor, I strode quickly toward my room, deftly avoiding the still-sleeping Humphrey.

Flinging open the door to my chamber, I saw my valise on a small, backless sofa positioned at the end of my bed. Closing the door behind me, I rushed to the bag.

This simply had to be the valise containing the blue velvet book. The scrapbook in which I keep poems I have written, drawings sketched by me and by my friends, mementoes, and letters.

Including the one letter I never should have kept.

The letter which would ruin Freddie's reputation if it fell into the wrong hands.

The letter which would destroy the life in Society I had worked so hard to make for myself, and leave me with no choice but to flee England and all I loved forever.

❧ 4 ❧

Was it just earlier this evening that I told you I could not fathom being unhappy in this room? How matters can change in a short span of time. For now I felt that every ounce of pleasure had evaporated from my life. The only thing left was a sharp pain I tried to ease with bottle after bottle of wine.

My dearest George,

You cannot know the disorder of my thoughts as I pen these lines. Friends have written me about my husband's behaviour of late, though their words can only confirm what I already know. The Duke has formed a strong attachment this time.

I knew by heart every word of the letter Freddie had written. Words put to paper at the very height of her distress over two years ago, when the Duke had made his relationship with Mary Anne Clarke public. I could recite the lines backward if I tried. Which makes me even more

of a jackanapes, guilty of an excess of sentimentality, for
having kept the letter.

Worse, much worse, I am no gentleman for having kept
it. A gentleman would have thrown the crested vellum on
the fire at once upon having read it, discerning its poten-
tial for scandal.

I had not done so.

All these years, I have thought of myself as a gentleman
if nothing else in this world. This predicament proves I
have deluded myself.

Taking another long swallow of wine, I surveyed the
bed where the scattered contents of my valise lay. My
burning, bleary eyes told me what they had told me each
of the four times I had gone through the bag, tossing its
contents across the bed: that the blue velvet book was not
there. Missing. No, stolen.

*Perhaps, George, a more charitable wife than I
could wish him the joy of Mary Anne Clarke. I fear
I am not so generous. Ours was once a tolerable
marriage, if not one of passion, but even that little
peace has been destroyed.*

I sat sprawled in a chair I had turned to face the bed,
my cravat tossed on the floor, my white linen shirt un-
buttoned to my waist, my hand reaching for the third bottle of wine. Perhaps if I drank another glassful, the book
would suddenly appear, having played a game of least in
sight with me all along. There it would be, tucked into
the folds of a pair of breeches, safe from a stranger's eyes.

The wine slid down my throat, dulling my senses a little
more. I immediately poured another glass, then tried to
focus on the mess of clothing on the bed. An evening coat
and silk breeches, buff-coloured leather breeches, shirts,
a pair of blue eyes in a dark brown face.

The latter, attached to a cat, looked at me accusingly.

Why, they seemed to ask, have you not cleared these things away and come to bed? Why are the candles still burning in the middle of the night? Why are you drunk?

"Because," I said to Chakkri, pausing to consume the contents of the glass, "because I hung on to that letter like a moonling of seven and ten years, a letter which any *gentleman* would have destroyed *immediately* upon having read the words. Not kept it selfishly in order to see the lines written in her handwriting whenever the need to know without any uncertainty the depth of our . . . our friendship . . . overcame me."

> *The situation is made worse by the guilt I feel. Yes, George, I know I have done nothing to dishonour my marriage vows. But is the thought as bad as the deed after all? If so, my dearest, dearest companion, my own conduct is shabby indeed.*

Chakkri's tail snapped up and down like a whip.

"Of course," I went on, pouring myself yet another glass with an unsteady hand, "we have known all along I am not really a gentleman, have we not, Chakkri? Certainly not a *titled* gentleman. I have never had a title except the one of Arbiter of Fashion, despite all of Father's plans for me, sending me to Eton and Oxford, demanding that I make aristocratic friends in the hope that one day a real title would be bestowed upon me.

"Still, I have always told myself that the code of honour that makes a man a gentleman has been mine all along, title or no. Members of the royal family trust me. The rules I live by are part of what enabled me to rise to the level of power and authority in Society that I currently enjoy. My identity in the world depends upon my being a gentleman of style, of grace, of manners and ethics.

"I believed I had succeeded in elevating myself in life. That I had earned the respect of men *I* hold in respect. I truly believed it, old boy. But this folly proves me wrong. I am, in fact, the worst of men."

The next glass of wine went down almost without my awareness. The room around me began to blur. My body felt blessedly numb.

I thrust a shaky hand into my pocket and pulled out the gold-framed miniature of herself Freddie had given me last Christmas.

> *For how I long to come to you despite the conventions of Society, to flee from the vows that bind me to the Duke. Never mind the certain peril to my honour. I would cast aside the beliefs I have forever held . . .*

"Freddie." My head slumped to one side. I held the miniature tightly.

> *. . . to render myself yours completely.*

"I did not let you," I muttered to no one but the cat. "And would never let you. I know the result of such immoral conduct would cause you even greater pain than your husband's behaviour. Not just from Society's censure, which would be scandalous enough, but from the censure of your own heart."

> *My punishment for these desires is the deepest of torment.*

> *Yours in truth,*
> *Frederica, Duchess of York*

The glass slipped from my hand. I slipped into darkness.

❧ 5 ❧

I woke slowly. The dryness of my mouth made it almost impossible to swallow. My head felt thick and heavy, and the effort of raising it from my pillow would be agony, I knew.

I was still in yesterday's clothing. How did I get in bed? I wondered, feeling the clean sheets beneath my palms.

"Good morning, sir," Robinson intoned from beside the bed.

I turned toward him slowly and squinted. "Is that tea?" I asked, indicating the tray he held.

"Yes, sir." Robinson set the tray on a table and poured hot liquid into a porcelain cup. "I thought you would be thirsty when you regained consciousness this morning."

The events of the evening before came rushing back to me. The letter. Hell and damnation, the letter. No one must know. I shut my eyes.

"Shall I ask Cook to prepare a tisane? Some laudanum to ease the pain?" Robinson asked with a mite of compassion. "Or do you just want breakfast?"

"No, thank you, on both accounts," I answered in a scratchy voice. I would have to face the world, face the problem of the letter with a clear head, not a laudanum-induced fog.

Last night's overindulgence could not be repeated either. This is an age of hard drinkers, and normally I can hold my own. But my present situation had caused me to go far beyond my usual consumption, evidenced by the fact that I could not even think of eating anything. Usually nothing deters my appetite.

I opened my eyes, carefully pulled myself into a sitting position, and accepted the cup from Robinson. Cautiously, I took a sip. "I do not remember getting into bed."

Robinson's lips pursed, a sure sign of his disapproval. "I expect you do not. The first time I entered the bed-chamber, you told me to—I believe your exact words were 'Go to the devil.' "

"Sorry."

"Since my sleeping quarters are in the dressing room accessible only through this room, I waited in the hall for an hour."

"Sorry."

"The second time I entered, you were out of your senses in that chair over there. I cleared the bed of your clothing and"—here Robinson's lip curled—"your cat. I now have a cat scratch on my left hand in addition to a dog bite on my right hand."

"Did you obtain a salve from Cook?"

"Oh, do not concern yourself with me, sir," Robinson said.

I pressed the fingers of my left hand to my temple and wondered why Robinson had not yet authored a pamphlet entitled "How to Inflict Guilt Upon Your Employer."

Without the sympathy that goes so well with tea, Robinson poured more hot liquid into my empty cup. "I set aside articles to be cleaned for this morning, then helped you into bed."

"Thank you."

"I have your leather breeches, your shirt, and your new cyanous-blue coat ready for after you have bathed."

"Perfect."

"Four and ten cat hairs were on the breeches, three and twenty on the shirt, and the coat had too many to count. I used a special cloth to rid the garment of the blight." Robinson glared past me to the opposite side of the bed.

Chakkri sat tall on the other bedside table, staring at me and twitching his tail back and forth. The look in his eyes rebuked me for my actions the night before. Good God, was the cat to be my conscience now as well? He need not be. My own conscience screamed inside my pounding head.

Robinson spoke. "Sir, if you are angry with me for losing your clothing, may I remind you that I, too, lost favourite garments in this disgraceful crime?"

I swallowed more tea and raised a hand. "No, you did nothing wrong, and your things will be replaced."

"Then what, if I may ask, was the reason you threw your clothing all about the bed where that animal could lay upon them, then imbibed enough wine for three men?"

"A whim," I answered nonchalantly. You do not think I am going to tell him the real reason, do you? I handed him the empty teacup. "What time is it? Have you ordered my bath?"

Robinson heaved a sigh. He picked up the tray containing the teacup and teapot and held it in a manner that mocked the consummate servant. Staring at a point above my head, he recited, "The time is eleven of the clock, the day is Wednesday, the seventh day of May in the year 1806. Today is her Royal Highness, the Duchess of York's, birthday. I shall return with your bath."

So saying, he turned on his heel and left the chamber,

shutting the door behind him with a *very* sharp click, deuce take him.

I eased myself out of bed delicately. With great care, I found I could walk with the room tilting only slightly. I stripped off my shirt and tossed it onto the chair. A glint of gold caught my eye. The miniature of Freddie lay in the corner of the upholstery. I picked it up, stared at her face for a moment, then placed the likeness on my dressing table.

Chakkri watched me walk to the window.

"I assume you have had your breakfast, else I would be hearing about it," I said to the cat.

He raised a brown paw, licked it, and gave his mouth a swipe.

"Good answer. Upon my oath you understand every word I say."

Chakkri leapt down and scrambled past me to get to the window first, hopping up on a table to better enable him to look out. He nudged the coffee-coloured draperies aside and stuck his head through the opening. Making sure the window was shut so he could not fall out, I stood behind him, not wishing to be seen by anyone outside.

The sun shone brightly. I nodded in approval even though the light hurt my eyes. Rain would not dare fall on Freddie's special day. Several people known to me, as well as others I did not recognize, strolled about the grounds. Standing near the drive, with another of her dogs, Hero—a black and tan little scamp—frollicking nearby, Freddie held a lead attached to the spaniel I had given her. She greeted and conversed with her guests.

I drew in a deep breath at the sight of her. She wore a very pale blue dress made of light muslin, crossed in front in the popular Grecian style. Her curly brown hair was covered by a straw bonnet with a matching blue ribbon. The distance from the window made it difficult to be certain, but I believe her necklace was of sapphires set in gold. I would wager the shade of the stones matched her eyes exactly.

"Reow," Chakkri said.

"Yes, she does look beautiful. How much longer, though, will I be able to enjoy the pleasure of her company? Not to mention my place in Society. If I lose that, what am I to do? Become a tailor in Jamaica? Who would patronise a broken Beau?"

Chakkri used a hind paw to scratch a spot behind his right ear.

My jaw clenched, and my brain struggled to function.

Freddie's letter had been written, as had all her correspondence to me, in French. What were the odds a common highwayman would understand it? Was there a chance of avoiding a raging scandal after all? Dare I hope that neither Freddie nor I would suffer the consequences of my folly in keeping the letter?

Robinson returned at that moment with footmen carrying my bath. Chakkri and I moved away from the window, he to the centre of the bed, and I to bathe and begin what Robinson and I have dubbed the Dressing Hour. Of course, it never is *one* hour, you know.

Once clean, I surrendered myself to the valet's ministrations. Soon my face was again free of stubble, my squared nails buffed to a shine, my light brown hair arranged to our mutual satisfaction.

After I donned my breeches, a pair of gleaming Hessian boots, and a spotless white shirt, I began the arduous process of tying my cravat. Wrapping the folds of snowy linen around my neck in just the right way, lowering my head so the starched material fell precisely as I wished, then tying the knot, could sometimes take several attempts. Fortunately, this morning we only had two failures before perfection was achieved.

Drawn as if by an invisible bond, I walked to the window and looked outside again while Robinson retrieved my coat. Freddie had moved away from the drive to speak with a strikingly handsome young man with black hair who stood next to a girl who looked to be the feminine equivalent of him. Roger and Cecily Cranworth, the quarrelling siblings? I wondered.

At that moment, an older, decrepit coach pulled into the drive. A man surely feeling the breath of his seventieth year on his neck moved slowly down the coach steps. A footman had to assist him. He wore a cheap brown coat with metal buttons, coarsely woven breeches, and a greasy periwig.

"That must be Squire Oxberry," Robinson said over my shoulder.

"How do you know these things?" I asked, marvelling at the valet's knowledge.

"Cook told me about the Squire. He is the district magistrate. Her Royal Highness will be speaking with him about the highwayman," Robinson replied.

Just then, the Squire looked about furtively, then moved to stand behind the coach, away from where guests mingled. Thinking himself unobserved by anyone other than the footman who had assisted him, the Squire took the opportunity to relieve himself.

I turned from the window in disgust.

Robinson unpursed his lips long enough to mutter, "He cannot even find a chamber pot, how is he going to find the highwayman and our belongings?"

Perhaps it would be better if he did not, I reflected.

"Has Viscount Petersham arrived?" I asked while Robinson helped me into my coat. The valet briskly straightened the material across my shoulders.

"He has, sir. I saw him last night while I was standing outside your room when you had cast me out."

Mentally, I rolled my eyes. I judged I would not hear the end of my crimes for weeks to come. My next statement was guaranteed to further irritate him. "The sad truth is, Robinson, that thanks to the highwayman, neither of us has enough clothing here at Oatlands for our stay. You must return home as soon as can be arranged and bring back additional garments. Later today, Diggie will help me get dressed for the evening. Robinson! Steady, now!"

He was suddenly using what I felt to be excessive force in smoothing out the material of my costly coat across my back. He eased off, but I could sense his anger.

You see, another source of conflict between the valet and me had been raised. Diggie, Petersham's valet, and Robinson are archenemies. The roots of their feud go back to the undeniable fact that Mr. Digwood flaunts in Robinson's face the fact that he, Diggie, serves a viscount. Robinson never refrains from reminding Diggie—and me—that Petersham has often extended the invitation to Robinson to come work for him.

"Mr. Digwood, sir?" Robinson said, tugging the sleeves of my coat in place. "I should hardly think him qualified to attend you on such an important evening as the Royal Duchess's birthday fête. You need me."

Chakkri snorted and snuffled in his sleep. I tell you it sounded like a laugh.

I took a step away and finished smoothing the coat myself. "Now, Robinson, you know I would prefer to have you here, but I need you even more to go to Bruton Street. Surely you would not want me to send a footman with word for Ned and Ted to gather our things, would you?" Ned and Ted are two Dorset country boys in my employ. They carry me in my sedan-chair when I am in Town. Robinson considers them bumpkins.

He levelled me with his most severe Martyr Look. "No, that would not do at all, sir," he said through stiff lips. "I shall go directly and arrange for transportation back to London."

"Good man," I said, attempting a smile. "Hurry back."

"Yes, sir," the valet agreed. He made quick work of

tidying the room—with a trifle more noise than might be warranted considering the fragile condition of my head—while I made the final adjustments to my cravat.

In truth the neckcloth was perfect. I was merely delaying having to appear downstairs as my usual mannered, charming self, when inside I felt like a trip to the gallows would provide more amusement.

I thought about what Robinson said regarding Squire Oxberry's inability to find the highwayman. Taking in a deep breath, I clung to the idea of the highwayman never being caught with his contraband. My mind took the further leap to an image of the villain going through his illegally obtained goods, and coming upon the blue velvet book. Flipping through the pages and finding nothing more than drawings and words he likely could not read, he would toss the useless thing onto the fire. In my mind's eye, I could see the flames engulfing Freddie's letter, transforming it to harmless ashes. Then all would be well.

That thought gave me the courage to bid Robinson farewell, tuck the miniature of Freddie into my pocket and exit the chamber to join the company.

Had I known the true fate of Freddie's letter, I might very well have made my own hangman's noose and put it to use around my fashionably clad neck rather than face what was soon to occur.

❦ 6 ❧

I had been correct in that the sapphire stones set in Freddie's necklace precisely matched the colour of her eyes. The shade was darker than the sky above us as we glided down the river Thames on a barge. Since Oatlands overlooks the Thames, the idea of an outing on the water was splendid, especially given the warm weather.

No simple flat-bottomed boat, the conveyance had been fitted out with every manner of luxury, from the Persian carpets under our feet, the numerous plump red pillows on which we sat, the footmen to see to our every need, and the sumptuous food and drink. About thirty guests enjoyed the balmy air and relaxed atmosphere.

At one end of the barge, a lone musician played a haunting melody on the violin. At the other end, Freddie and I sat together under a crimson-and-gold-striped canopy.

Sounds blissful, does it not? To tell the truth, half reclining on a pillow next to Freddie did make my head cease its merciless throbbing. I was even able to partake of a bit of Russian caviar and a drop of claret. More than a drop, I suppose. After the first half hour, one might say I was once more full of good spirits.

Though I managed to push the matter of the missing letter to the back of my mind and regain my cool composure, the outing was not without unpleasant complications.

One of them sat on the other side of Freddie.

"*Mi bella Duchessa,* allow me to tempt you with a cherry or perhaps a slice of pear," Victor Tallarico coaxed. He indicated a wigged footman standing nearby proffering a tray of fruit.

The Italian is my good friend Lord Perry's cousin, a cousin at least one hundred times removed, Perry often says. An incurable flirt, Tallarico's hidden—at least to me—charms are irresistible to ladies of any age. I glared at him over Freddie's head. He is not above trying to lead the Royal Duchess into a flirtation, and indeed, seems to live for romance. The man's trademark is a pink waistcoat. Need I say more?

Freddie smiled. "Signor Tallarico, you are everything considerate. I do favour cherries."

The Italian snapped his trim fingers at the servant, who lowered the tray to within Freddie's reach. In an instant, I perceived that the rakehell meant to lift the fruit from the tray with the intention of placing the cherries to the Royal Duchess's lips himself.

I elevated myself to a sitting position and raised my quizzing glass at the Italian. He paused, his hand over the tray. Then he smiled, showing off a set of magnificent white teeth, and gave an almost imperceptible nod of his handsome head. I allowed my quizzing glass to fall back to my chest.

Meanwhile, Freddie reached for a cherry and addressed me. "I did so dislike leaving Georgicus out of our party. But I could have no notion of how he would react to being on a boat. I did not want to upset the little darling's stomach on his first full day in his new home."

"Georgicus?" both Tallarico and I said at the same moment. I frowned at him. He shot me the very model of a sarcastic grin.

Freddie dismissed the footman and looked into my eyes. "That is what I named the spaniel you gave me for my birthday, George."

A rush of pleasure ran through me at this thoughtful sign of affection. Even if it was only a dog's name. She had named him after me, would think of me every time she petted him. . . .

Tallarico let out an expressive snort. "*Dio mio,* the Beau gave you a canine for your birthday, Duchess? I myself have a unique offering I shall give you later," he promised in silken tones, causing me to have some most disagreeable mental notions of what he would offer my Freddie. Then he looked at me. "What kind of gift is a dog, Brummell?"

"Exactly the sort her Royal Highness appreciates," I ground out. "One that touches her heart, I hope."

Freddie looked from one to the other of us with a smile playing about her lips, lips made even more pink from the juice of the cherries.

"Ah, I see. But of course that is what your Royal Highness would have told the Beau, gracious as she is," Tallarico said, *winking* at Freddie. Madman!

With studied calm, I looked about me at the gentle movement of the river and the swaying of the trees along the banks. Then I deliberately pinned my gaze on the Italian. "For some reason, you have suddenly reminded me that one of the great marks of the spring season is the well-known song of the cuckoo. How does the old Norfolk proverb go?" I looked off into the distance and began to recite:

> *In April the cuckoo shows his bill,*
> *In May he sings, night and day,*
> *In June he changes his tune,*
> *In July away he fly,*
> *In August away he must.*

I turned a bored expression on Tallarico. "June is not that far away, and August will follow eventually. What are your plans, Tallarico?"

The Italian shot me a murderous glance, but before he could challenge me to a duel, or something less civilised, we became aware of a lady and gentleman standing in front of us. Immediately we rose.

Freddie stood as well and performed the introductions. The gentleman was none other than the new Marquess of Kendrick, accompanied by his cousin, Lady Ariana.

I managed to say everything proper while observing his lordship. So this was "Connell," whom Miss Cecily Cranworth had been charged by her brother to make her husband. Lord Kendrick was short in stature, with blond curls forming a halo about his head. This cherub-like endowment was negated by cold blue eyes set in a hard face. You know the sort of countenance I mean, where the person appears to wear a perpetual smirk. While dressed well enough, he looked as nasty as Roger Cranworth had sounded last evening.

In sharp contrast, his cousin, Lady Ariana, was a wan, wispy thing, thin and almost unbearably fragile-looking. Everything about her was pale, her skin, her hair escaping its knot, her light eyes and colourless eyelashes.

My musings were interrupted when Lady Ariana artlessly asked, "Where is your husband, your Royal Highness? I have not met him, have I?"

A blush appeared on Freddie's cheeks.

Lord Kendrick turned sharply and gave his cousin a poisonous look, one she cringed under.

"The Duke of York is the military Commander in Chief, Lady Ariana," I replied smoothly. "He could not be here today." Not exactly a lie. I did not have to mention *why* the Duke of York was absent, that he chose to spend his wife's birthday abroad with his mistress.

"Lord Kendrick," Tallarico said, also aware of Freddie's embarrassment, "allow me to take a turn around the boat with your lovely cousin." Freddie smiled gratefully at the Italian.

The marquess nodded his consent. Lady Ariana turned her vacant gaze to Tallarico. She accepted his arm without question and the two strolled away.

Lord Kendrick, far from appearing chagrined at his cousin's social misstep now that she was gone, appealed to Freddie. "Your Royal Highness, may I, as your neighbour, beg the favour of an introduction to one of your guests?"

"Of course," Freddie replied. Only someone who knew her well could detect the chill in her voice at the marquess's boldness. "Whom do you wish to meet?"

"The lady seated next to the Duke of Derehurst, as well as the duke himself. I believe her to be his daughter," the marquess said, indicating a stately brunette. A footman held an opened parasol above the beauty's head, no doubt protecting her from the sun's tendency to freckle a lady's complexion.

"Indeed, Lord Kendrick, she is Lady Deidre, the duke's daughter. I shall be sure to introduce you to them both this evening at the dinner party. In the meantime, Miss Cecily Cranworth would be glad of your company, I am sure."

His lordship accepted this suggestion for what it was, a command. But he paused before obeying the order. "Yes, your Royal Highness. I am, naturally, acquainted with Miss Cranworth and her brother, Roger. Why, having practically grown up with the Cranworths, I consider them as close to me as a brother and sister." With a benign smile on his face, Lord Kendrick glanced over in the Cranworths' direction. Squire Oxberry stood with them.

The unspoken message was that Lord Kendrick would not consider Miss Cecily Cranworth a worthy candidate for his bride. I thought back to Roger Cranworth's insistence that his sister wring a proposal of marriage from Lord Kendrick. I reflected that Roger Cranworth was already making good on his threat to force his sister into the odious Squire's company. If Roger Cranworth and Lord Kendrick were such good friends, why did Roger not drop a hint in the marquess's ear? Perhaps he already had, to no avail. How would Roger react if Miss Cranworth failed to tempt Lord Kendrick into a betrothal? Doubtless he would be angry at her and at Lord Kendrick.

In front of us, Lord Kendrick bowed and then moved in the siblings' direction. Cecily Cranworth looked flustered at his appearance.

I noticed the arrival of the marquess on the scene prompted the Squire to retreat to the far side of the boat. He stood behind a footman waving a palm frond, cooling an older woman's flushed face. Remembering what the Squire had done when he thought no one was looking earlier, I turned to Freddie.

"Freddie," I said so she might look at me and avoid any offensive scene, "have you known the Cranworths very long? I think I heard them arguing last night. They are an attractive pair, but we may be in for some trouble. Roger Cranworth wants his sister to marry Lord Kendrick. In light of what the marquess just said about her being like a sister to him—"

"Tell me about it later, George," Freddie said urgently, placing her hand on my arm.

"What is wrong?" I asked, alarmed at her tone.

"Forgive me for interrupting you, dear. I hate to spoil our fun, but Lord Kendrick's cousin, Lady Ariana, has stolen my pearls and has them on."

❧ 7 ❧

The Marquess of Kendrick strode into the Oatlands
library. Though lacking in height, he did not lack pride.
Rather, he carried himself in a way that suggested a man
filled with self-importance. I closed the door behind him
and took up a position next to the chair where Freddie
was seated. Ulga sat in her usual place in the corner of
the room.

Lord Kendrick looked at Freddie. "You sent for me,
your Royal Highness."

Freddie sat regally, the picture of the *grande dame*. She
wore the light blue muslin gown she had on for the barge
party, its folds falling gracefully around her, but she had
removed her straw hat. "Yes, Lord Kendrick. I have a
delicate matter to discuss with you. You may be seated."
Freddie indicated a chair.

His lordship looked at me standing next to the Royal
Duchess and apparently decided not to sit. He waved a
careless hand. "If this is about Lady Ariana's unfortunate
mention of your husband—"

Freddie blanched.

"No, that is not what this is about," I said. Though my tone was even, I am certain my grey eyes resembled circles of iron.

Lord Kendrick looked confused. "What is it, then?"

"Reputations can be easily damaged, Lord Kendrick," Freddie said. "That is why I wished to speak with you privately. Are you aware of any thievery occurring recently?"

I watched the marquess's reaction carefully, wondering if he knew of his cousin's deed. He was suddenly all indignation.

"Why shouldn't I know about the highwayman striking again?" he demanded.

"Wait one moment," I said, startled into speech. "How *did* you know that? The attack occurred only yesterday."

The marquess folded his arms in front of him. "It's common knowledge in the neighbourhood that we've been plagued by the blackguards. I assumed that he had struck again and that was what the Royal Duchess was talking about. But if that's not the case, then of what thievery are we speaking?"

"The highwayman remains a menace, Lord Kendrick, but I am referring to your cousin. Lady Ariana had on a set of pearls this afternoon. *My* pearls," Freddie said. "I am sorry to tell you that I did not give them to her."

"What are you implying?" Lord Kendrick's eyes narrowed.

"Her Royal Highness is too discreet to come right out and say it, but I shall," I told him, disliking him more by the minute. "It seems Lady Ariana may have taken something that does not belong to her, pearls that belong to the Royal Duchess. We wish the necklace returned to their owner without delay."

Lord Kendrick looked at me, then turned to Freddie, the smirk that never leaves his face in full evidence. "This is preposterous. Are you saying my cousin *stole* your pearls, then had the audacity to wear them in front of you?"

Freddie gave a quarter-inch nod of her head. "I have no alternative but to think so."

"That is a ridiculous accusation!" Lord Kendrick exclaimed, colour rushing into his face.

Freddie sat with her head held high. "My maid, Ulga, set the pearls out in my dressing room to be polished. I received Lady Ariana there earlier this morning upon your arrival at Oatlands. We had an easy conversation about the weather and the animals here at Oatlands. Later, Ulga told me the pearls were missing."

"Well, the maid mislaid them," Lord Kendrick said in the tone of one speaking the obvious.

I glanced at Ulga. Her face was set. I could not conceive of her making such a mistake. "I do not think so," I said to the marquess.

"Nor do I," Freddie said.

Lord Kendrick let out an outraged breath, but I saw him rubbing his fingers together at his sides, a sign of uneasiness. Again, he addressed Freddie, his speech pitched to the tone of one voicing logic. "Your Royal Highness, how can you be sure the pearls Lady Ariana had on are yours? Pearls look much alike."

"They belonged to my grandmother and are a perfectly matched set of rose-hued pearls. If you inspect the clasp, I am certain you shall find a single diamond. Please examine the strand and then return them to me," Freddie instructed in a way which allowed for no argument.

Lord Kendrick lost all of his bluster. "Very well, I shall look into the matter." He bowed to Freddie, gave me a curt nod, and exited the room.

I watched him, thinking not so much about the pearls, but about his reference to the highwayman.

"That was most unpleasant, George," Freddie said, waving a silk fan in front of her face. "The new marquess is no better than his father, though I had hoped for more. As I believe you surmised, I thought he might do for Cecily Cranworth, but I can see now I was mistaken. Lord Kendrick's abrasive manner would shatter Cecily's sensitive nerves all to pieces."

I swung around to face her, having only been half listening. My brain was running down other paths where the Marquess of Kendrick was concerned. "Er, yes. Listen, Freddie, I think it would be interesting to see what the marquess does next. I am going to follow him." I made her a brisk bow and turned to leave.

"George! Is that really necessary?" Freddie called.

"I shall let you know what I find out." I hurried out the library door and down the corridor.

You may be wondering why I felt the need to trail Lord Kendrick. Did you not mark his reaction, nay, his *strong* reaction to Freddie's question about thievery? What about his immediate assumption that we were speaking of the highwayman? If there is even the slightest possibility that he knows anything about the robberies, I must know. I cannot miss a single opportunity, however remote, to retrieve Freddie's letter.

In the front hall, Old Dawe sat in a chair near the main door. "Did Lord Kendrick come this way?" I asked.

The elderly retainer rose to attention. "Yes, Mr. Brummell."

I raised a questioning eyebrow.

Old Dawe spoke in a low voice. "I'll tell you because I cannot like the new marquess, if you'll forgive my plain speaking."

I nodded. "Go on, man. I trust your opinions."

"He's not a man I can respect, Mr. Brummell. I don't like seeing him here at Oatlands. He is not worthy of his title and not worthy to be in the presence of her Royal Highness. He was always a nasty, greedy boy, and his ways haven't changed." Old Dawe nodded to himself, then drew a deep breath. "The marquess raced upstairs in quite a taking, but was back down here in the blink of an eye, asking where his cousin was. I told him she'd gone outside not five minutes ago."

"Thank you," I said. Stepping out the door, I assumed the air of one out for a casual stroll. Running my gaze around the grounds, I considered where the fragile Lady Ariana might have gone. Perhaps the gardens with the ornamental pool. A lovely, peaceful area, Freddie had a section near the water where she buried her treasured pets who have passed away. Each grave is marked with a stone bearing the dog's name and his virtues. A dreamy girl like Lady Ariana would surely be drawn to such a quiet, restful place. I turned my steps in that direction.

The parkland at Oatlands contains many beautiful pine trees and shrubbery. The area near the ornamental pool is no exception, and most convenient for one wishing to spy on another.

Yet, when the pool of water came into view, I was both satisfied and dismayed. There, indeed, were Lord Kendrick and Lady Ariana involved in what was a heated discussion if his posture were any indication. He had his hands around her neck, unclasping the strand of pearls she wore. All the while, he spoke angrily right into her face.

As quickly and as quietly as I could, I maneuvered my way into a discreet position behind a sturdy oak tree.

I heard Lord Kendrick's angry voice first. ". . . told you before to stop your foolish pranks."

Lady Ariana appeared whiter than she had on the barge, if that were possible. "It is not a prank!"

"What do you call it then, eh?" he asked, pocketing the pearls.

"I do not know, truly I do not, Connell," she replied in an anguished, little-girl voice.

"Do you expect me to believe that?"

"I have told you time and time again," Lady Ariana said, clearly not understanding her cousin's reaction. "I never remember when I take things. It just somehow happens."

"You took the Royal Duchess's pearls, you totty-headed female. How could you not remember taking them?" Lord Kendrick said in a furious voice. "I warn you, Ariana, my father took you in when you had no place to go, but now *I am marquess*. I have plans for the future that do not include a lunatic in my house."

"I am no *lunatic*," Lady Ariana insisted. "I just take things. How is it different from what you do?"

He grasped the girl's shoulders and shook her. "Cease your prattling! You're talking nonsense. And you'll stop 'taking things' at once, do you understand me? At once!"

With a little cry, she stumbled backward, but regained her footing.

Anger rose in me at this callous treatment of one not as strong as he. But then Lord Kendrick dropped his arms away from the girl.

In a menacing tone he said, "Don't interfere in my life, Ariana. How can I win the hand of a duke's daughter if you bring scandal on my head?"

"A duke's daughter? I thought you were going to marry Cecily. Then we could all be together, you and Cecily, and Roger and I."

Lord Kendrick shook his head. "You are mad. *I am the marquess now,* you idiot. How many times must I tell you? Can't you get it through your addled brain? I shan't settle for any female without a title. As for you and Roger"—here, Lord Kendrick let out a snort of a laugh—"I can tell you, Roger's taste in women leans toward the voluptuous. Which you are not."

Lady Ariana pulled a handkerchief from her pocket and wiped tears from her cheeks. "You are cruel. Cecily and Roger both expect our families to be joined."

"I don't give a farthing what they expect."

Lady Ariana's demeanor unexpectedly changed. She pocketed the handkerchief and twirled a lock of her pale hair between her fingers, looking away from her cousin. "I am sad for Cecily. You make me sad, Connell. What happened that day in the study with your father makes me sad too. Uncle had been kind to me."

With one hand, Lord Kendrick suddenly reached out and grabbed the girl's face. His thumb pressed hard on one cheek, his fingers on the other, forcing her to look at him. She let out a yelp of pain.

My muscles tensed. I was torn between intervening on Lady Ariana's behalf and the need to discover what their secrets were. What was going on? What did Lady Ariana mean when she asked her cousin how what she did was different from what he was doing? Could the marquess somehow be involved with the highwayman?

Lord Kendrick's face contorted with rage. "Shut up! If you ever dare say anything about Father, or if you dare take one more thing that doesn't belong to you, I'll have you committed to the Sussex Asylum for Lunatics. In fact, I've already written to them about you. They are ready to take you in at my word. *At my word, Ariana!* Do exactly as I say or I'll have you locked up for the rest of your life."

The girl gave a frightened little nod within the confines of her cousin's hold.

If he did not let her go immediately, or if he hurt her further, I must act. No sooner had I made the decision than Lord Kendrick roughly released his hold on the girl and strode away in the direction of the house.

Lady Ariana stood motionless for several seconds. Then, she reached up and rubbed her cheeks hard, over and over again. As if the action somehow had taken her pain away, her face abruptly cleared of all emotion. She idly picked a buttercup and sat on a bench, examining the flower's petals with minute concentration. I could hear her singing softly to herself.

Questions about the conversation I had heard crowded my mind, but for that moment I could not examine them. I could only stare at the child-woman on the bench and wonder what would become of her.

The fate of two women, Lady Ariana and Cecily Cranworth, now depended on the actions of the vulgar Marquess of Kendrick.

And if he were indeed involved with the robberies and stumbled upon that letter . . .

❧ 8 ❧

I returned to the house, but Freddie was no longer in the library. Instead, I found her seated on the sofa in the drawing room. As usual, several dogs lounged about the room. One was in human shape: Victor Tallarico.

For once I was grateful for Ulga's presence. She knitted away in her favourite chair, keeping an eye on the two.

The Italian perched on one knee in front of Freddie. His palm was outstretched, a piece of white velvet draped across it.

"Signor Tallarico, they are lovely," Freddie cried, unfolding the velvet to reveal its contents. "But you should not have brought me such a costly gift."

"Ah, but they must belong to you. Once I saw them at Christie's auction house, I could not help but think how your maid could arrange them in your hair. Perhaps, if one might be permitted to hope, a style which would show your *bella* neck to advantage."

"Thank you," Freddie responded and smiled, accepting the Italian's offering with pleasure.

I felt a surge of annoyance. Tallarico's persistence in

flirting with Freddie made me wish I could pack him and his pink waistcoats up and put them on a boat back to Italy. Or at least point him in the direction of a matron eager to indulge his propensity for dalliance.

Tallarico rose from his kneeling position to sit next to Freddie. "Will you not call me Victor? I long to hear my name on your lips."

"Your Royal Highness," I interrupted in a strong voice, unwilling to let the Lothario say another word.

The two looked up at me as I entered the room; Tallarico with annoyance, and Freddie with . . . could that be a flash of guilt on her face?

"George! Let me show you what Signor Tallarico has given me for my birthday," Freddie said, rising from the sofa. We met in the middle of the room. Tallarico stood frustrated by the sofa. Freddie held out her hand so I could see the gift. "Are they not charming?"

I looked down at a pair of matching antique hair ornaments, made of solid jet. The tops of the baubles were fashioned into cubes of jet decorated with gold inlay. Each ornament was about four or five inches in length, the jet narrowing from the cube and finally forming a sharp-looking point at the end.

"Pretty trinkets," I said. "Grecian?"

Tallarico strolled over, grinning. "Roman. Most difficult to find a matched pair in a condition *perfetto*. But the Royal Duchess is worth the effort."

"I thought the exact same thing when I had a dress made of Brussels lace for her Royal Highness last autumn," I said.

I could have kicked myself the moment the words were out of my mouth. Freddie studied the antique trinkets with intense concentration. Tallarico looked at me as if he were seeing me for the first time. The Italian would be sure to know that a Brussels lace dress would be worth much

more than hair ornaments. He would be bound to speculate as to the exact nature of my relationship with Freddie.

I know what you are thinking, that it was indiscreet of
me to boast of my extravagance. What excuse can I offer?
None, really. Tallarico's scorn of my birthday gift to Freddie of the spaniel still rankled.

I broke the awkward silence. "If you will excuse us,
Tallarico, I have something I wish to discuss with the
Royal Duchess. In private."

The Italian bowed low over Freddie's hand, kissing the
air an inch above it. "You must promise to save me two
dances this evening, your Royal Highness, else my misery
will be so great, I shall impale myself on my dress
sword." He grinned at her.

Freddie laughed softly. "You give me no choice, then.
I cannot allow you to do yourself an injury. Your request
is granted."

Impatiently, I marched over to the double doors and
ushered the smug Italian outside the room. He spoke to
me in a low voice, a strong measure of mischief in his
brown eyes. "She doesn't belong to you."

I snapped the door shut in his face.

Freddie placed the hair ornaments down on one of the
marble pedestals next to a bust of a dog named Trumpet.
Before she could remark upon my indiscretion regarding
the dress, I said, "I have news of your pearls."

"What happened?" she asked, her attention diverted.

"I followed Lord Kendrick to where he and Lady Ariana were engaged in an argument by your dog cemetery.
His lordship knew all along that his cousin must have
taken the pearls. Evidently, Lady Ariana is in the habit of
stealing things, though she claims not to remember what
she has done afterward."

"How terrible! Ulga, did you hear that? Lady Ariana
does have the pearls," Freddie said.

Ulga grunted. "I have never in all my years of service to your family lost anything."

"Oh, I know that, Ulga. Pray, do not give it another thought." Freddie took my arm and led me to the sofa. "Let us sit down and decide what to do now."

We seated ourselves, and I spoke. "Lord Kendrick will see the pearls returned to you, of that I am sure. Even so, he is an ugly fellow, Freddie, and I don't just refer to his physical appearance. He was rough with his cousin, he grabbed her chin, and spoke to her harshly. He even threatened to have her committed to a lunatic asylum if she continued to take things that do not belong to her."

"Heavens! I will not have such a man at Oatlands."

"I truly regret not learning what information Lord Kendrick might have about the highwayman, but—"

"About the highwayman?" Freddie interrupted. "You think the marquess knows something?"

My brows came together. "It is just a feeling I have. When you told him you wanted to question him regarding thievery, why did his thoughts leap to the highwayman instead of his cousin if she makes it a practice to steal? One would think her behaviour would be the first thing to spring to his mind."

"That is odd, I suppose. George, much as I would like to help Squire Oxberry identify the highwayman, we cannot allow Lord Kendrick to remain here hoping he will let some clue fall."

But then Freddie did not know about the missing letter.

"Regretfully, I agree. I do think it best if we ask him to leave in the morning and take Lady Ariana with him. It grows too late to do so today. It is almost time to dress for dinner. Besides which, I would not put it above Lord Kendrick to cause a scene, and I shall not have that on your birthday."

Freddie's face reflected contrition. "Oh, dear, George, I should have known better than to invite Lord Kendrick.

I refused to listen to neighbourhood gossip though, feeling it churlish to hold a party and not invite him."

"What gossip?"

Agitated, Freddie rose and began to slowly pace. I stood at once.

"The previous marquess was not a kind man. True, he offered his niece, Lady Ariana, a home about nine years ago, but that was because of some ghastly rumours that were circulating about her father, the old marquess's brother. The previous marquess wanted to stop the gossip at any cost. His brother was a widower living with his daughter, Lady Ariana, in Bath. I—I do not know quite how to say this, George. The gossip was that the man—the man had been using Lady Ariana in some abominable ways."

I put my hand on Freddie's arm, noticing she was trembling. "You do not have to say any more. Unfortunately, I comprehend your meaning."

Freddie nodded. "At first, when the old marquess brought the girl to live with him I thought it an act of kindness on his part. But, over time when he did nothing for her, ignoring her existence in his household, I came to realise he merely took her from his brother—who died a few years ago, by the way—to squelch the rumours."

"Family honour, eh?"

"Such as it were. Also, the old marquess was very tight-fisted with his money. He was single-minded and could think of nothing but getting the most out of his land."

"That is strange. His son does not seem the type interested in crop rotation."

"Oh, no, not the new marquess. His elder brother, who would have been marquess had he lived, was the one like his father. Maynard was his father's pride and joy, sharing as he did the old marquess's love of money and the land. Connell, as a second son, was left to find a way for himself in the world. His father gave him a miserly allowance and refused even to buy him a commission in the army."

Ah, I thought, and it was not unheard of for a younger son, eager for money, to take to the roads and rob coaches. Though, in my mind's eye, I had trouble picturing Lord Kendrick possessing the courage to carry out such acts. However, he could have an accomplice. To Freddie I asked, "How did the heir—Maynard, did you say?—die?"

"Yes, Maynard. A terrible tragedy. He was struck by lightning while riding out in the fields. The old marquess was literally destroyed by his son's death. He died himself of an apparent apoplexy less than a week later. That is how Connell came into the title about a year ago."

Coincidentally, about the same time the robberies had all but ceased. That fit. Now that Connell had the title and money, his need to continue the robberies would have ended.

"A small man with a small mind not up to the responsibilities of being a peer of the realm," I mused. How lucky for Lord Kendrick, long kept on a tight allowance, to unexpectedly find himself a wealthy marquess.

We fell silent for a moment, until Freddie said, "Perhaps I should not have told you all that, George. Repeating country gossip, or any gossip, is not normally my nature."

"I know that," I assured her. "This is different."

"And, oh, great heavens, George, I promised to introduce Lord Kendrick to the Duke of Derehurst and his daughter. How can I do so now in good conscience knowing Lord Kendrick to be a man without honour?"

"In a manner that lets the duke know you are merely performing the introductions out of a sense of duty as hostess."

"I expect that will have to be the way. I have no time to do otherwise."

"It will turn out all right, Freddie. Telling Lord Kendrick he is no longer welcome here—and believe me, I shall be at your side when you do so—can wait until tomorrow. As I said, we do not wish to spoil your birthday celebrations today."

Freddie retired to her room, leaving me to ponder what the Marquess of Kendrick would do when thrown out on his ear. His early departure was bound to cause repercussions among the guests. He would blame Lady Ariana for their banishment from Oatlands and his lost opportunity to court a duke's daughter. I hoped this would not cause Lord Kendrick to follow through on his threat to have the girl thrown into a madhouse.

What about Cecily Cranworth? Would she be forced by her brother to wed the aging Squire because she failed to wring a proposal from Lord Kendrick?

Whatever the outcome, I had a feeling it would not be good.

I did not know then just how bad it could be.

❦ 9 ❧

The ivory-painted square ballroom, seldom used at Oatlands, on this special evening blazed with candlelight. Old Dawe, bless him, had perhaps been overzealous in his desire to pay tribute to his beloved mistress on her birthday. Additional crystal chandeliers had been brought into the room, making the ivory walls glow and the numerous large, gilt-framed mirrors sparkle and glitter with light faceted by the crystals.

Colourful spring flowers perfumed one's senses, their number abundant as Freddie had endeavoured to bring nature indoors. The transition between nature and the indoors flowed smoothly, because the ballroom was on the ground floor. Four sets of double glass doors were open to the night air.

Mellifluous tones filled my ears from the quartet of musicians hired. The chatter of guests, whose number had swelled to close to one hundred, competed with the notes written by Bach. A royal guest arrived while we were enjoying drinks before dinner.

The Prince of Wales, son of King George III, brother-in-law to Freddie, and one of my closest friends, descended upon us with a group of his cronies to wish Freddie the joys of the day. He presented her with a diamond-and-sapphire bracelet during the lavish dinner we spent above two hours savouring.

The deep blue gems reminded me of a certain pair of accusing eyes. I made sure a servant took a plate upstairs to Chakkri. Lobster patties, his favourite and mine, had nestled among the delicacies. I imagined the cat pacing and muttering to himself until his dinner arrived. You know how particular the feline is about his food. He is even more discriminating than the Prince.

As for the Prince's decision to attend, I could only admire him for it. *Someone* had to represent the Royal Family on this occasion since the Duke of York chose to absent himself.

The Prince also showed a sensitivity to feeling that I approved when he left his "wife," Mrs. Fitzherbert, in London. While a good influence over Prinny, Mrs. Fitzherbert's true status can only be questioned, since the Prince married Caroline of Brunswick eleven years ago. As a whole, the Royal Family does not acknowledge Mrs. Fitzherbert. To have brought her to Oatlands would have put Freddie in an uncomfortable position.

In the ballroom with the assistance of Old Dawe, I presided over a table laden with a large bowl of a specially made liqueur. "Ladies and gentlemen, if I might interrupt the festivities for one moment."

Silence fell across the room. Guests moved closer to where I stood and waited expectantly. I smiled at Freddie and gestured for her to join me. She was a vision of regal beauty in the lace dress I had given her. I could hardly take my gaze from her. Yet, every time I did look at her, the situation regarding the missing letter niggled at the back of my brain, worrying me. I was beginning to feel like I was trapped at the bottom of a hill with a tremendous rock perched somewhere above me, ready to roll down the grass and crush me. Repeatedly, I had to push the matter of the letter from my thoughts.

Freddie at my side, I spoke. "Earlier today I began the preparation of a liqueur I formulated especially in the Royal Duchess's honour. Tonight we shall drink to her."

A murmur of expectation ran around the room. The Prince of Wales cleared his throat. "I say, Brummell, you've never made a particular concoction for me. I find I'm quite out of sorts with you."

I laughed and the rest of the company followed suit. Prinny loves food and drink, his excesses continually making themselves known in the form of his ever-increasing girth. The Prince joked, I knew, but nevertheless it would not do to give him even a hint of an insult. I am his friend and have been for many years. Indeed, if not for him, who knows if I would ever have reached the heights I have risen to in Society? But one must remember never to take a liberty with Prinny, however close the relationship.

"Why, your Royal Highness," I pronounced, "I am saving a secret recipe to prepare on your birthday in August. We shall call it Prince's Punch, eh?"

The Prince beamed at my words. "Capital idea. Mayhaps we won't need to wait until my birthday. Another occasion might arise which would require a special celebration."

A tremor of uneasiness fluttered across the room. Everyone knows Prinny burns with the desire to be named Regent. King George III's bouts with madness are common knowledge. However, every time Prinny tries to persuade Parliament to give him governing powers, his father's mental condition makes a remarkable turn for the better, frustrating his son's plans.

The fact that the Prince has those two wives might also be a factor in delaying a regency.

In any event, the Prince went on as if there had been no moment of awkwardness. "Meantime, tell us what you have prepared for Frederica."

Freddie smiled. About to name the ingredients of the liqueur, I heard the voice I least wanted to hear in all the world ring out over the gathering.

"Do explain in great detail, Brummell, in case we must give a report to our physicians later." Sylvester Fairingdale laughed at his own joke, but not many joined him. This spurred him on to say, "Go on, then, you are acting as host here tonight, it seems."

Freddie coloured at the insinuation that I took her husband's place.

This sly remark is typical of Fairingdale. The fop considers his own taste in clothing far superior to mine. He envies my position in Society and never misses an opportunity to try to discredit me in any way possible. The barb about my acting as host was particularly inflammatory.

I chose to ignore him, though I noticed to my chagrin that whispering began. I spoke to the gathering at large.

"I shall only give you an idea of the contents, as the exact ingredients will only be given to her Royal Highness. Brandy, lemons, currants, cloves, and a little cinnamon make it up," I said, while Old Dawe filled crystal glasses and passed them around. I waited until I caught Victor Tallarico's gaze. I looked at him deliberately and said, "I call it *Perfetto Amore,* because the Royal Duchess is such a gracious and generous lady. She is loved by all who know her."

"Hear! Hear!"

Tallarico's eyes burned with what I thought was a grudging admiration, but there was a hint of fury in their depths that I had chosen to name the drink in his language. He wore a dress sword, and I would wager at the moment he wished he could employ it on me.

I accepted two glasses from Old Dawe and handed one to Freddie. In ringing tones, I said, "To her Royal Highness, the Duchess of York, on her birthday. May there be many more birthdays to come so we might continue to enjoy the honour of her company."

"To her Royal Highness!" the company exclaimed.

"Thank you," Freddie said modestly.

Gloved hands held crystal glasses high in the air before the guests sipped the drink and then offered their compliments. But then, thoughts of the missing letter—and the Duke of York—intruded on my happiness. I took a large swallow of the liqueur.

"Delicious," the Prince declared. "I'll have another glass, then lead Frederica out for the first dance."

Curious glances slid my way. My face remained impassive while I sipped my drink. Mentally I prayed a sudden, ferocious attack of the gout would strike Prinny.

Yes, I wanted to be the first to dance with her. You probably suspected that. But, you are correct. It is not my place to do so. The Prince is the highest-ranking gentleman in the room, and Freddie's brother-in-law. He holds the right to the first dance.

I extended my glass to Old Dawe, who refilled it with what I interpreted as a sympathetic look.

The music began and Prinny took Freddie from my side. I was about to look for a partner when I was distracted.

"This liqueur is superb, Brummell." Lord Petersham, whom I have known for ages, sauntered up with his constant companion, Lord Munro. Petersham is tall, dark-haired and angular. Munro is smaller, with thin blond hair. The two frequently quarrel, but cannot remain apart. Last autumn, when Bow Street suspected Lord Petersham of murder and Lord Munro appeared to have supplied Bow Street with damaging evidence against the viscount, their break seemed permanent. However, their bond is strong, and they resolved their differences last Christmas.

"Good evening, Petersham, Munro," I said.

Lord Munro gave me a curt nod. He does not like me. Too bad for him, really.

I addressed the viscount. "Petersham, I must thank you for the use of Diggie this evening. His assistance in helping me dress is appreciated."

Petersham favoured me with his winning smile. "Robinson won't be happy. Say, your hair looks different. Diggie responsible for that?"

"Yes, I have let it grow. Diggie suggested the Apollo style."

"Are you going to continue wearing it like that?" Petersham asked.

"I might."

"O-ho, you're risking Robinson's wrath!"

"I cannot see this concerns us, Charles," Lord Munro said to Petersham, his gaze frosty.

Petersham looked uncomfortable, but quickly rallied. He is too lazy to remain upset for long. "By the way, what's the news on this highwayman everyone's talking about? Stole your things, did he?"

"Yes. Apparently he has struck in the county several times over the past years," I informed him.

"Egad, what if the highwayman had attacked our coach, Harold," Petersham said to Munro. "Why, I've got a dozen of my best snuff boxes with me. What if the blackguard had taken them?"

Lord Munro made soothing noises, then looked at me as if I were responsible for upsetting Petersham.

"I am certain the person responsible will be caught in time," I said reassuringly, though I felt far from certain that Squire Oxberry would help. What had he done so far?

Sylvester Fairingdale strode up. "Tsk tsk, Brummell. Had some of your clothing pilfered, did you? How will you go on without your additional garments—No, no, I've got the answer! It won't matter one whit that some of your things were stolen. All of your costumes look the same. You can wear the same one every day and no one will be the wiser."

I raised my quizzing glass and slowly studied Fairingdale's attire through it. Tonight he was all puce and chartreuse. Ugh! If Fairingdale were a good man, I would feel compelled to offer some discreet advice. Since he is a scheming care-for-nobody, altruistic thoughts did not enter my head. "Ah, but Fairingdale, I do not wear *costumes,* as *some* do. I wear simple clothing, cut to perfection."

Fairingdale possesses an elongated neck. That combined with the height of his neckcloth causes him to look down his nose at those around him, me in particular. "Simple?" He drawled the word. "That lace dress you gave the Duke of York's wife is anything but simple, I should say. Even you must agree."

Damn and blast! Tallarico had been talking. How else did Fairingdale know I had given Freddie that dress? Who knew what rumours about the Royal Duchess and me were, at this very moment, flying about the room?

And if the gossipmongers were hard at work over the dress, what would happen if they learned the contents of the missing letter? I looked at Freddie, dancing with the Prince, and felt a wave of dread.

❧ 10 ❧

Munro drew in a sharp breath. "You gave the Royal Duchess that dress, Brummell?"

Petersham pulled a gold initialled snuff box from his pocket and took a pinch, appearing bored.

Fairingdale looked smug.

I levelled the fop with a pitying expression. "When one is the Arbiter of Fashion, one's talent for design is often appreciated by royalty. Such was also the case when I helped the Prince of Wales plan uniforms for the Tenth Light Dragoons. But, do not worry, you could not be expected to know that, Fairingdale."

"Fie! People do look to me for style!" His face turned the colour of his puce coat. His eyes blazed with anger. "I'll take you down from your exalted post, wait and see. You are nothing more than the son of a secretary."

"Secretary and confidential advisor to the late Lord North, a former Prime Minister of England, to be precise," I replied in a blasé tone. "A highly respected and coveted position."

"Mushroom," Fairingdale spat.

Mushroom, you know, is slang for an upstart, someone above his station in life.

I frowned. "Were there? I do not recall seeing any on the dinner table, and I do delight in them, especially in wine sauce."

Petersham snickered. Munro looked thoughtful.

Fairingdale glared down the considerable length of his nose, then turned on his heel and minced away.

"I cannot think why the Royal Duchess invited him," I remarked.

"I don't think she could have, Brummell," Petersham said. "He came along with Lord Wrayburn. Fairingdale's still living at Wrayburn House, don't you know."

"No, I did not. I have not met Lord Wrayburn. Which is he?"

Petersham indicated a tall, thin man, the epitome of an Englishman, a bit pinched-looking. He was past his fortieth year with dark blond hair. He stood conversing with Lady Crecy, a woman anxious to marry off her daughter, Lady Penelope.

My mistake was looking their way. Lady Crecy immediately perceived my gaze and waved a pudgy hand in the air, commanding me to join her. "Excuse me, Petersham, Munro," I said.

Arriving at her side, I bowed and was greeted with much enthusiasm and a bouncing of Lady Crecy's too-tight grey curls. "Oh, Mr. Brummell, how delightful to see you! Here, Penelope, make a curtsey to Mr. Brummell, what can you be thinking? Do not mind her, my dear man, she is awed at seeing you again! She remembers well when you danced with her last autumn at my little party, do you not, Penelope?"

Before Lady Penelope could answer, her mother's tongue ran on wheels. "Have you met dear Lord Wrayburn, Mr. Brummell? Of course you remember all that unpleasantness surrounding his mother's death last year.

Such a scandalous crime. But here he is today quite re-covered," Lady Crecy pronounced with a fond smile.

I bowed and addressed Lady Penelope. "I am happy to see you looking well, my lady. Are you enjoying the Season?" This would be Lady Penelope's third Season. Her first two had been marred by her propensity to sniffle. I had passed along the name of a good doctor, and evidently her ailment had been brought under control, for she appeared in fine health.

"I am indeed, Mr. Brummell," she answered, smiling at me with a new confidence. With her expressive grey eyes and enticing dowry, I felt sure that this would be the Season she would find a mate.

I made Lord Wrayburn a bow. "Your lordship, may I offer my condolences on the death of your mother?"

"Thank you, Mr. Brummell. It is a pleasure to meet you. As you might be aware, I have spent most of my life away from England," he said.

His mother, you know.

"But he is home to stay now," Lady Crecy crooned.

As I exchanged pleasantries—when I could, since Lady Crecy dominated the conversation—I noticed the admiration in Lord Wrayburn's eyes when he looked at Lady Penelope. His regard seemed returned. As the next dance began, the couple headed for the floor under the shining approval of Lady Crecy.

While she watched them, I was able to make my escape. I strolled the perimeter of the room, watching the dancers and making observations. I wished to keep an eye on Lord Kendrick and his nimble-fingered cousin, Lady Ariana. He bothered me. She saddened me.

Again that one particular snippet of the conversation I had overheard between the two played in my mind. Lady Ariana had questioned her cousin as to how what *she* did—meaning her taking things—was different from what *he* was doing.

After seeing Freddie dancing with the Duke of Derehurst, I finally located Lord Kendrick at the edge of a
group of admirers surrounding the Duke of Derehurst's
stately daughter, Lady Deidre. She held court amongst her
swains with great ease, flirting with each one equally so
that no one would think himself ahead. I presumed that
Freddie had been forced into giving the introduction she
had wanted to avoid. Worse, I could see no way to talk
to him privately while he was busy pursuing his prey,
Lady Deidre.

Speaking of introductions, I had been presented to Cecily and Roger Cranworth just before dinner. To meet the
people whose voices I had overheard the night before was
intriguing.

To my regret, I have known men of Roger Cranworth's
type in the past. A dashing, reckless sort, he would not
be above using his dark good looks to connive and
scheme. Always on the watch for a way to gain money
without much effort, he was a gamester. And he bullied
his sister mercilessly.

Cecily Cranworth had rich dark hair like her brother's,
but unlike him she was attractive in a pretty, wholesome
way. Her big brown eyes nervously watched for her
brother's signals. His duty was to provide her with a way
to find a suitable husband, but his refusal to give her a
Season in London spoke volumes about his character.

Roger saw Cecily smiling shyly at a plainly dressed
man who approached her where she sat on a chair against
the wall. Roger broke from a group of young gentlemen
and quickly made his way to his sister's side. The plainly
dressed man saw him coming and reversed his direction.
The smile faded from Miss Cranworth's face to be replaced by a look of apprehension. Roger Cranworth spoke
in his sister's ear. A moment later, she got up and moved
toward Lord Kendrick, no doubt on her brother's orders.

Fingering my watch chain, I wondered again what was

going to happen when Roger finally realised his sister had
no chance with the puffed-up Marquess of Kendrick.

The dance ended and there was a pause in the music.
Here was my opportunity to dance with Freddie. I reached
her just as Signor Tallarico did. "Sorry, Tallarico, but the
Royal Duchess has already promised this dance to me."

He let out a theatrical sigh and put his hand to the hilt
of his sword. "Remember I told you, Duchess, that I
would impale myself on my sword if you did not save
two dances for me."

"You shall have the next, Signor," Freddie said, turning
to me.

"Victor, call me Victor," he beseeched.

I took her arm and led her into the dance before she
could reply.

"Are you having fun, Freddie?" I asked.

"Oh yes, George, dear. Your liqueur and all the champagne has made me quite giddy."

We could only have brief exchanges, as the steps of
the dance parted us frequently. Her face glowed with happiness. I found my ability to enjoy her pleasure vastly
diminished by thoughts of the missing letter. I could not
let her see my distress, though.

"Who is that plainly dressed man standing talking with
Old Dawe?" I asked when we came together again.

Freddie looked in the direction I indicated. "Doctor
Curtis Wendell. Recall I told you he is the county physician who also helps look after my animals."

"I remember." The dance separated us again.

Ah, Doctor Wendell must be the one Roger Cranworth
deemed unworthy for his sister. From the look in Miss
Cranworth's eyes when the doctor had been about to sit
with her, I judged the admiration she held for him high.
Surely he was to be desired over Lord Kendrick or the
vulgar and elderly Squire Oxberry. The latter had not
joined the dancing party, declaring it was well past the

time he normally retired in the evenings. Poor Miss Cranworth.

The dance went on for another quarter hour. I found myself wishing Freddie and I were alone. The dance, like life, kept parting us.

On one such occasion, out of the corner of my eye I saw Lord Kendrick take Cecily Cranworth through the open doorway leading outside. Here was a surprise. I thought he entertained no further thoughts of the title-less girl.

At that moment, the music came to an end. Freddie was once more across from me. "What is it, George? You are frowning."

"Lord Kendrick has taken Miss Cranworth from the ballroom. Miss Cranworth must be thinking this is her chance to secure Lord Kendrick's promise of marriage. From what I heard him say, she is sure to fail. Where is her brother?"

Freddie glanced about. "He is over there with Signor Tallarico and Lady Ariana."

The Italian saw Freddie's gaze and swiftly crossed the room, seeing his opportunity to claim his dance. Roger Cranworth remained with Lady Ariana, unconcerned about his sister. There was a definite look of admiration in Lady Ariana's eye as she spoke with Roger Cranworth. Certainly she appeared more animated in his presence than I had ever seen her.

"George, what should we do?" Freddie asked before Tallarico reached us. "Miss Cranworth's reputation will be ruined if she stays alone in the marquess's company much longer."

"I shall find her and be sure of her safety. Stay here."

Tallarico was only too happy to replace me at Freddie's side.

My progress toward the doors to the gardens was slow. People milled about, everyone seeming to want to greet

me. I maintained my usual aplomb and tried to look un-
hurried. To call attention to Miss Cranworth's predicament would only bring scandal on the girl's head. I
persevered in my quest to reach her, however. I could not
like the idea of her being alone with Lord Kendrick after
what I had seen between him and Lady Ariana earlier.

At last I was through the door and out into the night.
Cautiously, I walked across the neatly cropped grass and
looked around. If the two were engaged in a civil conversation, I would quietly withdraw.

The cry I heard coming from the direction of a large
pine tree was far from civil and not one of delight. I
quickened my steps to meet a disgraceful sight. Lord Kendrick held Miss Cranworth in a cruel grip, one arm linked
around her waist, the other capturing her wrists in front
of his chest. His lips crushed hers in a brutal kiss. She
averted her face from him, beseeching him to stop.

"Miss Cranworth," I said in a loud voice. That was all
I needed to do to break Lord Kendrick's hold on her. He
leaned back and lounged against the tree as if nothing had
happened. Miss Cranworth staggered. I said, "I believe
you promised me this dance, Miss Cranworth."

She was overcome and near to fainting. I rushed forward and caught her in my arms. She moaned and stared,
eyes wide, at Lord Kendrick.

"How dare you treat a lady thus?" I demanded, glaring
at the marquess and dropping any pretense of a chance
encounter.

Lord Kendrick smirked. "The chit wants to marry me,
if you must know. I was only giving her a taste of wedded
life."

"If that is your idea of lovemaking, I pity any lady
unfortunate enough to marry you," I told him.

All at once, Miss Cranworth found her strength. She
pulled herself from my arms and confronted her attacker.

"You may have the title of a noble lord now, Connell, but you have no honour!"

Lord Kendrick laughed at her. "Dear me, what a tigress."

Miss Cranworth's fear had changed to a raging anger. "I shall never marry you, Connell, *never,* no matter what!" she said in a furious voice. "I would rather die or see you dead first!"

The marquess's laughter rang out in the night air. He flicked his fingers at her in a dismissive gesture, then strolled in the direction of the ballroom.

Miss Cranworth's eyes blazed with hatred, her fists curled at her side.

"Take care not to find yourself alone with the marquess again, Miss Cranworth," I advised.

"Oh, I shall. Thank you for coming to my rescue, though, Mr. Brummell," she replied.

Then Doctor Wendell came hurrying out of the ballroom, looking left and right. With a glad cry, she rushed into his caring arms, calling out, "Curtis!"

Finding my presence unnecessary, I rejoined the party. Despite imbibing several glasses of champagne, I was preoccupied with the nasty scene I had witnessed. I would be happy to see the back of Lord Kendrick despite the fact I still had not been able to question him regarding the highwayman. I asked myself what he would be willing to tell me anyway. Nothing.

I saw Roger Cranworth take himself from the ballroom. No doubt he finally noted his sister's prolonged absence. I shuddered to think of what he would say when he found her with Doctor Wendell instead of the marquess.

Lord Kendrick remained a part of Lady Deidre's court throughout the evening. The duke's daughter bestowed little attention on the marquess, but I did observe her shrewd gaze linger on him appraisingly more than once.

In the small hours of the morning, the party broke up.

Ignoring Sylvester Fairingdale's inquiring look, I escorted Freddie upstairs. I was about to tell her what had occurred between Lord Kendrick and Miss Cranworth, but what happened next made my thoughts race in another direction.

When we reached her private sitting room, Freddie quietly opened the door. "It was a pleasant night, was it not, George?" She crossed into the room, with me following.

She turned and shut the door behind me. A branch of candles served as the only light in the room. We were alone. Not even a dog in sight.

I moved in front of her, taking her hands in mine. "You deserve to enjoy yourself, especially on your birthday."

"Did I deserve this?" she asked, removing her hands from mine and pulling a ribbon attached to a fan from her wrist. She opened the fan to its fullest. The orange silk sported a painted likeness of Sylvester Fairingdale.

Freddie's eyes glowed with amusement as they met mine.

"He had the nerve to give you that atrocity?" I asked.

"You do not think I shall find it useful?" she teased.

"Only if you want to frighten someone."

She tossed it onto a nearby chair. We laughed together, the excitement of the party and all the champagne making us lighthearted.

Abruptly, the atmosphere in the room changed. I took a step closer to her, holding her gaze. "Happy Birthday, my princess," I whispered. I reached out and caressed a curl lying against the lace of her dress.

"It has been happy with you here, dearest," she whispered back.

Her lips were but inches from mine, yet they might have been miles away. I could not kiss her. It would not be right. Married women took lovers, true, but not women of Freddie's integrity.

Yet, I could not bring myself to move away.

She is the Duke of York's wife, I reminded myself sternly, never taking my gaze from her blue eyes.

Then, with one beringed hand, she reached up and touched a lock of my hair resting on my starched cravat. "You have allowed your hair to grow. I like it this way."

"In that case, I shall keep the style. For you."

Her hand moved from my hair to my cheek. She stroked the side of my face.

All the while a voice in my brain—I expect it was my conscience—screamed that I must not kiss her.

She closed her eyes.

Well, I had meant to behave.

I bent down and kissed her forehead. I intended just one more small kiss on her cheek—I give you my word!—but somehow or another in a devilish mix-up at the last moment, she turned her head in the direction of my mouth.

My lips pressed against hers, gently at first, then I covered her mouth with mine.

But not for more than three seconds strung together.

The door connecting the sitting room with Freddie's bedchamber swung noisily open. Freddie and I drew apart.

Ulga with her bag of knitting stood in the doorway.

❖ 11 ❖

The next day, my arms were around Freddie again, but this time it was outdoors, in full view of the guests. In the back garden of the house, tables covered in white cloths had been laid out with food and drink served by liveried footmen. This afternoon people could enjoy the still warm weather while eating and gossiping. Two of everyone's favourite activities.

A short way down on the lawn, an archery range had been set up. Here was where I held Freddie close to me. I had promised her last autumn that I would teach her the finer points of the sport. I am a man of my word no matter how difficult the task. I breathed in Freddie's rose scent.

Three circular targets had been placed at a distance. Shooting at the first target were Doctor Wendell and Cecily Cranworth. That they enjoyed each other's company was obvious to all. Roger Cranworth was absent.

Freddie and I aimed at the second target. At the third, Signor Tallarico flirted with Lady Penelope under the unhappy gaze of Lord Wrayburn, and the calculating scrutiny of her mother, Lady Crecy.

My attentions were on Freddie. "Here," I said near her ear, remembering the taste of her lips. "Pull the arrow back while aligning it with the target."

"George, I must speak with you," she said, holding the arrow taut.

Damn.

"I expect I owe you an apology for my behaviour last night, Freddie."

She let the arrow fly. It fell short of the target. "Not about that," she said, her eyes downcast. "About Lord Kendrick."

Relieved, I selected another arrow from the case. "As soon as we can, we shall tell him he must leave Oatlands."

She looked at me. "George, I have already spoken with the marquess."

"But we were to do so together," I said, surprised. "I wanted to be by your side in case you needed assistance."

Freddie gazed off into the distance. "I would have appreciated your support. I had planned to make arrangements with you this morning at breakfast, but you did not come downstairs. Later, before the picnic began, I inquired after you. Old Dawe said you were still in your chamber."

"I am sorry. I slept longer than I had intended." The truth was, I had spent another night drinking myself into oblivion. Ulga's look of shock and disapproval upon witnessing the tender scene between Freddie and me acted like a hammer of guilt over my head. To cease its pounding, I resorted to an excellent smuggled French brandy. The unavoidable result was that I had traded the pounding hammer of guilt for the pounding hammer of a headache brought on by excessive drink.

Then too, visions of the blue velvet book and the missing letter kept popping into my aching head. If that letter were to fall into the wrong hands, Freddie's lips would never utter my name again, no less ever touch mine again.

I replaced the arrow in its case. "Did Lord Kendrick give you any trouble? Shall I speak to him? I do not see him outside, but I can find him."

"He has already departed Oatlands," she told me regally.

"What happened?"

She drew a deep breath. "After breakfast, I went to confer with Old Dawe regarding the picnic. In the hall, I saw Lord Kendrick enter the drawing room. I hesitated, then followed him. He was alone. I told him that he must leave Oatlands and why. It was not a comfortable scene."

"Why did you not wait for me, Freddie?"

"I rely on you too much, George," she said firmly.

So, she too felt guilty over last evening's kiss. "I am always at your service, your Royal Highness. You must never doubt that I have only your happiness at heart."

She smiled at me then. "Thank you, dear."

I relaxed. "What did Lord Kendrick say when you told him?"

"He was ugly about the matter, calling me irrational. But he agreed to leave and take Lady Ariana with him."

"Good. Then he is gone."

"There is more," she said, a troubled expression on her face.

"More? He did not touch you or hurt you in any way, did he? If so, by God I shall call him out—"

"No, no, George, there is no need to look fierce. After my meeting with Lord Kendrick, I retired to my chamber for a few minutes to compose myself. Something disturbing happened there as well, but I shall tell you about it in a moment. At any rate, when I returned downstairs, I heard Lord Kendrick's voice coming from the drawing room. He was still in there, with the doors partially closed. What caught my attention was that he was quarrelling with Roger Cranworth."

"I thought they were friends. Wait, were they arguing about Cecily Cranworth?"

Freddie nodded. "Yes. Lord Kendrick declared that nothing could induce him to marry Cecily. Then he said something about how if Roger put up a fuss, or went against him in any matter, that he would go to Squire Oxberry as well and tell him the way of things."

"The way of things? What way of things? And why would Roger tell Squire Oxberry that Lord Kendrick will not marry his sister? He cannot be thinking of a breach of promise suit?"

"I do not know. I surmised that was what Lord Kendrick meant. Roger became quite agitated and muttered what I think were threats. I could not hear clearly. Then I heard Lord Kendrick say, 'Why should I?' and Roger responded with 'Come to my room and I'll show you.' I sensed they were about to exit the very door near where I was standing, so I came directly outside."

"How interesting," I said. "There is something more going on, and I confess I am curious to learn what the two are about. Whatever it is, though, I want it to happen away from Oatlands."

"I agree. I am very relieved that Lord Kendrick and his cousin have gone."

"Freddie, you said that while you were in your chamber something happened that disturbed you. What was it?"

She let out a sigh. "Even though Lord Kendrick and Lady Ariana are gone, they have left behind another problem. Ulga told me she cannot find the antique Roman hair ornaments Signor Tallarico gave me for my birthday. She said she would continue looking for them, but, George, I feel perhaps Lady Ariana might have . . ." Freddie's voice trailed off, but I knew what she was thinking. "I just hope that Signor Tallarico does not ask me to wear them."

"Somehow I doubt you will escape that fate," I said dryly.

A breeze blew a strand of Freddie's hair across her face. She reached up to confine the lock. "His flirtations are harmless, George. I cannot lie to him, yet how am I to tell him that Lady Ariana—"

Freddie's voice broke on a gasp. One hand flew to cover her mouth. Her gaze focused behind me, toward the house.

I turned to see the cause of what had startled her and received a shock myself. For there, strolling out the garden door of Oatlands seemingly without a care in the world were Lord Kendrick and Lady Ariana.

Lady Ariana drifted over to Cecily Cranworth and Doctor Wendell. Cecily gave her friend a hug and commenced instructing Lady Ariana on how to hold the bow and arrow. I noticed Miss Cranworth ignored the marquess, who began walking down the side of the house. His objective appeared to be a shady oak tree where Lady Deidre sat surrounded by admirers.

"George, why has he not gone? How dare he remain after I told him to leave? How dare he?" Freddie questioned, infuriated at Lord Kendrick's defiance.

Before I could answer, the next few seconds threw all of us into turmoil.

With the help of Doctor Wendell and Cecily, Lady Ariana managed to shoot an arrow toward her target. Unfortunately, the arrow went off its mark—to the shoulder of Lord Kendrick. The marquess fell to the ground.

Chaos ensued as ladies screamed and fainted. Doctor Wendell rushed to the marquess's side. Freddie broke away from me to follow him.

I turned my steps to go with her, when I heard Miss Cranworth call my name. "Mr. Brummell, Mr. Brummell, please help me!"

I swung to my left to see her trying to manage an hysterical Lady Ariana. Alternately babbling incoherently and crying out Lord Kendrick's name, Lady Ariana worked herself into a fit. She dropped to her knees, her hands flailing.

Stepping over to assist her, I asked Miss Cranworth if she had a vinaigrette. While she retrieved one from her reticule, I helped Lady Ariana to her feet and placed a bracing arm around her thin shoulders.

"Do but look, Lady Ariana. Your cousin has merely fallen," I said, trying to reassure her. "I believe the arrow just nicked him. The unexpectedness of the blow must have knocked him down."

"My thoughts are bad!" Lady Ariana wailed. "I have killed him."

My gaze met Miss Cranworth's over Lady Ariana's head.

"No, my lady, you have merely killed *his coat*. See for yourself," I insisted.

"Mr. Brummell is correct," Miss Cranworth concurred while waving the vinaigrette under Lady Ariana's nose.

"No more, no more," Lady Ariana protested, coughing, and Miss Cranworth returned the vinaigrette to her reticule. "They are taking him into the house. He must be hurt!"

"Now use your sense, Lady Ariana," I said in a cajoling tone. "The Royal Duchess is *walking* with Lord Kendrick into the house. If he were mortally wounded, would he be able to walk? Here, Doctor Wendell comes to us. Doctor! Tell us of Lord Kendrick's condition."

The steadfast doctor waved his hand. "No cause for alarm. The arrow but grazed his right shoulder. It did not even break the skin. He'll have nothing more than a bruise. The Royal Duchess took him into the house where he'll change his shirt and coat, and be back with us in a trice."

Lady Ariana sobbed. I took my arm from about her,

confident she could stand on her own, and offered her my handkerchief.

At that moment, Signor Tallarico consigned Lady Penelope to Lord Wrayburn and appeared at our side. He took the handkerchief from my hand and dried Lady Ariana's tears himself, joking and teasing her the whole time as one would treat a girl of ten summers. An effective stratagem, for she soon managed a smile for him. Under the Italian's care, she walked away to the refreshment tables.

I wanted to see that Freddie was all right, but Doctor Wendell spoke before I could go. "In truth, I'm much more concerned about Lady Ariana than I am Lord Kendrick. Cecily, I hope you don't mind me being frank in front of Mr. Brummell."

She shook her head. "No, Mr. Brummell proved himself a friend last night when Connell—"

"Shh, you don't need to remember that villain's actions." The doctor pressed Miss Cranworth's hand. Then he said, "Lady Ariana has led a terrible life, if what one hears is to be believed, Mr. Brummell. Based on her behaviour, I'd say the rumours are true. Lord Kendrick neglects his duty where Lady Ariana is concerned."

"I wish there was something I could do for her," Miss Cranworth lamented. "I always thought that I would be able to if I—if I married Connell. Ariana would live with me. I would take care of her. Indeed, I love her as a sister. But now I am not to . . ."

Doctor Wendell tensed. "But now you are not to wed Lord Kendrick."

Miss Cranworth smiled at him shyly. "No."

The doctor relaxed and returned her smile.

"What can I do to help Lady Ariana?" I asked.

"Nothing more that I can think of at the moment, Mr. Brummell. If I may be so bold as to suggest, that your calm control would do her Royal Highness's guests the most good now. If you were to circulate amongst them and reassure them all is well."

"Yes, that is the very thing, Doctor." I pulled a silver card case out. "Here is my direction in London, if you should ever need me."

I left them and wandered about talking with people as Doctor Wendell had advised. The doctor was a man to be admired. He had kept a cool head and obviously cared for not only Miss Cranworth and Lady Ariana, but also Freddie. No doubt the years of helping look after her pets resulted in his loyalty.

His suggestion that I show by example that there was no need for distress was sound. Though it was not what I wanted to do. What I wanted was to find Freddie. I did not like the idea that she was once again forced into the marquess's company. There might be another confrontation.

Telling myself that Freddie would more likely return outdoors after turning Lord Kendrick over to a servant rather than enter into a debate with him alone—I would give her ten minutes before going after her—I bowed and made myself agreeable to the Duke of Derehurst and his daughter, Lady Deidre.

I cannot tell you the depth of my astonishment when, about five minutes later, Freddie and Lord Kendrick walked our way.

I had never seen Freddie so white in all the years I have known her. Her face was completely bloodless.

Lord Kendrick had changed his coat. He waved gaily at Lady Ariana and Signor Tallarico before joining us. With his perpetual smirk in place, Lord Kendrick gazed at me with a triumphant air about him.

Freddie addressed Lady Deidre. "All is well; however, Lord Kendrick has suffered a brush with death. You must promise to dance with him tonight, Lady Deidre. He is a brave man and would make you a fine partner."

I stood mute, staring at Freddie, hardly trusting my ears. What the devil had happened to make her say such a thing?

His Grace, the Duke of Derehurst, seemed almost as surprised. "Well, Deidre, if Lord Kendrick has received so high a recommendation by the Royal Duchess, I say one dance with the marquess is in order."

Lady Deidre looked appraisingly at Lord Kendrick. "I shall save you the first contra-danse." She plied her fan. "I have not seen you in London yet this Season, my lord. Will we have the pleasure of your company in Town soon?"

What the marquess answered to this query, I could not tell you. My attention was solely on Freddie. She stood as if turned into a marble statue. I could bear it no more. "Excuse us, please," I said, executing a bow and leading Freddie away. She did not protest the action, indeed, she complied in silence.

People were all around us, sipping drinks, strolling, and undoubtedly talking about Lady Ariana's unfortunate mishap.

I guided Freddie toward an unoccupied area of the refreshment table. "What happened? What made you say those things to the duke? Freddie? Freddie, what is it?" I whispered in growing alarm. I placed my hand on her arm, pressing it gently, willing her to speak.

She looked down at my hand and then up at me. "Please remove your hand from my person."

I felt as though she had struck me. Speechless, I obeyed the command at once.

Holding herself in rigid control, her Royal Highness would not look at me. Instead, she gazed at a point beyond my head. "Before he went upstairs to change his coat, Lord Kendrick demanded to see me in private. I would not have agreed, except that he began to recite these words to me: 'My dearest George, You cannot know the disorder of my thoughts as I pen these lines. Friends have written me about my husband's behaviour of late, though their words can only confirm what I already know. The Duke has formed a strong attachment this time.' "

❧ 12 ❧

Everything around Freddie and me remained normal; the guests nibbled food and chatted, players aimed at the archery targets, birds sang in the aviary, dogs begged for treats at the food tables. Yet, for a moment I heard nothing and saw nothing. I was numb with shock.

Freddie spoke again, her voice flat. "Lord Kendrick took me aside. He stated that he is in possession of that letter I wrote you, George. It is the one I wrote when my husband set up Mrs. Clarke as his mistress, and I was so very distressed—"

"I know the one," I managed to get out. The numbness began to leave my body. In its place, a profound self-loathing—what a detestable creature I was for keeping that letter!—along with a blazing rage at the marquess began to overtake me.

Freddie's voice, now grim, went on despite my silence. "Lord Kendrick said that unless I wanted him to send the letter anonymously to the *Morning Post,* I would do exactly as he said. At present, he is not blackmailing me for money. His father left a fortune. Rather he wants me to help him gain respect with the highest members of Society. Specifically the Duke of Derehurst and his daughter, Lady Deidre. Lord Kendrick desires her to be his wife, and he knows the duke holds my opinion in high esteem."

Without a conscious decision to do so, I turned my head in the direction of Lord Kendrick. He was walking away from the duke and Lady Deidre toward the Cranworths—Roger had finally appeared at the picnic—and Lady Ariana. Lord Kendrick's smirk was visible even from a distance.

Of a sudden, every nuance of my famous self-control deserted me. I left Freddie without saying a word and strode rapidly across the grass.

Before he could reach the others, I grabbed Lord Kendrick by the lapels of his coat. "You vulgar coward," I ground out. "Give me that letter or I shall deliver you to your Maker, I promise you."

Lord Kendrick's eyes reflected panic. Then he rallied. "I am not the only one who knows about the letter. Killing me will only result in my partner revealing all. The Royal Duchess will be the subject of a roaring scandal, and you will be hanged for murder."

"Better they take away my life than ruin my or the Royal Duchess's character. You are the highwayman, or you have employed someone to do your dirty work. Yes, that is it. You just said you had a partner. Not uncommon for the black sheep of the family to take on such an occupation."

"I'll not be involved with the robberies any longer," the marquess said. "I'll be too busy having you and the pretty little Duchess dancing on a string for me."

Fury overcame me. "By God, I shall find a way to stop you from hurting her, even if it does cost me my life."

"Heigh-ho, what's going on here?" the oily voice of Sylvester Fairingdale interrupted. His sharp gaze rested on the marquess, then my hands on Lord Kendrick's coat.

The fop acted as a catalyst to bring me to my senses. I looked about me at the curious glances directed my way. Lady Crecy had one hand to her ample bosom. Lady Penelope appeared taken aback. Tallarico reached inside his coat, probably to retrieve the jewel-handled dagger I know he keeps there. Doctor Wendell's jaw dropped.

For once, I was somewhat grateful for Fairingdale's tendency to meddle his way into my life. God knows what I might have done to Lord Kendrick had Fairingdale not appeared when he had.

I forced my muscles to relax, and my expression to reflect concern. My hands smoothed the lapels of Lord Kendrick's coat. "The marquess's valet had not adjusted the shoulders of his coat properly when Lord Kendrick changed clothes. I was just tugging the coat into place, helping him achieve the proper appearance."

Lord Kendrick smiled—meaning his smirk twisted a bit—at the company.

The others seemed to accept this explanation and returned to their own pursuits. All except Fairingdale.

"Is that so?" the fop said, clearly not believing a word I had spoken.

"Yes, it most certainly is," Lord Kendrick answered. "Brummell and I have become the best of friends. In fact, he will be putting my name up for membership at White's Club for gentlemen when we return to London."

I should sooner put his severed head up on a stake at the crossroads, but with every ounce of control I could muster I held my tongue and my temper in check.

"We will talk again later," I told Lord Kendrick.

"Indeed we shall," he replied in a superior tone.

I walked back toward the refreshment table, my mind racing. A plan to search Lord Kendrick's room for the letter immediately presented itself in my brain. Now would be an excellent time, while he was outside. Although his valet might be in his master's chamber.

First I wanted to say a few words to Freddie, namely words of abject apology, and give her my strongest assurance that I would get the letter back.

However, when I reached the long end of the refreshment table where we had been standing, she was gone. A wigged footman behind the table caught my attention. "I beg your pardon, sir, but her Royal Highness asked me to deliver a message to you."

"Yes, go on."

"Mr. Fishe came to her, asking for her assistance with the Royal Duchess's dog Phanor." The footman shifted, looking uncomfortable. "Her Royal Highness instructed me to tell you that she would be unavailable to see you until dinner this evening, sir. She asked that you respect her wishes."

"Thank you," I said, feeling as if I had been handed a one-way ticket on the Royal Mail-Coach to Hell. "Would you be good enough to pour me a glass of that Chambertin wine?"

Intent on searching Lord Kendrick's room, I went into the house and sent a footman for Old Dawe. The elderly retainer appeared in the hall and bowed. "What can I do for you, Mr. Brummell?"

I ran a hand through my hair, not caring about its perfect arrangement. "Which is Lord Kendrick's bedchamber?"

Old Dawe appeared undisturbed by the question. "His is three doors down on the left from yours, sir."

"Has he a valet with him?"

"Yes, sir. Thompson, who served the old marquess, now serves Lord Kendrick."

"Is Thompson, mayhaps, in the kitchens or the pantry just now?"

Old Dawe shook his head. "No, sir. I do not believe he has left the marquess's room since he helped him change his coat earlier."

"Did Thompson come down to supper with the servants last evening?"

"No, sir. A maid brought him his meal on a tray."

"Thank you."

Climbing the stairs, I decided there was no easy way I could search the marquess's room while his valet was about. I would have to find a way to divert the man. Quickly.

I reached my bedchamber, flung open the door, and found a possible co-conspirator; Robinson had returned from London.

Robinson dropped the clean towel he was about to drape over the washstand. "Sir! What has happened to your hair?"

"What? Oh, I think I must have run a hand through it. This has been a trying day." Good God, was that an understatement.

"No, sir, I mean, I knew it should have been trimmed before I left, but there was no time. Now you have got it in an entirely different style." Robinson's eyes narrowed. "Did Mr. Digwood do that?"

I closed my eyes for a moment. *You have allowed your hair to grow. I like it this way.*

Freddie. Freddie was angry with me with very good reason. Both our reputations were in jeopardy.

In that case, I shall keep the style. For you.

I must get that letter back. I passed a hand over my brow.

"Sir?" Robinson said, coming to stand next to me. "Are you quite well?"

Two chairs stood near the empty fireplace. I angled one toward the other. "Sit down, Robinson."

The valet did as he was told, his eyes bright with curiosity and, I think, concern for my well-being.

His expression changed when I lowered myself to the chair and a bundle of cat fur named Chakkri jumped into my lap. "Reow," the feline said, reaching up a paw to my chin.

"Good afternoon, old boy. Well, that is not precisely true, by God." The cat settled down, content to have me stroke his fawn-coloured back as was only his due in life.

Robinson sat, his lips pursed. He was no doubt gauging the number of cat hairs he would be forced to remove from my clothing.

"Look here, Robinson, I am in a bit of a fix. When the highwayman stole our valises, he got away with my blue velvet book. You know the one I mean?"

"Yes, I do, sir," Robinson replied, distracted from Chakkri by the question. "I have seen you placing sketches and such in it."

"That is correct," I agreed, wondering how much to tell him. I did not want to widen the number of people who were aware of the nature of the letter by even one. And that included my trusted valet, who liked to imbibe spirits and chatter at The Butler's Tankard in London. "Recollect that I was very upset when our things were stolen. The true reason was that I had placed a certain letter in the book for safekeeping. A letter which could prove, er, embarrassing if it fell into the wrong hands."

"Reow!" Chakkri shrieked. The cat stood up in my lap, his tail bristling. I stroked him from neck to tail, and after a moment, he settled down.

I, on the other hand, felt a sudden chill at the tone of the cat's cry. You may think me fanciful, but that feline understands every word I say.

Robinson leaned forward in his chair. "Was the letter from a young lady, sir?"

He is always trying to discover the details of my amours, and, as you might imagine, I thwart him at every turn. I raised my right eyebrow by way of censure. "I need your help, and I wish you would ask as few questions as possible."

"Very well, sir," Robinson said on a sigh. "Have they caught the highwayman? Does he have the book?"

"No, they have not caught him, but I have reason to believe his identity is Lord Kendrick."

"Lord Kendrick!" Robinson exclaimed, gripping the arms of his chair. "Sir, that was no member of the nobility holding a pistol on me, I assure you."

"I believe you. The marquess has a partner or an accomplice, if you will. A paid ruffian, most likely. Before you ask me why Lord Kendrick would stoop to robbing people on the road, let me say that the reasons people do evil things are numerous. To speculate at present would only cost us precious time. Let us just say that, as usual, money is the root of most evil."

Robinson thought this over. "Already there has been talk of his lordship in the servants' hall."

"Oh? What kind of talk?"

"When I returned from London this afternoon, I went to the kitchen to get a bite to eat. Everyone was angry and upset, especially Cook. It seems Lord Kendrick forced his attentions on one of the maids last night, Cook's niece."

Robinson and I looked at one another, a silent message of contempt for Lord Kendrick's behaviour passing between us. Housemaids are routinely accosted, make no mistake, but the frequency of a wicked activity cannot make it the slightest bit more acceptable.

"Look here, Robinson, what I must do is search Lord Kendrick's bedchamber. I would like to go straightaway, but I cannot see how at present. I must cool my heels until after dinner. I need your help."

"How can I serve you, sir?"

"Find Thompson, Lord Kendrick's valet, strike up a

conversation, a friendship. Convince him to take a drink with you downstairs, go for a walk in the cooler evening air, whatever comes to mind. That way, while Lord Kendrick is gathered with the guests after dinner, I can search his room. Send word to me when the way is clear. If Thompson questions you as to why you must apprise me of your whereabouts, tell him I keep you on a very short leash."

Robinson nodded. "I shall do it. After dinner, when the servants are clearing the table and washing up, I should be able to distract him then."

"Good man."

A sound like a snort came from Chakkri.

Robinson narrowed his eyes at the cat.

"Pour me a drink before we begin the Dressing Hour, Robinson."

❦ 13 ❧

I possess a good appetite, thankfully one yet to show itself on my lean frame. Little causes me to neglect my food. Tonight proved an exception. Somehow when one is placed *down the table,* well away from the object of one's affections, the result modifies the consumption of food. Not drink, only food, you understand.

As is the custom, after the covers were removed, the gentlemen were left to their port while the ladies retired to the drawing room. The Prince of Wales had departed Oatlands before the picnic, leaving the Duke of Derehurst the highest-ranking gentleman present. He would be the one to give the signal to rejoin the ladies.

He could, that is, if he would ever stop droning on about the pack of hounds he had carefully bred into the best fox-hunters in the south of England. Evidently he viewed sporting subjects the only suitable topic for conversation. The duke had not earned the sobriquet Stuffy for nothing. I sat, resigned to adding boredom to my current list of frustrations. Fox-hunting is one of the few popular gentlemanly pastimes I eschew, judging it only one better than shooting helpless birds out of the sky.

I had all I could do to keep from drumming my well-manicured fingers on the table, though I noted Lord Kendrick listened intently to every word the duke said. Smirking sycophant.

At last the duke rose. I swallowed the remainder of my port and was the first to exit the room. Crossing into the drawing room moments later, I saw that card tables had been set up. A pair of doors were opened, revealing a large gallery. A trio of musicians enticed couples to dance.

There had been no word from Robinson yet, so it was not time to search Lord Kendrick's chamber.

My gaze swept the drawing room until I found Freddie. I suppressed a groan. She sat on a small sofa with the garrulous Lady Crecy, Humphrey snoring away at their feet. Smart dog.

Though Lady Crecy's tongue ran on, I approached. I wanted to tell Freddie I would have the letter back that very night—I hoped—and I would most humbly beg her forgiveness for having kept it and propelled us into this mess.

I bowed before the two. "Ladies, I am pleased to see we have the privilege of dancing again this evening. May I solicit each of you for a dance?"

Yes, I was prepared to lead Lady Crecy onto the dance floor. No sacrifice was too great just now for a few minutes with Freddie. And I could not walk up and ask only one of them to dance.

"Oh, Mr. Brummell!" Lady Crecy simpered. "I should like to dance with you above all things. I remember how gracefully you danced with my Penelope. Such ease of movement, such dignity, such refinement."

Such ridiculous toadying.

Freddie's gaze turned to me for the briefest of moments. She was clad in an elegant royal-blue silk gown.

Sapphires sparkled at her wrists and neck. "I am afraid I must refuse you," she told me, while motioning to a footman. "I think I twisted my ankle this afternoon walking in the grass. I shall not be dancing this evening."

I stood amazed. What poppycock! Freddie loves the outdoors and is as sure-footed as a doe. I looked at her, willing her to meet my eyes, but she occupied herself with one of her dogs. Sparkles, named for his bright personality, took the opportunity to have his mistress pick him up and place him in her lap. Where was Georgicus? I wondered. Exiled as I seemed to be?

"Oh, dear Duchess, your poor little ankle!" Lady Crecy cried. "We must cancel our plans to visit the ruins tomorrow. We cannot have you traipsing about with an injured ankle."

Freddie asked the servant who appeared at her elbow for a footstool. "Do not fuss, Lady Crecy, I shall be fine by morning. We shall gather at noon and make the short journey to view the ancient crumbling stones on the other side of Weybridge, never fear."

"Well, if you are certain," Lady Crecy said doubtfully.

"Quite certain. You go ahead and dance with Mr. Brummell."

The footman returned with an embroidered stool. Freddie busied herself with the placement of her foot and arranged her skirts, avoiding my gaze. Lady Crecy rose, curtseyed to the Royal Duchess, and offered me her arm. I could do nothing other than make Freddie a bow and lead Lady Crecy into the gallery. I did not escape without hearing Lord Munro titter at my predicament from where he and Petersham sat at a card table.

Fortunately a spirited country dance was just starting up. The dance would be one which separated its partners frequently. I observed a bored-looking Roger Cranworth lead Lady Ariana to the floor. The pale girl actually had a glimmer of happiness in her eyes as she took the dashing Mr. Cranworth's arm.

Cecily Cranworth sat alone, biting her fingernails in the corner of the room. Where, I thought, was Doctor Wendell? Thankfully, it was past the Squire's bedtime so Miss Cranworth would not have to suffer his attentions.

Lady Crecy proved to be a lively dancer. Her exertions did not prevent her from a steady stream of conversation. "Oh, look. Dear Signor Tallarico has joined the Royal Duchess on the sofa. He is the most engaging man, do you not think so, Mr. Brummell?"

"I doubt he will ever allow himself to be trapped into an engagement," I muttered. Lady Crecy did not hear me and smiled adoringly in the Italian's direction. Another conquest for Tallarico! Apparently age was no barrier to his achievements. When it came to the females, Victor Tallarico brought a whole new meaning to the word *victor*. Devil take the man, I thought, watching him hold Freddie's hand to his lips.

"What is that you say?" Lady Crecy eventually asked.

The steps of the dance parted us. When we were in front of one another again, I said, "I saw Signor Tallarico helping Lady Penelope with her archery."

Lady Crecy's lips spread into a wide smile. She edged closer and snapped her fan open. Behind it she stage-whispered to me, "I think the dear man helped Penelope with more than her archery! Only look how marked Lord Wrayburn's attention is to my little dove. By the end of the Season, I expect my gal to be preparing to become a countess."

My gaze travelled briefly to where Lord Wrayburn handed Lady Penelope a glass of lemonade, then assisted her to a seat near one of the tall windows.

Lady Crecy snapped her fan shut in one fluid motion as if snapping closed the leg shackles of marriage around Lord Wrayburn's ankles.

Keeping an eye on Freddie while listening politely to Lady Crecy's chatter, I suddenly noticed a footman at the edge of the dance floor watching me and trying to catch my attention.

"Once my little Penelope is wed, perhaps I will try my skills at matchmaker somewhere else," Lady Crecy said, nodding in the direction of Lady Ariana. "My Penelope says the gal is quite without prospects. The naughty marquess is too busy pursuing his own interests to secure a husband for his cousin. Lady Ariana is making eyes at Mr. Cranworth, but surely a titled lady can look higher."

I listened to these plots and plans with every indication of attention, waiting for a chance to make my escape. Finally, the dance ended. After extricating myself from Lady Crecy, I crossed to where the footman stood. "Mr. Brummell, sir," he said.

"Yes?"

"Mr. Robinson desires me to say"—the footman cleared his throat and recited—"The bird has left its cage."

"Er, thank you."

Mentally, I smiled. This must be Robinson's idea of the lingo of a spy.

As quickly as I could without attracting notice to myself, I left the gallery and slipped up the stairs. Counting backward from my bedchamber, I located Lord Kendrick's room. Before the cat could lick her ear—or in this case before the dog snoring in the corridor could raise his head—I entered the marquess's room.

Not knowing how long Robinson could keep Thompson away, I made quick work of the contents of the wardrobe, the bedside table, his lordship's portmanteau, the desk, and—with great distaste—the bed. Then I methodically looked in, around, and over every piece of furniture in the room, growing more anxious as the minutes passed. I even moved a chair in front of the wardrobe, and climbed up on it in order to see the flat surface of the top. After all, a letter in such a place would not be seen by the casual eye.

Lord Kendrick's bedchamber did not contain a dressing room for his valet as mine did, merely a cot in the far corner. Thus, when I had completed my search, I had nowhere else to look. Standing in the middle of the chamber, I tried to think of any stone I might have left unturned.

I heaved a sigh. There was none. Damn and blast, Lord Kendrick must have the letter on his person for safekeeping. Hmmm. Would not that be more dangerous, though, than hiding it?

Just then, I heard Robinson's voice, pitched louder than normal, in the hallway.

With a coolness I was far from feeling, I opened the door to the bedchamber and stepped briskly out into the hall.

A plump, white-haired man in a black coat walked in front of Robinson. When he saw me, he started, then gave me that universal stare of the intimidating butler or manservant.

Hah! He had picked the wrong victim for this manoeuver. I raised my quizzing glass in his direction for the merest of moments before addressing Robinson. "Mingling with *country* servants, Robinson? I cannot fathom you falling so low. Step along and fetch me another handkerchief. I have lent mine to a lady. All these blessed doors are the same on this hall and I mistook my chamber. Once I was inside, and saw the smallness of the room, I comprehended my error."

This was said before the outraged Thompson could even voice a question as to why I was in his master's room. Robinson and I were down the hall and through the door to my chamber before Lord Kendrick's man could draw breath.

Robinson closed the door. "Did you find the letter, sir?"

"No."

"I am sorry, sir."

"So am I. You did your part, though. Now I must get back downstairs before my long absence is noted."

"If there is anything more I can do—"

"I shall tell you at once," I said, leaving the room.

Entering the drawing room while adjusting the sleeve of my coat, I looked to the sofa that Freddie had been seated on with Victor Tallarico. In her place, the Italian now flirted with Lady Ariana. Freddie was nowhere to be seen. Instead, I watched Lord Kendrick dance attendance on Lady Deidre.

"What a murderous expression you have on your face, Brummell," crooned Sylvester Fairingdale at my side, about as welcome as the plague.

I did not reply.

"You don't care for Kendrick, that's a fact," Fairingdale said in a more conversational tone. "You didn't fool me this afternoon with that story about his coat needing adjustment, and you're not fooling me now."

"You are fool enough all by yourself."

"Tsk tsk. What *can* this all be about? Do you want Lady Deidre for yourself? I wouldn't put it past you to think you could become the son-in-law of a duke."

"Why do you not fly away, Fairingdale? You look like a bee in that yellow and brown *costume* and are twice as annoying."

Fairingdale leaned closer and narrowed his eyes. "Mayhaps you already have a lady. Society thinks you feel no ordinary woman is good enough for you. Are they correct? I think they are. I don't think a *lady,* even a duke's daughter, will do for you . . . only a *princess.*"

I yawned behind my hand, strongly suppressing a desire to swat Fairingdale. "Pity I find your opinions about as worthy as that of the bee you so resemble. Now go take your stinger and place it—ah, Old Dawe, just the man. I am going above stairs for the night. Is there a spare bottle of port about?"

Leaving Fairingdale with a calculating look on his face, I quit the room and waited in the hall until Old Dawe returned with a decanter on a tray.

"Sir, I am sorry. I would have brought it up to you."

"No need. Tell me, has the Royal Duchess retired for the evening?"

"I believe she has, sir. She seems especially fatigued tonight."

"It has been a long day. Thank you for the port."

Too irate at Lord Kendrick's monstrous nerve in black-mailing Freddie and too exasperated by Freddie's avoid-ance of me to be tired, I climbed the stairs to my bedchamber only to pace.

"Do you want me to help you get ready for bed, sir?" Robinson asked, sending a look of animosity toward the bed where Chakkri already slept.

"No." I lifted the stopper on the decanter.

"We could work on your hair, then. With just a few snips of the scissors, I could restore it to—"

"No." I put the port on the table between the chairs. There might not be anything more I could do about Lord Kendrick tonight, but I was damned if I were going to wait until morning to see Freddie. I would see her now, no matter what her Prussian behemoth of a maid said.

"Go to bed, Robinson," I said curtly, then exited the room, leaving the valet with his mouth hanging open. I advanced down the corridor to Freddie's sitting room, my need to see her increasing with every step.

I gave only the briefest of knocks before entering. It was empty. I heard sounds coming from Freddie's bed-chamber.

Never in all my visits to Oatlands had I been in there.

Impulsively, I knocked, then opened the door and strode into the room. I had a brief impression of shades of blue before several of the dogs draped on chairs and sprawled on the floor woofed and growled at me.

Ulga paused in the act of brushing her mistress's hair. Her eyes grew wide, outrage at my intrusion in every feature.

Freddie sat at her dressing table, attired in a robe of exquisite white satin trimmed with tiny diamonds and fastened in front with a large diamond clasp. She hushed the dogs, then spoke to me. "What can have prompted this unprecedented action on your part?"

I stood tall and proud as if we were at Almack's Assembly rooms, not like the uninvited guest in her bedchamber that I was. "I must speak with you. Privately."

Freddie rose. "Privately? We are as private as we *can* be, George."

Damn!

"Freddie, there are some things better spoken without an audience—"

She waved a hand. "Ulga is always with me, you know that. If you have come regarding Lord Kendrick and the letter, you may speak freely. Ulga already knows the situation. She was in the hall when I came indoors, and I had her attend me during my interview with the marquess. I trust her. Ulga is loyal to me. *She* does not keep letters that ought to be destroyed."

Again, she used a tone of voice which made me feel like I had been slapped.

Still, I waited to speak until the maid retreated to the corner and pulled out her knitting. "Freddie, I know that keeping such a personal letter was wrong of me. But cannot you try to understand?"

She said nothing.

"My scrapbook is so treasured that I will not leave it at home. How was I to know it and your letter would be stolen? I ask for your forgiveness, Freddie. Pray believe me when I say that it is only the great fondness I feel for you that prompted what I know was a selfish and stupidly careless action on my part."

"Fondness?" she asked coldly. "You are responsible for making me the object of blackmail, and you call this fondness?"

I paused a moment. She had been the one to write the letter in the first place. How could she be so icy now? Where was her usual generous spirit? "I give you my vow that I shall retrieve the letter," I said.

Her posture remained frigid. "Ulga tells me the gossip in the servants' hall is that you were in Lord Kendrick's room tonight without his lordship's permission. His man, Thompson, questioned the servants as to your identity. I do not see the letter in your hand, so I assume you failed to find it. Tell me how you intend to keep this vow you make me."

I closed my eyes. I could not bear to see the condemnation in hers. I could not bear the wall she had put between us, one greater than the wall of her marriage. And mostly, I could not bear to see this unforgiving side of Freddie.

I opened my eyes and fixed my expression to one of determination. "He must have the letter on his person, or I expect there is a possibility that he took it, or had it taken, to his estate for safekeeping." No need to tell her the marquess claimed he had a partner and cause her to worry more. "Freddie, I shall do whatever is necessary to get the letter back immediately. Even if I have to obtain a pistol, find the marquess and shoot him dead unless he gives me the letter. On my oath, I shall."

"You will do no such thing," Freddie stated unequivocally. "There would lay the road to certain scandal. And, George, make no mistake, I shall not have scandal brought down on my head. For to do so would bring scandal to the royal families of which I am a part. My brother is the King of Prussia. My husband, lest you have forgotten, is the son of King George the Third."

Cut to the very core, I nodded stiffly. "It shall be as you say, your Royal Highness."

"Yes, it shall indeed. Do not forget it." She pressed her fingers to her temples then, the only sign of the weight of distress she was under.

Ever watchful, Ulga put her knitting aside to dip a cloth in water. She waited with it in hand by Freddie's bed, worry written across her features.

"Good evening, George," Freddie said.

I reached for her hand that I might place a kiss on it.

Her hands were clenched into fists at her sides. She pressed them further into the folds of her robe.

"Good night, your Royal Highness," I said with dignity before leaving her.

❦ 14 ❧

Robinson woke me at ten the next morning. We would need plenty of time to ready me for the excursion to the ruins at noon. Glancing into the mirror after bathing and dressing, I thought the company need look no further than my face if they wanted to view a ruin.

Yes, as you must have suspected, I consumed the entire contents of the bottle of port when I returned from my frosty interview with Freddie. Now the signs of my recent excesses began to catch up with me. My breeches could barely be fastened, my eyes were shot with red, and dark circles had formed under them. I must remember to drink less if I lived through this current ordeal.

Robinson seemed more dismayed than I was at my appearance. "Sir, if I might suggest a touch of a special tinted lotion I have procured. It would hide that darkness under your eyes—"

I raised my right eyebrow severely, silencing him. "Do not be absurd. Hand me my dog's head walking stick, my hat and my gloves."

"Yes, sir," was the gloomy reply. Then, "While everyone is out, do you wish me to try to search Lord Kendrick's room for your missing letter? Two sets of eyes can be better than one."

I smoothed the sleeve of my Persian-blue coat. "True. If you feel you can do so without Thompson knowing, go ahead."

"Sir," Robinson said, his tone somber, "I know it is not my place to question you—"

"Has that stopped you before?"

"Perhaps not, sir. But all this plotting and effort for one letter. Is it so very important, then?"

I looked into his eyes. The genuine concern I saw there caused me to be more forthcoming. "The letter was written by the Duchess of York to me. She would be . . . flustered . . . having her private thoughts made public."

Robinson nodded in comprehension. "Just so, sir. This makes all the difference in the world. I shall indeed do my best to help you recover her Royal Highness's letter."

"Thank you. Now, I think the marquess either has the letter on his person, or he may have sent it to his estate for safekeeping. My plan, unless I kill the blackguard first, is to search his house. I gather that after a few hours outdoors in this heat, the guests will be drooping. Everyone will return to Oatlands. It will not be remarked upon if I retire to my room to rest before dinner. Then I shall slip out and ride to Lord Kendrick's estate."

"Would you like me to come with you, sir? Surely the house will be large, and you will need help," Robinson asked in a brisk tone I sensed he employed to lighten the serious tone of the conversation.

"No, the absence of both of us would be remarked. I need you here in case anyone should come to my door. You can tell them I am sleeping and must not be disturbed. In addition, someone must look after Chakkri. I do not wish a maid coming in here to clean and leaving the door open where the cat could slip out."

Robinson looked thoughtful, sliding his gaze over to where Chakkri stood on a side table monitoring activities from the window. He had been unusually quiet this morning—Chakkri, not Robinson.

I could almost see the devious plans forming in the valet's brain. "Robinson," I said casually, "you do know that if anything were to happen to Chakkri while under your care, you would find yourself accepting Petersham's frequent offer of employment."

Robinson adopted his Martyr Act. "So I have assumed. Your affection for the animal grows with the passage of time."

And Chakkri's affection for me remained constant, unlike some *people* whose affections were withdrawn if one made a mistake. I grasped the dog's head walking stick Freddie had given me last year. Silver, with sapphires for the dog's eyes, the cane contains a deadly swordstick that can be triggered by a twist of the dog's head. I wondered if the walking stick was to be the last reminder of her attachment to me. I pocketed the gold-framed miniature of Freddie—yes, I do always carry it—and left the chamber.

Downstairs in the drawing room, many guests had gathered waiting for the outing to begin. My gaze immediately scanned the room for Freddie. She was not there. Signor Tallarico, in his trademark pink waistcoat—today under a dark, greyish-brown coat—sauntered over to me.

"That is a handsome-coloured coat, Tallarico," I said grudgingly. I stood next to a pedestal with a bronze dog statue, holding my hat, cane, and gloves in one hand. "It almost makes up for the pink waistcoat. What do you call the colour?"

"*Gràzie*. I do not know if the colour has a name. Stultz made the coat for me."

"Stultz? Ah, I imagine the man's hands must shake while cutting material. That could account for the quality

of his tailoring. Have you not been in London long
enough to know that Weston is the best tailor?"

"Stultz is the better man, Tallarico. Don't listen to
Brummell," Sylvester Fairingdale said, mincing up to us.
Today he sported a lime-green coat and canary-coloured
waistcoat over forest-green breeches. I could not decide
if he looked more like a parrot or an oversized leprechaun.

Tallarico grinned, showing off his gleaming set of teeth.
"I am glad to know that. Stultz charges less, that is why
I have been giving him my custom. I shall see your Mr.
Weston immediately upon my return to London."

"You *pay* your tailor's bills?" Fairingdale asked,
amazed.

"Obviously, Tallarico, with Fairingdale running around
telling people Stultz is his tailor, the man is desperate for
money," I said mildly. I raised my quizzing glass to get
a better look at Tallarico's coat. "Still, an excellent colour.
London smoke. That is what it will be known as. I shall
see that Weston obtains the shade. By the way, what are
we waiting for? It is past noon."

"*La bèlla duchessa,*" Tallarico said. "But you must
know she has not come down yet, for you looked for her
the moment you entered the room."

"Did he?" Fairingdale feigned shock.

I swung my quizzing glass on its length of black velvet
ribbon, ignoring the taunts. "Ah, there she is," I said, indicating a window. "She has already been outdoors."

Freddie's form, clad in an apricot-coloured muslin
gown, could be seen passing by a window.

Tallarico frowned. "Why is she not wearing the hair
ornaments I gave her? The day is warm. She must show
her neck."

Fairingdale reached and plucked something from the
pedestal I leaned against. "What's this?" he asked, holding
up one of the jet hair ornaments about which Tallarico
had just been speaking.

With a cry of dismay, Tallarico snatched it from his hand. "What is this doing here?"

Unfortunately, Freddie, pale and looking like she had not enjoyed a good night's rest either, chose that moment to enter the room and approach us. She saw the hair ornament in the Italian's hand.

"Oh, there they are!" she cried. "Now I remember placing them there the other day. Victor, I was terribly afraid that I had mislaid your beautiful birthday gift. I am so glad to have them once again."

Victor?

Fairingdale eyed the length of jet appraisingly. "There are two of those? I don't see another."

Freddie furrowed her brow. "I know I put them both there. I shall have the footmen search for the other. Perhaps it fell to the carpet." She appeared distracted. "In the meantime, I must address the company. There will be a delay in the morning's outing, I am afraid."

Tallarico took one of Freddie's hands. "The news was not good?"

Freddie shook her head, tears forming in her eyes.

Tallarico, Fairingdale, and myself all immediately offered her handkerchiefs. She accepted the one from the Italian. "What is the bad news?" I asked.

Freddie wiped her eyes. "Fishe came to me this morning while Victor and I were breakfasting in the dining room. Phanor's condition had worsened during the night. I went to him, but only in time to have him die in my arms."

"Mío bèlla duchessa," murmured Tallarico. "Do not cry."

"Who was Phanor?" Fairingdale asked.

"One of her dogs, you oaf," I replied. "Your Royal Highness, may I offer my condolences? Perhaps it would be better to cancel the outing so that you may be private with a close friend or two in your grief."

Freddie dried her eyes. "Thank you, George, but we must carry on with the day. Phanor had been sick for a long time. He is not suffering any longer. I must take my comfort from that fact." She took a moment to compose herself, then turned to the gathering.

"Ladies and gentlemen," she began. "I beg your pardon for this delay in visiting the ruins. We shall be underway within the hour, I assure you. One of my dogs has passed away this morning—"

Expressions of sympathy ran through the room.

Freddie held up a small hand. "Thank you. My trusted footman, Old Dawe, will select a special place in my dogs' cemetery for Phanor to enjoy his eternal sleep. I beg you will forgive me, but I feel the desire to see Phanor laid to rest personally."

"We know how you love animals, your Royal Highness," Doctor Wendell's voice rang out in the room. "They are fortunate for your care."

Freddie's eyes grew misty again. "Thank you, Doctor. Old Dawe should be preparing the grave as we speak. He will return to tell me when all is ready. I will be but a short while. In the meantime, I have rung for tea and sandwiches."

At these words, footmen filed into the room bearing trays laden with food. Conversation became general, with several guests coming up to Freddie to express their sympathy.

I noted that Lord Kendrick was not amongst the company, but it was Tallarico who gave voice to the observation. He said, "I do not see Lady Ariana this morning. Or her cousin, Lord Kendrick, for that matter. I hope the two have not left the house party. Lady Ariana mentioned to me that they might have to do so."

The air around us felt suddenly tense. Usually I consider my words before speaking, but this time, I am sorry to report, distress caused me to be careless. "I daresay that the marquess's smirk would be something few of us would regret never seeing again."

Fairingdale's gaze flew to me. "As I said last night, Brummell, it appears you don't like the marquess—"

But he got no further.

The sounds of sharply indrawn breaths, shocked gasps, and cries of alarm went around the room. I turned to see what had happened.

Old Dawe stood on the threshold of the drawing room, dirty, a sheen of perspiration on his forehead. His face was ashen. "Your Royal Highness!" he cried out in an unsteady voice, his hand to his chest. "In the cemetery. There is a fresh grave. Someone tried to conceal it with clumps of grass, but I saw. I did not know what to think, so I looked. There is a body. Not a dog, Duchess!" He took in a great gulp of air. "A human corpse, your Royal Highness!"

❧ 15 ❧

Freddie rushed to her manservant, Doctor Wendell and I right behind her.

But before any of us could reach Old Dawe, he collapsed. Freddie called for footmen to carry the elderly retainer to his room. "And get Ulga," she instructed.

Doctor Wendell supervised the men. "Yes, Ulga, and Mr. Fishe as well. They are both good assistants to me."

Tallarico, Fairingdale, and—appearing from nowhere—Roger Cranworth and I all watched as the footmen carried Old Dawe to the servants' quarters. Ulga came running down the steps and joined them.

As they seemed to have the situation in hand, I spoke to Freddie. "I shall go to the dog cemetery and see what has Old Dawe all worked up."

"I shall go with you," Freddie said.

"Do you think that best?"

"Yes, I do," she said shortly. "Victor, will you come as well?"

Suppressing my irritation at Freddie's marked attention to the Italian, I tossed my cane on a nearby chair and was the first out the front door. I strode in the direction of the ornamental pool, the place where I had observed the marquess and his cousin argue.

Coming upon the scene, I observed a pile of dirt and grass under the shade of a pine tree. A shovel had been thrown down a few feet away.

Freddie, Tallarico, Fairingdale, and Cranworth caught up with me just as I reached the spot. A length of bloodied linen could be seen unearthed from the dirt and grass. Old Dawe had evidently dug only a little deeper, uncovering the shallow grave. The merest sliver of a human shape was visible.

Ignoring Freddie's muffled scream, I donned my gloves, crouched down and began pushing clumps of grass and dirt away from the victim's face, head, and neck. Blood was mixed with the earth and was caked on the dead person's skin and shirt. He had been laid in the grave on his side. I felt my heartbeat accelerate as his golden curls came into view.

The remainder of the dead man's cravat, heavy with wet blood, hung limply around his shirt, the ends of the length of white linen coming untied. This left his neck exposed, revealing the wound.

And a square of black jet.

"Well, there is your missing hair ornament, your Royal Highness," Fairingdale said.

The sharp length of jet had been plunged to the hilt into the Marquess of Kendrick's neck.

A moan escaped Freddie before she fainted into Victor Tallarico's arms.

I shot to my feet. "Give her to me."

"No!" the Italian denied me, lifting Freddie's small form as if she weighed no more than one of his pink waistcoats. "Look at your hands. They are covered in dirt and blood. I'll take her to the house and have Ulga attend her."

The sight of her in his arms unnerved me. "She has never fainted before to my knowledge."

"Perhaps your knowledge of her is incomplete," Tallarico threw over his shoulder as he walked away.

Sylvester Fairingdale raised a handkerchief—scented, no doubt—to his nose. "Someone certainly didn't like the marquess." He eyed me down his nose, his expression filled with meaning, then followed Tallarico.

Damn Fairingdale. I wondered how long it would be before he started braying to whoever would listen about how much I disliked the marquess. I glanced back to the body.

"My God, I never thought..." Roger Cranworth looked to be the next candidate for swooning. He stood shaking, his gaze fixed on the body in the grave. Beads of sweat dotted his forehead, making the dark locks of his hair cling to his skin.

"You never thought what, Mr. Cranworth?"

He looked at me then, but he did not appear to see me. "I never thought that smirk could be wiped from his face."

"Someone has accomplished the task. I think you should go to the house and find Squire Oxberry. As the local magistrate, he should be apprised of the murder at once."

With a glance back at the corpse, Mr. Cranworth said, "Why don't you go, Mr. Brummell? I'd like a few minutes here with Connell. He—he was a friend of mine, you know."

I knew it, but I had other plans. "I am afraid I cannot. My soiled gloves and grass-stained breeches would shock the company. You must go. There will be opportunity enough to say good-bye to Lord Kendrick when he is laid out for viewing." Without giving him a chance to reply, I returned to the grave and continued to unearth the body.

Out of the corner of my eye, I watched Mr. Cranworth head for the house. Once he was far enough away, I began to work rapidly, moving the dirt away from the body. My mind worked faster than my hands. You may think it uncaring of me, but for this one moment I had to put aside the question of who had killed the marquess. At present, I had to seize the opportunity to search the body before anyone else did. If the marquess had Freddie's letter on him, I wanted to be the one to find it.

At last, feeling like a graverobber, I was able to reach into the pocket inside his coat. Nothing. I moved more dirt, averting my gaze from his face. I tugged at the tails of his coat where another pocket was sure to be. At last the earth released her hold on the cloth. I plunged my hand into the pocket. Nothing.

"Mr. Brummell, you don't need to dig him out!" Squire Oxberry called, making his way to the site with two strong footmen in tow. "I've brought servants for that."

Puffing in exertion, the Squire raised his quizzing glass at the dead marquess with detached interest. "Wonder who did this, eh? Nobody liked him, no indeed. He wasn't the man his father or even his brother was. Won't be missed by anyone other than that cousin of his. Finish digging him out, boys, and put him on this blanket." Squire Oxberry heaved a sigh as if he were the one doing physical work. "I expect I'll be put through a great deal of trouble trying to identify the culprit, curse it."

Lady Ariana, I suddenly thought. The angry scene between Lady Ariana and Lord Kendrick which took place a few steps away from where we presently stood flashed in my mind. Had she absently picked up one of the hair ornaments—as Freddie had first thought—and then later used it to end her cousin's life?

Or what about Roger Cranworth? Freddie had told me of the argument between the two men in the drawing room. Roger was angry that Lord Kendrick would not marry Cecily.

"What's happened?" Doctor Wendell asked, arriving at

my side. He looked at the marquess's body being heaved
out of the grave. "Great God!"

"Did you see her Royal Highness?" I asked him. "She
fainted."

"The Royal Duchess regained consciousness. Ulga is
with her," the doctor replied. He bent over the body, now
on its back on the blanket. "Who did this?"

"We do not know yet," I replied.

I must admit, it was a gruesome scene. Watching Doctor Wendell's professional fingers running over the marquess's bloodstained throat, brushing dirt from his eyelids
so he could open the eyes, made me wish for the wine
decanter. I suddenly looked at my filthy gloves in something approaching horror. I stripped them off.

"That sharp length of jet went right through his neck.
From the condition of the body, I'd say he was killed
sometime early this morning. Perhaps before dawn.
Doesn't look like there was a struggle. No broken fingernails, torn clothing, or anything of that sort. Taken by
surprise, mayhaps, and likely killed right here. There's no
trail of blood coming from the house, only some near the
grave," Doctor Wendell said. "At least, that's my opinion,
Squire."

"I've no reason to doubt you, Doctor Wendell," the
Squire said. He took a moment to pace a few steps around
the scene.

I turned to Doctor Wendell. "The Royal Duchess must
be shielded from as much of this scandal as possible."

He nodded. "So must Miss Cranworth." The doctor
looked me in the eye, his gaze beseeching. I was reminded
of Cecily Cranworth's impassioned speech that she would
rather see Lord Kendrick dead than marry him. Had something happened which caused her to resort to dire action?

Squire Oxberry rejoined us. "That fancy thing in his
lordship's neck belongs to the Royal Duchess, I hear."

"That is true," I said. "There are a pair of them. Her

Royal Highness received them as a birthday gift from Victor Tallarico. She mislaid them on one of the pedestals in the drawing room. In fact, she had forgotten she had done so until today when Sylvester Fairingdale found the other one."

"So they have been in the drawing room since Wednesday, eh? Anyone could have pocketed one of 'em. A bad business. I'll ask the Royal Duchess what she wants done." He scratched his wigged head. "A lot of trouble it will all be, though I don't see as how we can claim it was an accident, with him buried here like this."

Accident! I exchanged an incredulous look with Doctor Wendell.

Just then, Thompson, Lord Kendrick's valet, came hurrying from the house. When he saw his master on the ground atop the blanket, he threw himself down and began to weep.

I felt sorry for the older man. Some time passed before we could calm him. He had served the family since Lord Kendrick had been in short coats. He insisted on helping to carry the dead marquess back to the house, maintaining that his master must be cleaned and the instrument of his death removed from his throat.

His overwhelming grief was exactly the excuse I needed to accomplish another task which might lead to retrieving the missing letter. "Thompson, you must not wish his lordship to remain in those clothes any longer than he must."

"No," the stricken valet said. "He should be in full Court dress befitting a man of his rank. He should not be viewed in this foul condition."

"I shall ride to his estate and gather the clothing directly after I have changed and seen the Duchess." The missing letter and Lord Kendrick's murder merged into one horrible mess, but there was more to it than that. I had despised Lord Kendrick, but his murderer must be found.

My plan to obtain the formal clothing for the marquess was quickly agreed on by all concerned. I strode in the back way of Oatlands and made my way to my bedchamber, my brain reeling. Robinson must have been in the servants' hall getting the news, as he was nowhere to be found.

Chakkri laid on the bed, his long brown tail curled around his hind leg, an alert look in his blue eyes.

"The immediate threat to Freddie has been silenced in a way I could never have predicted, old boy," I said to the cat. "But where is the letter? I have searched Lord Kendrick's room and his person. Or, his corpse, I should say. That leaves only his house, unless his partner has it. Who that person is, I cannot say. Lord Kendrick must have been referring to the ruffian who actually held up the coach."

The cat said nothing. He merely watched me with his knowing blue eyes.

I stripped off my coat, washed my face and hands in a basin of water, and changed into fresh clothes, all in record time without Robinson's help. He would have been appalled.

Presenting myself at the door to Freddie's private sitting room a scant twenty minutes later, I knocked briskly.

Ulga opened the door and stood, arms akimbo, a solid barrier against my entry.

"I must see her," I said.

"You vill not. She is lying down vith Hero to comfort her. I had to give her a drop of laudanum in a glass of sherry, so upset is she," Ulga said. The maid looked at me as if it were all my fault that her mistress was in such a condition. She felt the little dog a more loyal companion than me, no doubt.

"Her Royal Highness asked for laudanum?" I asked in

some surprise. Freddie is not one for strong hysterics and never doses herself with drugs. I would not have thought even finding a corpse on her property enough to make her resort to laudanum.

Ulga took her hands from her hips and clasped them in front of her. "After all these years, I know vhat is best for her Royal Highness." Here, the Prussian maid looked at me severely. "That is vhy you cannot see her right now. You vill upset her even more talking of that letter."

I had to agree. "Inform your mistress that I am riding to Lord Kendrick's estate to search for the letter."

"You have not yet found it?" Disapproval of my ineptitude was written across her face.

"No, but I shall. I am going under the pretext of getting Court clothes for Lord Kendrick's body. Thompson has given me instructions and his blessing to do so. While at the house, I will search for the letter."

"Good."

"Tell the Royal Duchess. Her concern might be lessened." I turned to go, but Ulga's next words stopped me.

"I think she vill feel better once Mr. Lavender has arrived from London."

I swung around, astonished. "Mr. Lavender? She sent for Mr. Lavender of Bow Street?"

"Yes." Ulga shut the door in my face without another word.

I strode down the stairs and outside, noticing that guests were leaving the house party in droves. Not that I cared. I walked toward the stables positively seething. Ordering a horse to be saddled, I paced the stable yard, considering Freddie's action.

Very well, I told myself, a murder had occurred on Oatlands property. The killer must be identified and apprehended at once. I could understand all this, indeed, I agreed with it. Even if the killer turned out to be Lady Ariana or Cecily or Roger Cranworth. But what of Squire

Oxberry? Was he not the appointed magistrate for the district? Could he not work with the constables and the county coroner to uncover the murderer?

I accepted a fine chestnut horse from a stableboy, mounted after obtaining directions to Lord Kendrick's estate, and galloped away.

The springtime English countryside passed my view unappreciated as I made the long ride. All right, Squire Oxberry was not the brightest man. Had I not wondered if he were even capable of finding the highwayman? But why had Freddie chosen Mr. Lavender, of all people? Jack Townsend was the Bow Street man usually called upon in criminal matters relating to the Royal Family.

To my knowledge, Freddie has only once met the toothpick-wielding, finger-pointing, brusque Scotsman known as John Lavender. That occasion was during the investigation of another murder, the one last autumn at the Royal Pavilion. I told you the whole story another time, remember?

You might recall that Jack Townsend and Mr. Lavender both were involved in that case. You might also recall that Mr. Lavender holds a strong aversion to my being involved in any of his investigations. Well, I did not want him at Oatlands either, so this time our animosity would be mutual.

A warm, dusty ride later, I arrived at Lord Kendrick's estate. The house and grounds were smaller than I had imagined. Knocking at the door, I found myself in the awful position of being the messenger of bad news. The butler looked at me in horror as I explained what had happened and why I was there. I admit I did embellish matters a bit, saying that I was also there to obtain some of Lord Kendrick's papers. That would account for my being in rooms other than the marquess's bedchamber.

The butler did not question me further and wasted no time in gathering the servants in the kitchen to apprise them of their master's death. They remained huddled together belowstairs, each perhaps going over what his or her future held. I was left with the freedom to go about the house at my will.

I shall not bore you with details. Believe me when I say that I spent the rest of the afternoon and into the early evening searching the house. A letter is a small item, easily concealed in any number of places. I assumed the letter had been separated from the blue velvet book, though I could not be certain of anything.

Thankfully, I was not disturbed by anyone after the butler offered me tea, which I declined.

Near five o'clock, tired and frustrated beyond words, I had to admit defeat. Standing in Lord Kendrick's library, I turned the last book upside down, letting the pages fall free. No letter.

I sagged into a chair, tapping my fingers on the armrest. Assuming I had covered the house, I was at a loss as to where the marquess had hidden the letter. I tried to put myself in Lord Kendrick's place—and thought hard. The letter was not on his person, not in his room at Oatlands, not here at his estate unless he had buried it somewhere. No, he would not have had time for any such elaborate scheme. In addition, he would have wanted to have the letter close at hand, to produce it for Freddie had she asked for proof.

Which left only two possibilities: one, that his accomplice, whoever he might be—and he might very well be the killer—had the letter in his keeping, or two, there was somewhere else at Oatlands the marquess had hidden it.

I vaulted to my feet. Lady Ariana's room! The perfect place, close at hand, yet safe.

Cursing myself for a fool, I dashed up the stairs, retrieved the Court dress I had gathered earlier for Lord Kendrick to be laid out in, and exited the house.

I rode at a tearing rate back to Oatlands. I could search Lady Ariana's room at dinner, if not before, should the young lady be absent from the chamber. She had brought no maid with her; indeed, I doubted her cousin had ever provided her with one. My way would be clear. Though perhaps, I thought, riding into the Oatlands stable yard, Lady Ariana was so overset at the murder of her cousin she had taken to her bed.

Unless she had a different feeling altogether regarding her cousin's death. One of relief.

While my mind had not yet been free to contemplate the array of possible suspects, Lady Ariana's name had been the first to strike me when I saw the murdered marquess. The girl was not in her right mind. Furthermore, her very freedom had been in jeopardy when Lord Kendrick threatened to have her placed in a lunatic asylum. Though I could not rule out Lord Kendrick's partner in his highwayman scheme, nor, sadly, could I rule out Cecily Cranworth or her brother, Roger.

But I would explore those possibilities later.

Entering Oatlands, I was in time to see Freddie, trailed by four dogs and Ulga, coming down the stairs. Old Dawe was not at his post at the door. I hoped he was resting after the shock he had received. A younger footman was stationed in his stead. I handed him the parcel of Lord Kendrick's clothes with instructions to give them to Thompson.

I bowed to Freddie. She looked at me anxiously.

"Your Royal Highness, I would not ask for much of your time, standing here as I am in all my dirt from the road, but there is a matter—"

"Step into the drawing room, George." Freddie motioned. Once the three of us were inside, she closed the doors behind me, and we found seats. "Almost everyone has departed, so we can count on a few moments of privacy. What did you find? Ulga tells me you went to Lord Kendrick's house."

"I did not find the letter, I am sorry to say."

Ulga let out her breath in an aggravated rush, then returned to her knitting. Freddie's complexion paled over her aquamarine-coloured gown.

"All is not lost, Freddie," I said. "I have another idea where the marquess could have hidden the letter, in Lady Ariana's room. How did the girl take the news of her cousin's murder? Is she in her chamber?"

Freddie looked at me intently. "Lady Ariana was in shock, as one might imagine. She had no relatives other than her cousin, Lord Kendrick. Lady Crecy kindly took the girl under her wing. Her ladyship astutely stated her belief that Lady Ariana should not be subjected to the burdens of a funeral. They have left for London."

I passed a hand over my forehead. "It is still worth a look into Lady Ariana's chamber. Another curious thing is that none of my stolen clothing was to be found at Lord Kendrick's house. He has a partner, Freddie, he told me so himself. I am sorry to have to tell you and cause you more concern. But if I can find the accomplice, I might find the letter."

"Unless," Freddie said stiffly, "he finds us first in order to continue the blackmail scheme."

This idea had already occurred to me, but I did not want Freddie to worry. "Surely not. Robinson said the person who held him up was no gentleman. The cohort must be a paid ruffian, one who would not know the value of what he held."

"We must hope that to be the case. However, I shall not be able to have a moment's peace until that letter is returned to me, George."

"Freddie, I have given you my vow to return it to you and I shall. Now we have the marquess's murder to contend with as well. I shall do everything in my power to resolve both matters."

If possible, her face grew even whiter.

"Ulga told me you sent word to Mr. Lavender. Why have you asked him to come? He and I are far from the best of friends, while I do admire his work. Why not Jack Townsend?"

"Jack Townsend, while well enough in his way and discreet, cannot be relied upon to get to the truth. Mr. Lavender's excellent reputation for justice is precisely why I have asked him to Oatlands," she replied, her bearing rigid. She swallowed hard. "I cannot bring scandal on this house. The murderer of Lord Kendrick must not, on *any* account, be left to go free. The duke would want me to do everything possible to avoid scandal."

I tensed at the mention of Freddie's husband. "The Duke of York? Avoid scandal? While parading his mistress through the streets of London and, at the moment, the streets of Geneva?"

Freddie rose to her feet.

I followed suit, taking a step toward her. "I apologize. I ought not have said that, Freddie. It is just that I do not want you to feel you must bear all this alone. I will find the letter and uncover the murderer. You can count on *me* to help. You can always trust that *I* will be available to you."

Her Royal Highness looked at me through doubtful eyes. "Can I count on you, George? For the first time, I wonder if that is true. And if it is true, to what lengths will you go—"

Her voice broke off.

The appalling idea that she thought *I* might be responsible for Lord Kendrick's death presented itself in my brain. I suppose I could not blame her, as I had threatened Lord Kendrick's life just the night before in her bedchamber. Still, she should know me better. Before I could disabuse her of the notion that I had killed the marquess, the door to the drawing room opened and Signor Tallarico entered the room.

Freddie walked past me and held out her hand to him. "Victor, how glad I am to see you."

The Italian murmured something close to her ear, and she nodded at him.

I marched from the room, more determined than ever to find the letter. And the killer.

❖ 16 ❖

"*Sir! I have* been awaiting your return. I have laid out your evening clothes," Robinson said, his gaze running over me critically. "Er, would you like a bath first?"

"Yes. Immediately," I replied, stripping off my coat and tossing it on the back of the chair where Chakkri rested. The cat sat with his tail curled around his hind leg.

"Robinson, which was Lady Ariana's chamber? The one before or after Lord Kendrick's?"

"After, I believe, sir. If you are looking for the lady, I am afraid she departed a short time ago with Lady Crecy's party."

"Thank you."

Robinson exited the room to give orders for my bath.

I followed him out the door and stopped at Lady Ariana's chamber. Done in cheerful shades of yellow and white, it nevertheless managed to depress me when I found nothing whatsoever of interest within its walls.

Shuffling back to my room a quarter of an hour later, I addressed the cat, "Well, old boy, now what? That scandalous letter is still missing, we have a dead marquess found in the dog's grave, and Mr. Lavender on his way from Bow Street. If he discovers Lord Kendrick's hold over Freddie and me . . ."

"Reow," Chakkri cried urgently, shifting his position a bit and re-curling his tail around his hind leg.

"Devilish bad situation in which to find oneself, I tell you." I poured myself a measure of wine, drank it, then resumed my conversation with the cat. "What are you doing with your tail? Looks like an initial *C* curled about like that. Is that *C* for Chakkri?"

"Reow!" the cat said. He licked a spot over his left shoulder.

"A clever trick. You will be practicing it at Astley's Royal Amphitheatre, though, if Mr. Lavender finds that letter and thinks I murdered Lord Kendrick to protect Freddie. As if I would ruin the marquess's cravat while doing so."

The cat made a garbled sound.

"Just so. I would not have killed him despite my angry threats. I believe the idea that I might have done away with Lord Kendrick has crossed Freddie's mind. However, I cannot say with any certainty what Freddie has been thinking. Our relationship has been strained since I kissed her on her birthday."

"Reow!" he said again.

"I suppose you think I should not have kissed her, eh? Ah, Robinson," I said at the valet's entry. "Good timing, man. I need a hot bath to clear my head."

After bathing and dressing in black satin knee breeches, pristine white shirt and white waistcoat, I tied my cravat and glanced at the coat Robinson had selected. "No, let us have the Scotch-blue coat this evening, Robinson. Appropriate since we are expecting Mr. Lavender."

Robinson hurried to the wardrobe and extracted the desired coat. "I heard in the servants' hall that the Scotsman is on his way. He could use a hand in dressing."

"I have tried, I give you my word. One can only make suggestions, that is all. Some people do not believe, as I do, that dressing is an art."

Once properly clad, I was about to leave the room when the question I had been waiting for Robinson to voice all during the dressing process finally came out into the open.

"Sir, who do you think killed Lord Kendrick?"

I pulled on a pair of spotless white gloves. "I do not know. The marquess seemed to have more enemies than friends."

"Sir, the thought presented itself to me that Cook or her niece might have done it."

I swiveled around at that. "What? Oh, yes, I recall your telling me that Lord Kendrick had forced himself on Cook's niece. Hmmm, that would be motive indeed."

"I think so, sir. Shall I find out what I can? I know you do not like to discuss your part in resolving the two other murders that have touched our lives—"

"No, I do not want my investigations to become general knowledge amongst Society."

"That is just as it should be, I am certain, sir," Robinson agreed. "One would not want it known that you were associating with persons at Bow Street, either."

Or their daughters, I suddenly thought, remembering the Scotsman's lovely daughter, Lydia Lavender. The Bow Street man did not want me near her, I think because of the difference in our stations in life.

"In truth, Robinson, I had not yet considered Cook or her niece as possible suspects. Other members of the house party have come to mind. Find out what you can and report back to me."

"Yes, sir."

I walked out of the room, noticing that Robinson positively glowed with pleasure at the idea of inquiring into the matter. For my own part, I felt my mind split in two.

One part of me was preoccupied with finding the missing letter. The other part recognized that the letter was irrevocably tied up with the marquess, which made me more determined to find his killer. Adding to these motivations, I was incensed at the thought that the killer had struck at my dear Freddie's Oatlands, had buried the body in her dogs' cemetery, and appeared to be one of the very guests at her house party.

And that she might entertain the thought that I had been the one . . .

I stopped that line of thinking. I must tread with the greatest of care in this delicate situation, and act from intellect without allowing my emotions to cloud my judgment.

Later that night after a quite unsatisfactory dinner, due to Cook's upset, I surmised, Old Dawe announced the arrival of Mr. Lavender. The bluff Scotsman was clad in his customary salt-and-pepper game coat worn over corduroy pants tucked into scuffed boots. Stockily built and past his fiftieth year, he entered the green drawing room and stood on the threshold, studying the occupants. I noted his clothes were exactly as I had expected. Indeed, I had never seen him in anything different. I let out a sigh, which alerted him to my presence.

I thought I heard him utter a disgusted "ach" but he may have just been clearing his throat. He considers me naught but a foolish dandy. I admit I sometimes encourage this view to my own ends.

Freddie greeted him. "Mr. Lavender, how good of you to come. Please sit down."

Mr. Lavender bowed to the Royal Duchess, then saw that every chair in the room was taken up by either a human or a canine. He moved to the chair where Humphrey lay and bent to scratch the top of Humphrey's head. The hound gazed at him with soulful eyes. "Here's a trusty lad," Mr. Lavender pronounced in his Scottish burr. "Mayhaps he'd share this chair with me."

"I am sorry," Freddie said. "I did not even notice there was no empty chair. These past two days have been so distressing, I am afraid I am preoccupied."

Old Dawe offered Mr. Lavender a glass of wine from a tray. The Bow Street man accepted it and took a sip. "There's no need to be fretting yourself over me, your Royal Highness. I believe I met this fine hound in Brighton last autumn."

"Indeed you did." Freddie managed a smile. "How kind of you to remember."

"I have a head for remembering things." Mr. Lavender had the dog out of the chair and placed at his feet within moments. "I may be acquainted with Humphrey, and I do know Mr. Brummell here . . ."

Obviously the dog ranked higher in his opinion, but I nodded in the Bow Street man's direction.

". . . and I recollect meeting you also, haven't I?" Mr. Lavender said to Signor Tallarico.

"*Si,* I am Victor Tallarico," the Italian responded. "We also met at Brighton."

Mr. Lavender nodded. He placed his wineglass on a nearby table. Then he pulled a tattered notebook from one of his coat's copious pockets, extracted a stub of a pencil from another, and began making notes.

"Mr. Lavender, let me introduce Doctor Wendell and Squire Oxberry. The Squire is our local magistrate," Freddie said.

The men half rose, greeted one another and regained their chairs. You risk losing your chair to a dog at Oatlands if you leave it for long.

"Now, your Royal Highness, I received your missive and came straight out. I'd be pleased to help you with this matter. You wrote that your footman found the body of the Marquess of Kendrick buried in your dogs' cemetery earlier today."

"One of the Royal Duchess's dogs had passed away this morning and Old Dawe went to prepare a grave," I said.

Mr. Lavender slowly turned his head in my direction. I was the only one standing, refusing to sit anywhere other than at Freddie's side. Since Tallarico had beaten me to the coveted place, I stood next to a marble pedestal, one arm propped next to a dog statue.

The look Mr. Lavender gave me spoke volumes, volumes on letting him have control of the interview, but I have suffered those looks before and survived in one piece. Thus far.

"Unseemly place for a marquess to be buried, and a great deal of trouble," Squire Oxberry pronounced. "A great deal." Clearly the Squire disliked trouble of any sort. Why he had agreed to the position of magistrate, I cannot tell you.

"Old Dawe found the body, reported it to us, and we went out to inspect the scene," I said.

"What time and who went?"

"Myself, Sylvester Fairingdale, Roger Cranworth, Tallarico and the Royal Duchess. It was shortly after noon. We were all preparing to visit some local ruins."

"I know Fairingdale. Who is Roger Cranworth?"

"One of my neighbours, as were Lord Kendrick and his cousin," Freddie told him. "Mr. Cranworth and his sister were here for my house party."

"House party?" Mr. Lavender repeated, a bleak note in his voice. "Were there many people here?"

"Not really," Freddie mused. "Only about a hundred for my birthday celebration on Wednesday. Less than half of those were actually guests at Oatlands."

The Bow Street man looked like he had swallowed a lemon. "Where is everyone now?"

"The murder cut short our entertainments. People went back to Town, of course," Freddie answered, surprised at the question. "We are in the middle of a Season."

"Parties, assemblies, afternoon breakfasts, trips to Vauxhall, and the theatre are all so much more amusing than dead people buried where they are not supposed to be," I pointed out, shooting a mocking look at the Scotsman.

"One day there'll be a law against people leaving the vicinity after a murder has been committed," he muttered. "Let's get back to the body. How had the marquess been killed?"

Freddie looked at the floor.

I adjusted the sleeve of my coat.

"Hideous way to die," Squire Oxberry mumbled.

Doctor Wendell spoke up. "I examined the body, Mr. Lavender, and can tell you that a sharp instrument impaled Lord Kendrick's neck."

"What sharp instrument?" Mr. Lavender asked.

Freddie moaned. Tallarico took her hand.

I gritted my teeth.

Ulga appeared from her corner, poured her mistress a glass of wine and handed it to her, causing Freddie to remove her hand from the Italian's. Freddie took a swallow and waved the maid away. "The murder weapon was a hair ornament that belonged to me, Mr. Lavender."

"Antique Roman they are, made of solid jet," Tallarico said. "I know because I gave them to the Royal Duchess for her birthday."

"Them?" Mr. Lavender inquired.

"Yes, there was a matching pair," I said. "The Royal Duchess had left them right here." I indicated the top of the pedestal next to which I stood. "We found one. The other, well . . . you know where that one was discovered. The problem is, anyone could have come into the drawing room and slipped the thing into their pocket."

"Anyone with a motive to kill Lord Kendrick," Mr. Lavender stated.

"That is what I meant," I said, noting that more of the Scotsman's red hair had gone to grey since the last time I had seen him. I wondered if I had anything to do with the loss of colour. If so, his hair would be as white as snow before this investigation was over.

Doctor Wendell said, "I wonder why the hair ornament was selected as the murder weapon."

"The choice of weapon is interesting, I agree. Perhaps the killer acted on impulse. He or she noticed the hair ornament, and saw an opportunity," Mr. Lavender said. "Who do you think wanted Lord Kendrick dead, Doctor?"

Doctor Wendell looked startled. "I'm sure I don't know. I did think the murder happened outside, near the makeshift grave. There was blood on the grass and dirt around the grave, but no trail of blood leading from the spot. I find it impossible to imagine the killer could have thrust the hair ornament into Lord Kendrick's neck in the house without leaving a trail of some sort. Surely there would be evidence. Squire Oxberry and I looked around and could find none."

"He's right," the Squire pronounced. "We searched carefully, out in the hot sun this afternoon. It was while you were over at Lord Kendrick's estate, Mr. Brummell."

Mr. Lavender's gaze swung to me. "At the murder victim's house?"

"Er, yes, the man could not be laid out in the same clothing in which he was murdered. His cravat was soaked with blood," I said in my best foolish dandy voice.

Mr. Lavender nodded, his light green eyes mocking. "Bloodied cravats not being the fashion."

"Right. No more than bushy side whiskers and large mustaches."

The Bow Street man stroked the enormous growth of hair above his upper lip. "So you went to Lord Kendrick's house to get him fresh clothes, did you, laddie?"

"With the permission and gratitude of his valet, a man who had known the marquess from the time he was a boy."

"Name?" Mr. Lavender asked, pencil poised above the notebook.

"Thompson," Freddie said. "He and some of my servants took the body back to Lord Kendrick's estate just before you arrived. As Mr. Brummell said, Thompson wished his master to be cleaned and dressed in his Court clothes."

"There was no need to keep him drenched in all his blood," Squire Oxberry explained.

Freddie reached for her wineglass with trembling fingers.

"Squire, what about you? Do you have any opinion as to who killed the marquess?" Mr. Lavender asked.

The Squire scratched his head. "Opinion? I can't say I do. Though there have been stories aplenty about Lord Kendrick's family swirling about for some time."

"I do not think we need to repeat old gossip," Freddie said firmly.

"With all possible respect, your Royal Highness," Mr. Lavender said, "we need to start somewhere."

Freddie gave a little shake of her head, but the Squire plowed on. "Lord Kendrick's cousin, Lady Ariana, has bats in her attics, don't you know," he said, tapping a finger to his temple. "Her father was uncommon cruel to her while he was alive. She came to live with the old marquess several years back. Walks around in a fairy world, if you ask me."

"Did she have reason to want her cousin dead?"

I held my tongue silent. I was not ready to divulge Lady Ariana's stealing nor Lord Kendrick's threat to have her confined to a lunatic asylum.

The Squire's old face twisted. "Not that I am aware,

but you never know what a dotty person will take into their head."

Mr. Lavender's pencil flew across the pages of his notebook. "Where is she now?"

Freddie answered, "Out of sympathy, Lady Crecy took her to London to stay in their house. Lady Ariana was surprisingly unruffled about the news of her cousin's death. Lady Crecy and I agreed the girl must have been in shock."

"Why did she not go to the Cranworths'?" I asked Freddie. "I thought Lady Ariana and Cecily Cranworth were friends."

"Roger Cranworth decided suddenly that he wanted to go to London too," Freddie replied. "I cannot think he has the means to support Lady Ariana as well as himself and his sister, Cecily, in Town."

"He did take Cecily with him, though," Doctor Wendell said gloomily.

"Who will benefit financially from Lord Kendrick's murder? His cousin?" Mr. Lavender asked. "And who is marquess now?"

"It would depend upon how the letters patent were written," Freddie said. "Though unusual, it would not be impossible for the title to pass through to Lady Ariana's son, should she have one. In the meantime, a trustee would be appointed and she could have an allowance and the house. Though that may not be the way of it at all. I have no idea."

I had not even considered that motivation for Lady Ariana to do away with her cousin. Was she even capable of thinking that far ahead? I could sooner imagine her killing him more out of a desire to be kept from that lunatic asylum.

Mr. Lavender made notes. "Anyone else? Someone who quarrelled with the marquess?" he asked the room in general.

Tallarico looked at Freddie. What had she told him? How much did he know? Surely she would not have confided in him regarding the letter.

Doctor Wendell shifted in his chair. Other than Freddie and me, the marquess had quarrelled with both the Cranworths. I knew the doctor was worried about my saying something about Cecily Cranworth's passionate statement that she would rather see the marquess dead than to marry him. Again, I refrained from telling Mr. Lavender anything. I had no clear plan at this point. Better to say nothing than steer the investigator in a direction which might ultimately lead to Freddie. At least until I found the missing letter, I would have to keep Mr. Lavender in the dark as much as I could.

Unfortunately the Squire had no reason not to speak. "I think Roger Cranworth was angry with Lord Kendrick."

"They were friends," Doctor Wendell said hotly.

"Now, Doctor, I know about you and Cecily Cranworth. She told me herself she'd never marry me. I've got eyes in my head and could see she had formed a *tendre* for you."

The doctor's face went red.

"What does that have to do with Lord Kendrick?" Mr. Lavender asked impatiently.

The Squire enlightened him. "Roger Cranworth took it into his head that Lord Kendrick would marry his sister. He was furious when it looked like the marquess would not comply with this plan. I had offered for the girl, but Roger Cranworth wanted Lord Kendrick to wed his sister. She, er, had other ideas," he ended, glancing significantly at Doctor Wendell.

Mr. Lavender made notes.

At that moment, Freddie rose, causing the rest of the company to follow suit. "This is ridiculous! Neither Lady

Ariana nor Cecily nor Roger Cranworth would be capable of murder," she cried fervently.

"Then who would, your Royal Highness?" Mr. Lavender asked reasonably. "No stranger would have had access to the hair ornament left here in your drawing room. You must face facts. The killer has to be someone who was here at Oatlands."

Freddie's voice shook. "This is all exceedingly upsetting. I cannot bear much more—"

I was at her side, muscling my way between her and Tallarico. "I think you have learned all we know of the situation, Mr. Lavender. Let the Royal Duchess have some peace."

The Bow Street man pressed on. "To speak bluntly, I'd like to know more about the nature of your distress, your Royal Highness."

"She has had a violent murder occur on her property, cannot you understand that?" I said in an angry voice.

"Yes, I can, laddie. 'Tis only that when I first arrived in this room, the Royal Duchess said that she'd been distressed for the past *two* days. The murder happened today. What were your troubles yesterday, your Royal Highness? Did they involve the marquess? Do you have any suspicions as to who might have murdered him?"

Freddie looked at me.

Then she swooned into my arms.

❖ 17 ❖

Ulga tried to take Freddie's limp body from me. Tallarico let forth a burst of Italian protests, but I ignored them both. I carried the Royal Duchess upstairs to her bedchamber, Ulga following in our wake until we were at the door. The maid swung open the portal, then lit candles at the bedside and burned feathers to wave under her mistress's nose.

Hero and Georgicus looked up at our entrance from their place at the foot of Freddie's bed. I recognized two other dogs, Legacy and Minney, slumbering by the empty fireplace with three of their puppies.

I laid the Royal Duchess tenderly upon her bed. The skirts of her aquamarine gown with its small train spread across the coverlet. As I let her head fall gently on her pillow, every protective instinct in me cried out with the desire to remove all the unhappiness from her life. I could start by discovering the whereabouts of that blasted letter and the identity of Lord Kendrick's murderer.

If only I could do these things, I told myself, then Freddie and I could close the distance that had sprung up between us. We could return to the way things had been the evening of her birthday.

Even as the thought formed in my mind, a doubt crept in behind it.

"Excuse me, please," Ulga said. She carried the smoldering feathers held over a porcelain dish.

The dogs sat up, sniffing the air with interest. Hero moved to nudge Freddie's hand with his wet black nose, then licked it hopefully. He cocked his head at his mistress, who did not respond. Georgicus adjusted his position so that he laid against Freddie's limbs.

I took a step back while the maid administered to Freddie. On a table stood a decanter of sherry. I poured a small amount into a crystal glass.

"Ulga," Freddie murmured a moment later.

"Do not try to get up, your Royal Highness," Ulga advised. She put the dish with the feathers aside. "You fainted and are safe in your bedchamber now."

"Oh, dear. I cannot remember ever fainting before today. Now I have done it twice. What will people think?" Freddie said, her hand automatically going to stroke Hero. Her touch triggered a direct response via the enthusiastic wagging of his plumy tail.

"That you were overcome from the events of the day," I answered quietly. Ulga's lips folded at my intrusion.

Freddie gave a start, her hand dropping from the dog, then she looked at me. Her expression was guarded. "George, did you carry me upstairs? I must rise."

"Yes, I did carry you. Stay where you are comfortable, and do not concern yourself with the proprieties. I shall remain but a few minutes. Here, drink a bit of this sherry."

Ulga moved to place another pillow behind her mistress's head. As Freddie lifted herself to a sitting position, the dogs slid closer. Freddie accepted the glass from my hand, her fingers like ice.

Watching her take a sip, I said, "I wish you would

leave the matter of the marquess's demise and the letter
to me." I held up a hand against any protests. "Now I
know you have hired Mr. Lavender to uncover the killer,
and while I cannot think it wise, I accept it. We shall all
have to go back to London, even Mr. Lavender. That is
where everyone who attended the house party will be,
with the exceptions of Doctor Wendell and Squire Oxberry. Old Dawe will be here to forward any correspondence to you in Town. With him doing so, and the two
of us in London, we will be aware if anyone attempts to
continue Lord Kendrick's blackmail scheme."

Freddie shuddered. "I know I said I would come to
Town after the house party, but you cannot expect me to
keep that promise after what has happened."

Ulga nodded her agreement, then subsided into a chair
under my hostile gaze.

"Freddie, you must listen to me. As unpleasant as it is,
word of Lord Kendrick's murder at Oatlands is probably
all around London already. You must appear in Town,
above suspicion, above reproach, with your usual air of
dignity."

She looked away and began to pet Hero again. "I do
not want to go to London. I want to stay here with my
dogs. They love me. I can trust them."

Only with the greatest of self-control did I refrain from
comment on yours truly's feelings and trustworthiness.

A moment passed, then she said, "Very well, I shall
remove to St. James's Palace on Monday. I need the next
two days to organise the household. I should also pay my
final respects to Lord Kendrick. It would look odd in the
neighbourhood if I did not."

"I agree," I said.

"George," she said, turning her gaze to me. "I think it
best if you leave Oatlands since almost everyone else
has."

What of Victor Tallarico? I wanted to shout. Are you

going to tell him to leave as well? "I shall return to the drawing room and inform everyone you are recovered and resting. You will find me gone in the morning."

"You may call on me at the Palace to apprise me of your efforts to obtain the letter."

I made her a bow.

Ulga stood waiting with the door open. Happy to see me go, no doubt. I paused next to her and spoke in a low voice, "Take care of her."

Ulga's shoulders went back. "I alvays do."

Not like you, was the silent message I read in the maid's eyes.

I walked down the corridor, hearing the door close behind me.

Downstairs, Mr. Lavender, Victor Tallarico, and Doctor Wendell sat in the drawing room.

I told them of Freddie's condition, adding that she would arrive in London on Monday.

Mr. Lavender said, "That's good news." He pulled a small ivory box from one of his pockets, darting a look at me. I knew the box contained toothpicks. I also knew it had a tiny round turquoise stone in the centre of the lid. How did I know this? Because I personally had gifted the Scotsman with it after he once saved my life.

He popped a toothpick in his mouth and was about to put away the box when he examined it more closely. I knew what was coming next and tried not to cringe. Sure enough, Mr. Lavender spat on the top of the box, then rubbed it on his sleeve to clean it before putting it away. I shuddered.

He spoke around the toothpick. "Squire Oxberry has gone to bed. He is cooperating with me regarding the investigation and will let me know of any developments here in the countryside. I needn't stay overnight."

"You are going to set out for Town at this late hour?"

Victor Tallarico asked. "What about the highwayman who has been plaguing the area?"

"Highwayman?" Mr. Lavender sat forward in his chair.

I waved a careless hand, wishing I could choke the Italian. But wait, Tallarico's mention of the highwayman surely meant Freddie had not confided in him about the letter. If she had, he never would have broached the subject.

I answered the Bow Street man's question. "A mere country nuisance. He will not bother a man dressed as you are, riding on horseback. Er, I assume you came on horseback."

Mr. Lavender's bushy eyebrows came together. "I did. I'll go now, but when I get back to Town, I'll want to speak with you again, Mr. Brummell."

"I hold myself flattered," I replied, giving him my most elegant bow.

He scowled. "I'll want to talk to *everyone* involved in this again, and will be asking the Royal Duchess for a list of all in attendance at the house party. Not until Monday, though," he said, jamming a hat shaped like a coal-scuttle on his head. "Tomorrow I'll find out where the people mentioned here tonight are residing in London. Sunday is the Sabbath. We honour the Sabbath in the Lavender household."

With that remark he was gone. I turned my attention to Tallarico. "I expect you will be leaving in the morning."

"I had not decided."

"Now you have," I said.

He met my steady gaze and shrugged. "*Dio mio*, there's no need to have an apoplexy. I'll go tomorrow and prepare for her Royal Highness's arrival in Town. She will need to be kept amused once she arrives." With a wide smile, he strolled from the room.

Alone with Doctor Wendell, I poured myself a drink. "Wine, Doctor? I hear it is good for a man."

The country doctor looked as if he needed something to console him.

"Thank you, no. I must return to my home. The county relies upon me for medical services. There might have been a note asking for my assistance left at my door."

"Then I suppose you will not follow Miss Cranworth to London," I said.

The doctor shook his head, looking miserable. "There is another doctor in the area, but he is miles away and his wife has been ill. Perhaps in a day or two when she improves . . ."

"You may find that the Middlesex Hospital is holding a series of lectures you think beneficial for you to hear," I suggested.

He looked up at that, a light of hope in his eyes. "Indeed, Mr. Brummell, indeed I shall. In the meantime, if it's not too much to ask of you, I must beg a favour."

"Please do. I am at your service."

"Can you look after Miss Cranworth in London?" he asked earnestly. "She is not used to Town ways as it is, not to mention the events of the past few days. With her brother the only one to offer her comfort and guidance, she might be unhappy."

My plan was to watch both of the Cranworth siblings, in fact, to call on them, but for different reasons entirely. However, there was certainly no need to alarm Doctor Wendell. "You may be assured I shall. In the meantime, you have my card in case you wish to direct a letter to me."

"I do, but I hope to be in London before long."

We parted company on the best of terms. He could not know that the thought crossed my mind that his obvious love for Miss Cranworth might provoke him into doing away with the thorn in her side, that thorn being Lord Kendrick.

I made my way through the quiet house up to my bedchamber. "Robinson, we must leave tomorrow," I said as he helped me remove my coat.

"Sooner than expected, sir. What time shall I wake you?"

Was that a hint of a smile on Robinson's face? Was he perhaps anxious to return to his mysterious lady friend in London? Or just happy to be leaving Oatlands' dog hair behind?

"There is no need to rush. You can bring my tea around eleven."

"I shall notify the stables to have your coach ready to depart around one o'clock. Am I to ride with you, sir?" he asked, clearly torn between wanting to do so and knowing he would have to share my company with that of the cat. He darted a look at Chakkri, who laid on his stomach, his paws tucked under his breast and his tailed curled into a *C*.

"Yes, you will come with me this time," I replied, reminded of the highwayman and the letter. "By the way, did you have an opportunity to find out about Cook and her niece?"

"Yes, sir. We must eliminate them as suspects."

"Oh?"

"Someone might have told me earlier, but it appears Cook's niece, Jane, needed medical attention. Jane had been in shock after Lord Kendrick forced himself on her, then last night she took to uncontrollable crying. Cook sought Doctor Wendell, and the two of them stayed up watching over the girl all night and into this morning."

"Good God."

"Indeed, sir. One of the maids said that Doctor Wendell only left the room to change clothing in Mr. Dawe's room just before everyone gathered for the trip to the ruins at noon. As for Cook, the maid said that she found her dozing in the bed with Jane. The girl's hand clutched her aunt's even in sleep."

"That would explain both the difference in quality of the meals served and Doctor Wendell's haggard looks today," I mused.

"It appears so, sir," Robinson agreed.

It also appeared that my last hope the killer was not one of the guests at Oatlands had vanished.

❖ 18 ❖

Ah, London at the height of the Season. Is there anything to compare to it? Provided one is wealthy or powerful, and not preoccupied with a murder investigation.

The grand balls, parties, assemblies. The theatre, the plays, the opera. Almack's, the most fashionable of gathering places where so many matches between members of the cream of Society are made. Hyde Park, where birds fly overhead while Birds of Paradise, Soiled Doves, Peacocks, Cocks of the Walk, and Pigeons Ripe for Plucking stroll the grounds or show themselves to advantage—in their new high-perched phaetons—alongside the members of the *Beau Monde*. One must be seen, admired, envied.

Alas, I had other things on my mind.

Saturday near the hour of three o'clock, I arrived home at No. 18 Bruton Street. Crossing the black-and-white-tiled hall, I ascended the stairs to my bedchamber, lidded basket in hand. Robinson trailed behind lugging my valises.

The occupant of the basket, heretofore silent, commenced a shuffling, murmuring, and finally a loud "reow!"

sensing he was home at last. The supreme happiness of his feline heart knew no bounds.

No longer would Chakkri be disturbed by the disagreeable sounds of dogs barking, whimpering, howling, woofing, or growling. No clicking of dog paws on the hallway outside where the Prince of Fur slept would interrupt his slumber. No stray dog hairs would float through cracks into His Catly Highness's realm to cause a delicate sneeze or ten. No barbaric canine sniffing at the bottom of the door to his chamber would cause Lord Feline to lift his dark nose into the air and his mouth to open an inch, the whisker pads curled back a bit in haughty disdain. A cause for celebration indeed.

"Here we are, Chakkri," I said, opening the door to my bedchamber and releasing the cat. He hopped out of the basket with the agility of a ballet dancer. After a quick, satisfied survey of the room, he disappeared behind a black-lacquered screen set up in one corner. This area contains his sand-tray.

The selection of the tray where Chakkri conducts his private business had been left to Robinson when the cat first joined our household last autumn. The valet had chosen a particular porcelain container given to me by a member of the merchant class who hoped to gain my favour. The thing is ivory-coloured with gold trim. In the exact centre, the artist has painted a detailed likeness of yours truly complete with tall hat, perfectly tied cravat, and raised quizzing glass. Robinson's idea of revenge.

I stripped off my gloves and laid my dog's head walking stick on a table between two high-backed chairs angled toward the cold fireplace. My chamber contains every luxury a gentleman of fashion could want: a spacious, tented bed with ivory silk hangings, a handsome dressing table, a set of mahogany wardrobes marching in a row down one wall, a fine floral-patterned Persian carpet, engravings and paintings upon which to gaze, as well as my superb collection of prized Sèvres porcelain resting on a crescent-shaped console table.

Furthermore, the chamber runs the length of the house, with large windows on either end from which Chakkri can monitor the activities of passersby both human and avian.

Speaking of the devil, Chakkri emerged from behind the screen, stretching his fawn-coloured body to its utmost length. He walked on elegant legs to the bed, elevated himself to the top of the coverlet, and rolled around on his back enjoying the smooth feel of the satin. At one point during this performance, he looked at me upside down. I could not resist reaching out and stroking his incredibly soft fur. This seemed to relax him enough to shed his inhibitions, curl into a ball, and, after a sigh of deep contentment, drift into sleep.

While Chakkri might loll about, there was no time for me to enjoy the comforts of home. I had some investigating to do. All during the ride back to London from Oatlands, I had concentrated on the matter of the missing letter and Lord Kendrick's murder. Questions formed in my mind, some of which I hoped to have answers for today. I had thought of a plan which might lead me to the identity of Lord Kendrick's accomplice in his high-wayman scheme. If I could find that ruffian, I might find the letter.

When Robinson entered the room carrying a second set of valises, I was already extracting an Egyptian-blue coat out of the wardrobe. "Robinson, after you have put those down, bring me some water so I might wash before changing clothes."

"Very well, sir. You are going out?"

"Yes."

"Then my services will not be required for the next few hours?"

I glanced pointedly at the valises. "After everything is unpacked, I daresay you will be free. Why?"

"I wish to take a walk, sir," the valet replied stiffly.

Going to see his lady friend, I surmised. I wonder who she is. "All right. Just return in time to help me dress for the evening. That reminds me. While you are downstairs getting the water, examine my invitations and see who is holding entertainments tonight. I need to know what gossip is flying."

"Very good, sir."

"Oh, and Robinson?"

"Yes, sir?"

"I also need to know where Roger and Cecily Cranworth are staying in London. Should you by chance happen upon any other domestic staff while out on your walk, please inquire."

Robinson picked up a Chinese bowl from the washstand, nodded his agreement, then exited the room.

About an hour later, I hailed a hackney coach to take me to my destination in Covent Garden, outside Mayfair. Ned and Ted, my chairmen, were away from the house, so I could not ride in the extravagant comfort of my sedan-chair. Their absence was understandable. They did not expect my return until Monday, and were probably off enjoying themselves. I chuckled to think of what the two farm boys—identical twins of muscular build nearing their twentieth year—would be doing. Viewing the Menagerie at the Tower? Attending a balloon ascension? They had only arrived in London last autumn, seeking employment and money to send home to their "mum," who worked a pig farm.

As it turned out, Ned and Ted were indulging in neither of these treats. They were, in fact, loitering outside my very destination, Miss Lydia Lavender's shelter, Haven of Hope, with a pretty girl. The two blond-haired boys flanked the dark-haired girl like bookends.

Ted was the first to perceive my arrival. "Mr. Brummell, sir!" he cried in astonishment. He adjusted the sleeves and collar of his blue-and-gold livery. He knows how particular I am in regards to their appearance. "We thought you'd be away 'til Monday night."

His brother, Ned, swung in my direction and gaped at me as if he were all of seven years old and had been caught pilfering blackberry tarts from the larder.

The girl who had been flirting with the twins giggled. Then, holding her skirts up a good two inches higher than necessary, she hastened down the street.

Ned gazed after her longingly. Then he looked at me, a frown between his eyes. "I don't mean to be rude or nothin', Mr. Brummell, 'cause you've been awful good to Ted and me since we come up to Town. But it don't seem fair that just when I was goin' to get Miss Molly to walk out with me, you come along and spoil my chance. It feels like the time back home at the county fair when I thought I'd won the prize for holding the most pickled eggs in my mouth—"

"You never had a chance with Miss Molly, Ned," Ted interrupted before his brother could begin one of his long-winded stories. I was surprised at the tone in which he spoke, a manner quite unlike any I had heard either of the good-natured brothers employ.

Ned glared at Ted. "You're wrong about that, you are! Miss Molly slipped me one of them fancy candied violets the girls make at the shelter and sell to the grocer. She likes *me*, I tell you."

Ted snorted. "She gave *me* one of them violets too, so what do you say to that, Ned?"

"Knave!" Ned shouted.

Before the two could resort to fisticuffs and possibly damage their well-tailored livery, not to mention their persons, I intervened. "In my experience, girls of about six and ten years, as Molly appears to be, rarely know their own minds in regards to men. Add to that the fact the

pair of you look exactly alike, and well . . ." Here I spread
my hands in a helpless gesture.

The twins scowled at each other.

I sighed. "Knock on the shelter door, Ted. I have business inside. The two of you need to return to Bruton Street
and be ready to take me about in my sedan-chair this
evening."

Ted followed my order, then he and his brother walked
away into the crowded streets. I could hear their argument
over the girl begin again.

"You always think girls like you better than me," Ned
complained.

"I'm smarter than you," Ted boasted. "Females like that
in a man."

"You aren't smarter than me! We're wearin' the very
same livery!"

Ted gave his brother's arm a punch. "Half-wit! I meant
what's in my brain-box."

Ned shoved him back.

Meanwhile the shelter door swung open. Expecting to
see Miss Lavender, or one of the females inhabiting the
house, I was taken aback when my gaze travelled down
to a young boy, about eleven years old, standing in the
portal. Exceedingly thin and gawky-looking, the lad had
a thick mane of light brown hair, blond on the top layers
where the sun had faded it. A cowlick made the hair above
the centre of his forehead stand straight up. Since this was
directly above his nose, it only called attention to that
unfortunate appendage, which was short and turned up at
the end.

My surprise was nothing, though, compared to the
shock writ across the boy's face as his gaze ranged slowly
from my shiny Hessian boots to my snowy white cravat.
His mouth hung open, but no words came out.

"Lionel, who's come to see us?" Miss Lavender's Scottish lilt sounded from the hall behind the boy. "I told you

that if you open the door to anyone, you must collect me or Miss Ashton."

"Must be the Prince 'isself," breathed the boy. He dropped down and knelt on one knee, head bowed.

"No, no, no, halfling," I said, stretching out my hand to help him rise. "I am not the Prince of Wales. You must not bow and scrape to me."   Lydia Lavender appeared at the door. I swept off my hat and made her a bow. "Good afternoon, Miss Lavender. Is this young man your butler?"

Standing once more, the boy beamed. "Naw, ain't nothin' so fine as that!"

"Mr. Brummell! What a surprise to see you, but a nice one to be sure. It's been too long since we've met," she said. "Please come in. This is Lionel. He came to live with us about a fortnight ago and helps with the heavy work around the shelter."

The boy looked worshipfully at his saviour.

"Is that so? He does appear strong," I said, earning a bashful grin from the youth. I observed the scruffy but clean homespun brown breeches and neatly darned shirt, which were both much too small for the boy. I wondered how he came to be a part of Miss Lavender's household.

Suddenly, the youth's blue eyes opened to their widest. "Are you *the* Beau Brummell?" he gasped with the large measure of awe managed only by persons of his age. Immediately he answered his own question. "O' course it's you, sir. I 'ear tell the Prince is a fat man, and old too. He don't dress as fine as you neither."

I stifled a laugh at this assessment which, if he were to hear it, would propel Prinny to his bed for a week. I crossed the threshold into the house. "Delighted to meet you, Lionel," I said, netting another shocked look from him.

"That's enough, Lionel," Miss Lavender said in firm tones, negated by the way her hand affectionately mussed the top of his hair. "Go back to the kitchens now and see if they need more water pumped."

"Yes, ma'am," Lionel said. He stared at me a moment more, as if memorizing my appearance, then took to his heels and raced from the room at top speed.

"You are full of surprises, yourself, Miss Lavender. I did not know you housed boys," I said, removing my hat.

Miss Lavender's shelter is for women fallen on hard times, or as she is wont to say, "destitute and downtrodden females." She had used an inheritance from her mother to open the house, but is always in need of funds to keep it running. Her father has informed me he would prefer to see her wed, and himself with a grandchild to bounce on his knee.

She closed the door behind me. "I don't normally take in boys, you're right. But Lionel is an exception."

"Tell me about him."

"Let's go into the sitting room. Miss Ashton is teaching a class in mathematics in the front room."

The Scottish woman led the way, while I availed myself of the view. Not of the contents of the small house, but of the appearance of Miss Lavender's person. For the Bow Street investigator's daughter is most attractive. Her hair, which I once had the privilege of seeing loose, is a dark red. If one observes closely, one can see flecks of gold in the strands. Today, she wore the pretty tresses in a careless knot set at the crown of her head. Several tendrils escaped their confinement, running freely down her neck to lie on her straw-coloured, sensible gown.

"Can I get you some tea?" she asked. I noted she wore the spectacle-glasses I had designed for her. Other than being gold-framed, they are simple and delicately feminine. The case I presented them to her in is a different matter. Black velvet, the top features two *L*'s embroidered in gold thread with two small emeralds—the exact shade of her eyes—after each letter.

"No tea, thank you. I will not stay long."

We crossed into the sitting room. This is a tiny area cluttered with books. A few shabby upholstered chairs are placed around the fireplace. A dilapidated desk stands in one corner. Indicating I should sit, Miss Lavender closed the door behind her. She is not one to follow the proprieties which state an unmarried female must not be alone behind closed doors with a gentleman.

I waited for her to be seated before taking a seat close to her, observing that the stuffing was coming out on the arm of my chair. "Thank you for seeing me without prior notice. I would have sent you a note, but I have just returned from the country and did not have time."

Miss Lavender gave me a saucy grin and removed her spectacles and put them in her lap. "Now, Mr. Brummell, when have I ever been one to stand on ceremony?"

I returned her smile. She can be strong-willed and is the most independent female I have ever known, yet I have occasionally felt a warmth for her that her father would not approve. Indeed, the Bow Street man does not wish me to associate with his daughter, so conscious is he of the difference in our stations in life. There is something else as well. I cannot put my finger on what it is, but Mr. Lavender is exceptionally protective of his daughter.

As her translucent skin glowed like the finest Sèvres porcelain, I did not feel like complying with Mr. Lavender's wish for me to stay away from his daughter. Besides, I needed her help.

"Never in the time I have known you have you been, let us say, overly concerned with the conventions," I answered.

She laughed in her full-throated way. "Faith, I believe your man, Robinson, follows more of the rules of Society than I do."

I chuckled. "You may be right. What about Lionel? How did he come to live with you?"

Miss Lavender let out a sigh. "His father sold him to a chimney sweep when he was a tot. Lionel's never seen him since. His mother died in childbirth."

"Eventually his shoulders grew too wide for him to get up the chimneys, I expect," I mused in a cheerless voice. "The rest of him is as thin as a peppermint stick."

"Precisely. He ran away from the sweep when the man wanted to begin selling him for other services." Miss Lavender's hands balled into fists.

"Good for Lionel," I said, trying to lighten the mood. Inside I felt enraged that anyone would so abuse a mere child. Though I know in the stews of London, many such atrocities take place. "The boy has spirit. What happened after he ran away?"

"Funny you should say 'the boy,' for Lionel had no name. The sweep referred to him as Boy. Lionel and I decided on his name when I took him in. He'd been living in the streets for over a year. The little soul survived on his wits."

"And a bit of thievery, perhaps?"

"What else?" Miss Lavender asked me, defiantly.

"And is that how he came to your attention?"

She nodded. "By chance, I happened to be at Bow Street bringing Father some of my special stew when the constable brought in the poor, frightened boy. Oh, he tried to be brave, as boys will when they are half scared to death, you know, Mr. Brummell."

"Yes," I replied, thinking of some of the behaviour I had witnessed while attending Eton.

"At any rate, there was something about Lionel that touched me. I see a goodness in him, despite the life he's been forced to lead. Lionel promised he could run like the wind and that he would practice running faster and faster every day so he might one day work for Bow Street. He begged for a chance to help out at the office, but Father said he was too young. That's when I realised I could use the lad here. Later, as he grows older, he might very well become a runner or even a constable. Father argued with me at first—"

"I should wager he did," I said.

"But I prevailed."

"Naturally."

We looked at one another for a long moment. Miss Lavender's chance act of kindness in bringing her father a meal had resulted in nothing short of a miracle in a young boy's life. I reflected that Miss Lavender probably never stopped to think of what might have become of the boy if not for her kindness.

Miss Lavender held my gaze, then pushed a stray lock of hair from her temple. "Now, Mr. Brummell, you did not come here to hear about Lionel. What has prompted your visit? You've been at a place called Oatlands, owned by the Duke of York, weren't you? My father told me someone was murdered there, and that her Royal Highness has engaged his services."

I was called back from my thoughts. "Yes, that is true."

She cast me a mocking look. "Seems to me that one member of Society isn't exactly adhering to good moral practice, are they? Unless murder is suddenly the fashion. But it comes as no wonder to me. As you know, Mr. Brummell, members of the nobility are most often the ones who cause the downfall of the girls here."

"And I shall continue to drop a word in the ear of any gentleman who I think may feel his conscience eased by making a contribution to your shelter. Right now, though, I need your assistance."

"Concerning the murder?" she asked warily. "You know I don't get involved in Father's business."

"Oh, this is no concern of your father's," I dissembled. "While on route to Oatlands, the coach containing my valet and my things was set upon by a highwayman. The thief made off with several of my belongings."

"Gracious heavens! Never say so! Who would commit such a heinous crime?" Miss Lavender exclaimed, those green eyes of hers sparkling with humour. She clutched her throat in a dramatic way.

"Sadly, I speak the truth. Ahem, I think it likely the thief took my clothes to a, to a . . ." I raised a hand to my brow, unable to get the words out.

"A rag-merchant, Mr. Brummell?" Miss Lavender asked, a smile playing about her lips.

"Yes," I said with a profound air of tragedy.

She laughed out loud. "As if any of your fine garments could be termed rags!"

"You see the pain I am in," I said, helplessly.

"Impossible man. What can I do to help?"

"I am not familiar with the sort of person who would accept stolen goods and sell them. I do not know where to begin looking. I thought perhaps you—"

"Might know who the rag-merchants are and tell you?"

I smiled. "One can never accuse you of being slow, Miss Lavender."

A line appeared on her ivory forehead. "But whatever would you want with the clothes now, even if you were to find them? Surely you couldn't wish to wear them again."

I assumed an air of haughty disdain. "Of course not. I shall never wear the garments if I find them. Rather, I wish to see if the rag-merchant remembers the person who sold him my things. If he does, I might be able to trace the highwayman."

Miss Lavender slanted a look at me. "That's very clever. But why put yourself to the trouble? Surely there is a local magistrate in Weybridge who will find the thief?"

"There is indeed. But the highwayman has been preying on travellers near Oatlands, the home of her Royal Highness, the Duchess of York. She is my friend. I cannot allow the thief to continue lest she be put in danger."

"Oh." Miss Lavender straightened her shoulders. "I see. The Royal Duchess. Of course you would be concerned for her."

"So you will help me?"

"I'll tell you what I know," she said, rising and crossing to the desk.

I admired her, er, posture as she walked. She seated herself behind the desk and drew out paper and pencil.

"Most of the cast-off shops are in Monmouth Street. You could try the scavengers, but I think no barker would have one of your fine coats. Here are the names of the merchants who carry more valuable items."

I stood next to the desk as she continued to write names and directions. Her slender hands worked efficiently. At last she put the pencil down and handed me the slip of paper. With luck, one of these people would lead me to Lord Kendrick's accomplice.

"If you don't find anything at those places, come back and tell me. But unless the items have already been sold, you should find at least one of your things."

"Thank you. I am in your debt, Miss Lavender. By the way, before I go, I wanted to tell you that I think my chairmen, Ned and Ted, are enamoured of one of your residents. Molly?" I raised an inquiring brow.

Miss Lavender let out an exasperated sigh. "That girl! Are your men the twins I've seen hanging about?" She smiled suddenly and answered her own question. "But of course *you'd* have *matching* chairmen."

"Yes. If they have caused any trouble—"

"No, no, Molly brings it on herself, I'm afraid. She's an incorrigible flirt, though there's no harm in her. The agencies I work with trying to find positions for the girls have each told me the same story. They send Molly out for an interview and either the prospective employer will not hire her because of her beauty, or she is hired and then subjected to advances by the men in the household. Invariably, she returns here."

"And you take her back?"

"I can't leave her to the fate of the streets," Miss Lavender said, her amusement fading and her voice rising a bit. "You've no idea the horrors awaiting an unprotected woman who finds herself at the mercy of a man—" She broke off abruptly, then drew in a deep breath. "This shelter exists to help those in need, which Molly is."

I tilted my head and studied her. "You know, Miss Lavender, I do not believe I have ever met anyone with as much concern and caring toward unfortunate girls as you show. Your charity is remarkable."

"Thank you," she said, her attention suddenly on putting paper away in her desk.

"I confess I wonder what drives your plans and ambitions for the shelter and your protective nature toward its occupants. Do you somehow feel a sort of kindred spirit with the girls?"

Miss Lavender shut the desk drawer with a trifle more force than was necessary. When she looked up at me, there was a closed expression on her face I had never seen. Clearly she did not want to discuss her past nor her motivations.

Of course, this attitude only made me want to know more. Miss Lavender is so unlike the females of my acquaintance, you see.

"That's a long list I've given you, Mr. Brummell. You'd best start now if you hope to find your fine clothes before the shops close."

"Just so," I said, donning my hat and turning to leave.

"Mr. Brummell," she said, making me pause. "Good luck to you. Let me know if you find your clothes and the highwayman."

I inclined my head. "I shall."

A short time later, a hackney coach dropped me in Monmouth Street. I travelled on foot from there, my dog's head cane with the concealed swordstick in hand, to each of the establishments on Miss Lavender's list. My presence in this part of London was met with a clamour of attention. While I was forced to endure the calls of the peddlers, "What do you buy?" whom I ignored, the cries of "Please, sir!" from the street urchins I could not brush aside until I ran out of shillings. I was approached by prostitutes smelling of gin, stared at insolently by most of the grubby men, and eyed by slithering pickpockets at every turn.

Upon entering the next to last stop on my list, a shop whose weathered sign proclaimed it to be Kirkhead's Fineries, I stopped just inside the door, staring in complete shock at the heavyset man behind the counter. No doubt he was the proprietor, Mr. Kirkhead. His rheumy gaze fixed on me, then he beamed, revealing an incomplete set of teeth. "Come in, me fine gennelman! I 'ave jest what yer lookin' fer, and iffen I don't, I'll get it." One sagging eyelid dropped in a wink.

"I believe you do have what I seek," I replied in a muted voice, feeling my head spin from the atrocity I beheld. For stretched to the very limit the cloth would allow, and still not meeting across his huge stomach, atop a shirt Grimaldi the clown would shun, was one of Weston's finest creations.

My Saunders-blue coat, to be exact.

❧ 19 ❧

Regaining my composure, I stepped up to the counter. "That coat you are wearing belongs to me. It was stolen."

The small eyes narrowed. "Git out o' me shop!"

I gripped my dog's head cane and banged the tip down hard on the floor. "Do you know who I am?"

"Bloody 'ell, what's it to me? I won't 'ave nobody comin' in my shop accusin' me o' stealin'," he blustered. But he made no move to evict me from the premises.

My gaze held his. "I am George Brummell. *Beau* Brummell."

Mr. Kirkhead's little eyes popped within the loose folds of his eyelids.

I continued smoothly, "Weston made that coat for me under my specifications. Shall I send for him, along with someone from Bow Street—"

"No!" the merchant howled. He raised his hands, palms outward. Then lowering his voice he let out a nervous laugh and adopted a friendly tone. "Lookee 'ere, I don't want no trouble. I didn't steal the coat, I tell yer. I bought it fair and square. 'Ere, ye can 'ave it fer what I paid fer it." He struggled to remove the garment.

"I think not," I said, freezing him with my words.

A hurt expression spread across his fleshy features. " 'Twouldn't be gennelman-like o' ye to take it without payin' somethin' for it. I'd be losin' money through no fault o' me own."

"You purchase stolen goods at your own peril. Now tell me where you got my coat."

"Where I got it?" Mr. Kirkhead said nothing for a moment, thinking hard. Then he slammed a meaty fist on the wooden counter. "I knewed 'e would be trouble. Didn't 'e 'ave the mark of the devil 'isself on 'is face? I shouldn't 'ave dealt with 'im." He licked his lips suddenly, then said, "Mr. Brummell, sir, I be a business man. I buy a lot o' goods and don't ask no questions, see? This 'ere was the only thing I did git off 'im who came to me offerin' it. Fancied it for meself, I did."

Lying, I thought. Probably tallying up how much he could get for the rest of my things now that he could use my name in connection with them. But did he have the blue velvet book? I looked closely at the contents of the shop. A jumble of clothes, hats, some battered-looking canes. Not a book of any sort in sight.

"What is the man's name who sold you my coat?"

"Didn't get no name. Not the usual practice, yer know."

"What did you mean when you said the man had the 'mark of the devil' on his face?" I asked.

Mr. Kirkhead looked frightened. Perhaps he believed in spells and curses and thought Lord Kendrick's highwayman capable of inflicting them on him because of some birthmark.

"I am waiting for a reply," I stated. "I want a description of the fellow. Give it to me, and I shall not apprise Bow Street of this misadventure."

The merchant weighed his options.

"And you may keep the coat," I added magnanimously. Not that I would wear the dirty thing now.

That settled it for Mr. Kirkhead. " 'E were black-haired, thin, an' wiry but a tough sort. 'Cross one side of 'is face there were a red mark." Mr. Kirkhead raised his hand and placed it flat against his cheek. " 'Bout 'ere it were. Like 'is skin were stained red by the hand o' the devil."

The tinkling of a bell announced the arrival of another customer. An older woman, obviously well bred but in reduced circumstances, carried a pretty gown from the last century in her hands.

"One more thing, then I shall take my leave," I said in a low voice. "Did the thief offer you a book to sell? One covered in blue velvet?"

The threat of Bow Street gone, the merchant's eyes were on the brocade finery in the woman's arms. "Book? Don't carry nothin' like that. Wouldn't be able to sell it."

I left the shop thinking that this particular book would certainly sell. And for a price higher than Mr. Kirkhead could ever imagine.

But even with his distinctive facial abnormality how would I ever discover the identity of Lord Kendrick's highwayman and where in London he was? I was hardly familiar with thieves' dens. Time was precious. Days could pass before I found the man. And were I to wander about in low places, my presence in the less-fashionable parts of London was certain to be remarked upon.

I hailed a hackney cab and sat down after wiping the seat with my handkerchief. The rhythmical sound of the horses' hooves on cobblestone faded from my mind as I contemplated my dilemma.

Robinson would hand in his notice on the spot were I to ask him to venture into the low side of London to help me find the thief. Though I could inquire if anyone fitting the description given had been seen about Oatlands.

Ned and Ted were apt to only find trouble.

Dash it. If only I could trust Mr. Lavender with this new information about the highwayman. He would have plenty of contacts among thieves. But I could not risk the Bow Street man's tracing the blackguard and finding out about that blasted letter.

Then I thought of Miss Lavender's Lionel.

By the time I arrived home in Bruton Street, the hour was advanced. I would need to see if, from the mountain of invitations received, Robinson had discovered which entertainments were being held tonight.

My plan was to see Lady Crecy, in hopes of setting a time I could call on her and visit Lady Ariana. I was anxious to question the girl and see for myself how she was taking the death of her cousin. Of most particular interest was her mental state.

I also wanted to question Lady Crecy to find out where the Cranworths were residing in Town. The siblings might even be attending a party tonight, though Roger Cranworth did not move in the highest circles of Society.

Before I did any of this, I would need to try to speak to Lionel in private. I felt a bit of a cad, not letting Miss Lavender know I wanted the boy's help. But that intrepid female would ply me with questions I did not want to answer at present.

My best chance was to return to the shelter, perhaps with a bouquet of flowers for Miss Lavender and a note of thanks telling her I had located my clothes. I would deliver the tribute myself, but at the kitchen door, where I was most likely to find Lionel. No doubt he would be thrilled to execute such a simple commission as asking in the neighbourhood about a thief with a particular birthmark. A commission for which I would be sure to reward him.

Pleased with these strategies, I closed the front door behind me and called for Robinson, wondering why he had not perceived my arrival in the hall.

There was no answer. I deposited my hat and stick onto the hall table. Robinson could not still be out with his lady friend, could he?

I walked into my book-room. Perhaps Robinson had left out the cards of invitation for tonight's events.

Seating myself behind my desk, I was happy to see five invitations laid out for my inspection. Scanning the lines rapidly, I came to the conclusion that two of them were lesser parties given by newly rich members of the merchant class. The other three were all being held by members of the *Beau Monde*. I considered their hosts, knowing instinctively that Lady Crecy would choose the one whose standing in Society was the highest.

There was no question who that was: the Marchioness of Salisbury. I smiled. Lady Salisbury is one of my favourite people, and I am fortunate enough to call her my friend. She is also one of the patronesses of Almack's, someone Lady Crecy would be sure to toady to.

Upon my soul, I thought suddenly, Lady Salisbury would give me a rare set-down if she learned I was in Town and did *not* attend her party. The matter was decided.

At that moment, Chakkri, who had entered the room soundlessly on his velvet brown paws, leapt onto my desk. This is a habit I cannot like. He invariably is interested in my letters, he adores sniffing and even nibbling at my quill pen, and his lashing tail has often threatened the inkstand.

Holding Lady Salisbury's invitation in my hand, I spoke to the cat with heavy sarcasm. "Well, Chakkri, thank heavens I had this murder investigation and the matter of the missing letter inspiring me to go about tonight. Otherwise I would surely incur Lady Salisbury's displeasure."

Chakkri sat tall, with his tail curled around his hind leg in a *C*. He let out a loud "reow."

Across the room, a gasp and a shuffling sound startled me. Rising, I saw Robinson stretched out on the long sofa which rests against one wall. He had been sleeping there the whole time I had been in the room!

"Robinson! Good God, man, what are you doing?" I stepped across to peer down at him. His hair was mussed, his shirt was not tucked into his breeches properly, and his neckcloth was straggly. One foot was shoeless. In short, he had been sleeping in his clothes and looked like it.

He struggled, but it seemed an effort for him to open his eyes. "Sir? Th-that you?"

Chakkri leapt onto the side table. He stretched over the arm of the sofa, his neck elongated, and stared down at the valet. That Robinson did not even react to this movement on the cat's part should tell you just how far out of his senses Robinson was.

"Have you and your lady friend been drinking?" I asked in a severe tone, though he did not smell of spirits.

"No. Fanny gave me a tisane. For my nerves," he murmured, closing his eyes as if against a bright light.

Fanny!

"A tisane for your nerves! What nerves?"

Robinson's eyes opened again. "Fine in a few moments. Help you dress for the evening."

"The devil you will! Sleep off whatever your ladylove has given you. I shall dress myself."

At this, Chakkri turned his attention from the supine valet to look at me skeptically.

"And I do not wish for any comment from you!"

"Reow!"

With that, I marched upstairs to my bedchamber, chose a dark blue coat, the colour of the midnight sky, and laid it on the bed. I turned back to the wardrobe, selected a crisp shirt, a white waistcoat with faint lines of silver thread running through it, and a pair of black breeches.

When I turned, musing that I would have to either try to rouse Robinson or heat water for washing myself, a sight met my eyes which caused me to shout, "You devil-cat! Get off my coat this instant. That is a bad-cat thing to do!"

Chakkri yawned.

A complicated manouever ensued, where I extracted the cat from the coat without his claws nicking the expensive cloth, the feline muttering the whole time.

Suffice it to say, the hands of the clock were striking nine before I was ready to be seen in public.

First, I needed to visit Lionel. This presented a bit of a problem in the form of transportation. I did not want Ned and Ted possibly seeing Molly and fighting over her. Thus, I instructed them to wait for me outside my town house, sedan-chair at the ready, to take me to Lady Salisbury's after I returned from an errand.

Hailing yet another hackney, this one thankfully cleaner than the last, I gave the direction to the Haven of Hope. I instructed the coachman to drop me at the entrance to the alley behind the shelter, and commanded him to wait for me. Coins changed hands, and the driver agreed. On the way, we stopped once at a flower-stall.

Reaching my destination, I rapped on the back door with my dog's head cane. I hoped Miss Lavender would not be the one to answer my knock. I had the excuse of the flowers, though that would not explain my coming to the back entrance.

Luck was with me. After a furtive glance from behind the curtains, Lionel himself opened the door.

I pressed a finger to my lips and motioned him to step outside.

"Who's there, Lionel?" an unfamiliar female voice called from inside the house.

"Er, jest a friend o' mine. Be back in a trice to wash out the big stewpot." He eased the door almost closed behind him.

"Well done, Lionel. I see you are awake on every suit, and have realised I wished to speak with you privately," I praised the boy. My gaze travelled to his neck. What looked like kitchen linen had been twisted and wrapped around the boy's throat, the ends tied, in an imitation of my own cravat. I suppressed a smile. My style of cravat is often copied, but never had I felt so honoured.

The boy's mouth dropped open as he took in the glory of my evening dress. One hand reached up to the linen around his own neck. He blushed and made as if to take it off.

I tucked the flowers in the crook of my arm. "No, no, do not take it apart." With one hand I gently stayed him, while the other reached for my quizzing glass. I studied the attempt, allowed the glass to fall to my chest, then made a few rapid adjustments to the boy's "cravat." "Your fingers are nimble, Lionel. I have no doubt that with the proper linen, the result would be one that would not disgrace a nobleman."

The boy's eyes shined. "Truly, sir? My hands are quick, that I know."

They would have to be in his former profession as pickpocket. "Truly."

Lionel looked at the flowers. "Have you brung those for Miss Lavender?"

"Indeed I have. I wanted to thank her for her assistance this afternoon."

"She's gone home already, but I reckon I could give

'em to her in the mornin' when she comes in." Lionel glanced up to see my reaction to this idea.

"Thank you." The floral bouquet changed hands. I pictured Miss Lavender in the neat little set of rooms she shared with her father in Fetter Lane. He would be smoking one of his pipes and she would be making tea or coffee.

"I seen you makin' sheep's eyes at her. Sweet on her, ain't you?" Lionel asked with a crooked smile.

I cleared my throat, a bit startled by this statement. "I hold Miss Lavender in high esteem," I replied stiffly.

Lionel guffawed. "She's a purty lady and awful nice. She don't have no beau, other than you, and you're Beau Brummell!"

"Yes, well, er," I managed, feeling on shaky ground. Better to get on with my proposition. "Lionel, I hoped you might help me with a small task. I would compensate you, of course."

Lionel scratched his head. "I'll do as you say seein' as how you're Miss Lavender's beau."

"I am not—" I broke off. It suddenly occurred to me that Lionel did not understand the word *compensate*. "Look here, I need to find out the name and location of a particular thief." I pulled coins out of my pocket. "If you could find out for me"—here I pressed the money into the boy's hand—"I shall give you this same amount again."

"Odsbodikins!" the boy exclaimed, seeing the coins.

"And," I cautioned, "if you return to me without a single scratch or bruise on you after completing the errand, there will be an even higher reward. You must be careful of your person while executing this task."

Lionel snorted a laugh. "I know Seven Dials like the back of my hand."

Inwardly I groaned at the mention of the notorious area

of London where criminals and the lowest sort of persons reside.

Lionel must have sensed my dismay. He said, "Leave it to me, sir. I ran those streets for over a year, now didn't I, and didn't come to no harm. Who be you lookin' for?"

"All I know is that he is dark-haired, wiry, and has a large red mark on his right cheek, some sort of birthmark."

Lionel nodded. "Right. I'll jest be puttin' these flowers inside, washing the rest of the supper pots, then when the ladies be at their sewin' "—this last was said in a tone of disgust—"I'll slip out and be off. Remember, sir, I can run like the wind."

Once again, I stayed him with a hand. "You must give me your word of honour as a gentleman that you will take no unnecessary risks."

The boy glowed at being called a gentleman. "My word on it, sir," he replied solemnly.

I studied him a moment longer. He meant what he said. "Very well then. When you have the information, bring it to me at Number Eighteen Bruton Street."

Lionel grinned and backed into the house. Just before he closed the door he whispered, "And tomorrow mornin' when I see Miss Lavender, I'll be sure to give her the flowers and your very bestest admirations, 'ffections and such."

I opened my mouth to contradict him, but he quietly closed the door in my face.

Muttering a silent prayer for the boy's safety, I returned to the waiting hackney and, eventually, to Bruton Street. The twins were ready with my sedan-chair. After paying off the hackney driver, I entered the elegant vehicle and gave orders for No. 20 Arlington Street.

During the short ride, I reasoned that I had done all I could about the missing letter for one night. Now I must concentrate my efforts on finding out what I could about

Lady Ariana and Cecily and Roger Cranworth.

Specifically, I wanted to know if one of them had driven the sharp length of jet into the Marquess of Kendrick's neck.

20

❧ 20 ❧

I entered Lady Salisbury's elegant town mansion to find the festivities in full swing. Here, at the height of the London Season, was the cream of Society in all their finery. A press of at least five hundred people crowded the large ballroom and the adjoining anterooms.

The frenzy of parties and entertainments during the Season are designed not only to entertain the bored members of the aristocracy, but also to bring young ladies to the attention of eligible gentlemen.

Feminine figures draped in the finest and sheerest of muslins, the styles inspired by ancient Greece and Rome, were admired by the gentlemen, myself included. The ladies wore their hair in the Roman style of a top knot with loose curls falling from it. Most attractive. Long white gloves, fans with scenes from mythology painted on them, and, of course, a plethora of jewellry completed their apparel.

I took in the opulent scene and allowed myself a moment of satisfaction at the attire of the gentlemen. With few exceptions my innovation of well-tailored dark coat and crisp, clean cravat was adopted by the gentlemen. True, some took my advice to the extreme and starched their shirt points so high they could not turn their heads, but I could only lead by example.

One whose shirt points threatened to cut off his ears thought *he* could lead fashionable Society. I gave him an austere look in an attempt to ward him off. I had no desire to speak to him, but my efforts were to no avail. I waited in patient resignation for my certain fate.

Sylvester Fairingdale, clad in a particularly vile shade of lobster red, minced up to me. A large, brown enamelled pin in the shape of a horse's head with tiny rubies for the eyes rested in the folds of his overdone cravat. His fingers, heavy with rings, sported one in the shape of a horseshoe. Toadying to the horse- and hunt-loving Lady Salisbury, I thought. The milksop.

"Brummell, I'm surprised to see you here," oozed Fairingdale. "I'd have thought you'd still be enjoying the attractions of Oatlands. Never say you have arrived alone. Where is the Royal Duchess?"

Since Fairingdale has a voice that tends to carry when he so desires, and the ballroom was crowded with people, several heads turned in our direction. I made a slight bow in Mrs. Creevey's direction, aware that she is a woman who prides herself on knowing the latest *on dits*.

"Why, I left the Royal Duchess at Oatlands, as did you," I replied smoothly, then changed the subject. "Is Prinny here tonight? I did not have a chance to call on him at Carlton House today."

"No. Word is an excess of buttered crab at Lady Jersey's yesterday brought on an attack of the gout. Our Prince does love his food."

"I hope he is improved tomorrow," I said and made to move away, but Fairingdale continued.

"Will the Royal Duchess be coming to London?" he asked, his voice rising. "I'd think after the shock of a murder at Oatlands she'd want to get away."

A battery of eyes looked our way.

"I am not certain of her Royal Highness's intentions," I told Fairingdale. And everybody who was listening. "If you will excuse—"

"Oh, come now, Brummell. You don't expect me to believe you are ignorant of the Royal Duchess's plans. What a fellow you are! Why, everyone knows you're the *closest* of friends with the Royal Duchess. You acted as host at the Oatlands house party!" Fairingdale taunted.

Aware of the hard faces, the hard eyes looking at me sideways, over the tops of fans, from under lowered lashes, I pretended an imperturbable poise I did not feel. "Whatever her Royal Highness does, I am certain it will be in line with the manner in which she always conducts herself: that of honour, principle, and kindness. Now, while I would not willingly lose an *instant* of your company, Fairingdale, I have just arrived and must see my hostess."

I walked away inwardly seething, outwardly calm. Friends hailed me, but I did not feel like chatting. Fairingdale was spreading rumours about me and Freddie. Just how widespread was the damage? If I knew anything about Society, by now everyone in the ballroom had heard the fop's prattling.

I wove my way through the crowd.

"Brummell! Good to see you out and about. Care to join me at a prizefight Monday?"

"Another time, eh, Yarmouth? I know you will enjoy yourself, though. Pick the winner."

"There's a great horse race getting up this Thursday, how about it?" Scrope Davies asked.

"I shall let you know," I said, clapping him on the shoulder, but continuing on my way.

The musicians began playing. The crowd moved back to allow couples room on the dance floor. I could see

Lady Salisbury standing in conversation with her husband, James, Marquess of Salisbury.

"Egad, Brummell, have you heard?" Lord Petersham called out. Nodding to several more of my acquaintances, I turned my steps toward the lazy viscount. He and Lord Munro were sipping claret.

"What is the news?" I asked, wishing for some liquid refreshment myself.

"We were at White's earlier, and the word in the club was that Lady Perry's confinement has come."

"Ready to deliver the heir," Munro put in.

I believe I told you that Lord Perry is a good friend of mine and is Signor Tallarico's cousin. Unlike the Italian lady's man, Perry is devoted to one lady only, his wife. "Is that so, by Jove? What good news, indeed. Perry is most likely beside himself with pride. I shall call on them tomorrow. I might even be able to see the babe."

"Has Lord Kendrick's killer been identified?" Munro asked.

"Not that I am aware," I replied shortly and turned on my heel. I did not want to give Lord Munro, who has never been my friend, a chance to begin questioning me.

Conscious that my movements were being watched by many, I finally reached Lady Salisbury. She is a small woman, over fifty years of age, with a strong-willed face and heavy black eyebrows.

"Hmpf!" she barked as I made an elegant bow in front of her. "Just in time. James left me for the pleasures of the card room."

"Good evening, my lady," I said. "How fortunate I am to find you with a few moments to spare for me."

"Where have you been?" asked the gruff marchioness. "Haven't seen you at all this Season."

"I have been at Oatlands, and—"

"Oh, I know about that! The whole world knows. I meant before then, but never mind. Come, the dance is ending. We can promenade around the room. Take my arm."

"It would be my honour, Lady Salisbury." She linked her hand through the crook of my arm, and we began to stroll about the perimeter of the dance floor. The look on her ladyship's face dared anyone to interrupt us.

"You'd best tell me exactly what's going on," she said.

"I did not feel like participating in Society after the Duchess of Devonshire died."

"Pity she's gone. Too young to die. But that's in the past. What's going on between you and the Royal Duchess?"

With an easy smile fixed on my face for the curious, I said, "I do not know what you are talking about. Her Royal Highness invited me, and several other guests, to Oatlands—"

"You gave her an expensive lace dress for Christmas, didn't you?"

"Yes." Fairingdale the Tattler.

"And you've been out at Oatlands teaching the Duchess archery with your arms about her?"

"Yes." Fairingdale the Lout.

"And you fixed up some special punch just for her, and gave her one of Blenheim's spaniels?"

"Guilty on all counts." Fairingdale the Soon-to-Be-Newly-Deceased.

Lady Salisbury guided me through to a corner in the refreshment room and looked at me frankly. "You know I'm fond of you, George," she said in a low voice.

"My lady," I said, placing a hand across my heart.

"Stop that at once! I am serious. My ballroom is teeming with gossip about you and Frederica."

"Put about by that horse's ass—he is wearing his head in the form of a pin in his cravat—Fairingdale. You cannot credit anything he says, my lady."

"Everyone else is! Lud, you're a gentleman, George,

and you've risen high in the world despite your lack of title or great fortune. Don't ruin it now with this type of scandal. For, mark my words, you're sure to be the greatest loser. Frederica might be banished to Oatlands, but she wouldn't care two straws for that. Loves the country and all her dogs. She'd care about the shame of it, though. Got a great bunch of morals, you know, more than the Duke of York deserves in a wife the way he parades that Clarke woman up and down the streets of London."

"You are correct. The Royal Duchess is more than her husband merits."

"But that won't make a shilling's difference, and you know it," she insisted. "Men can do as they please, dally with married women, set up as many mistresses as they want and go about Town with them. But it's different for a lady. She can take a lover only after she has provided her husband with an heir and only if she is discreet. For a lady, to be *found out* is the biggest crime of all."

A mental image of that lethal letter came into my mind. Everything Lady Salisbury was telling me was true. Though nothing had happened between Freddie and me. All right, that one kiss. But I ask you, was that really so bad? Quite the contrary, it felt—er, in any event, the truth would not matter in the judgmental eyes of Society. They would think the worst and act accordingly. Even Prinny could not continue our friendship if it were thought I had cuckolded his brother. And if I lost his favour, I might as well pack Chakkri up and head for Siam.

Unconsciously, my hand reached inside my coat to touch the pocket where my miniature of Freddie rested. "Lady Salisbury, you know I hold you in the highest respect."

"You have a reputation as a man of impeccable taste," the marchioness said with a wry little smile.

I smiled back, then looked into her eyes. "I am most

fond of her Royal Highness and would never wish scandal attached to her name. Our relationship is not unseemly."

Lady Salisbury nodded. "Good. What about Lord Kendrick's murder right there at Oatlands? Why would someone kill him?"

"I want the answer to that question myself."

"Fairingdale says you didn't like Kendrick. He thinks the nature of your aversion to his lordship has something to do with the Royal Duchess."

"Fairingdale wants to discredit me."

"That he does. He's a fool and a boor, but dangerous, George. His tongue wags more than all of Frederica's dogs' tails combined. Watch yourself. This is a bad business. The quicker they find out who killed Lord Kendrick, the better. In the meantime, you need to stay away from Frederica."

"I cannot promise you—"

"There you are, Lady Salisbury! I have looked everywhere," trilled Lady Crecy, dropping a curtsey. "Oh, and dear Mr. Brummell, too!"

I bowed. "Good evening, Lady Crecy."

"Indeed it is a wonderful evening, Mr. Brummell," Lady Crecy whispered dramatically. "And a special one. Very special. Now, my dear Lady Salisbury, you said I might make the announcement at your ball?"

"Yes, yes, go ahead," Lady Salisbury answered impatiently. "I'll instruct the butler to have the footmen bring out additional glasses of champagne."

Both ladies hastened away before I could say another word. I regretted the chance to speak to Lady Crecy about Lady Ariana. I would seek her out later.

In the meantime, I watched as Lady Crecy got everyone's attention from her position on the raised platform where the musicians played. "Ladies and gentlemen, Lord Wrayburn has an announcement to make."

A murmur went through the crowd. I made my way

toward the front in time to hear his lordship announce his engagement to Lady Crecy's daughter, Lady Penelope. Everyone clapped politely. Lady Crecy beamed with triumph. I imagined several mothers with marriageable daughters mentally crossing Lord Wrayburn off their list of eligible bachelors with an angry slash of their mental pencils.

Just as I accepted a very pleasing glass of champagne and drank the contents, I was surprised to see Cecily and Roger Cranworth amongst those wishing a radiant Lady Penelope the best in her forthcoming marriage.

❧ 21 ❧

The siblings turned after toasting the bride-to-be and walked directly into my path. I heard Cecily Cranworth say to her brother, "Why not tell everyone your own good news?"

"Miss Cranworth, Mr. Cranworth, what a pleasant surprise to see you in Town," I greeted the pair. "I was not aware you planned a visit to London." Or that they could travel in such exalted circles as Lady Salisbury's ball.

Cecily Cranworth looked out of place in her country-made dress. Roger Cranworth, on the other hand, wore a fine coat and seemed at his ease.

"Good evening, Mr. Brummell. How convenient to find you here. Has her Royal Highness the Duchess of York come to London as well?" Roger asked with a smile.

"No," I said.

"But she will," Roger stated.

"Good!" I responded cheerfully, within an ames ace of throttling the next person who spoke to me in that familiar way regarding Freddie.

"I am happy to see you again, Mr. Brummell," Cecily Cranworth told me.

"And I you, Miss Cranworth. You do not often come to Town," I remarked.

"Things are different now," she said quietly.

Roger looked at me. "After Connell's death, I wanted to leave the countryside and enjoy London. It's a way of easing my sorrow."

Odd, he did not appear grief-stricken. Just the opposite. In truth, he had an air about him of renewed confidence. Almost like one who has a delicious secret they are just bursting to share. And was it not his custom to leave his sister languishing in the country while he tried to cut a dash in Town?

"Did I hear Miss Cranworth say you had something to tell everyone? Good news, I believe?" I exchanged my empty glass of champagne for that of a fresh one and raised it. "If so, I stand ready to drink to your success, whatever it may be."

Cecily's brown eyes sparkled. "Roger is to wed Lady Ariana."

I trust I kept my expression bland. Roger to marry Lady Ariana? That very first night at Oatlands I had overheard Roger declare he would never marry the girl. Why the change of heart?

"Cecily," Roger hissed at his sister, causing her to shrink from him. But when he turned his gaze to me, her chin came up in a little rebellious gesture. She had somehow changed, too.

Roger said, "As the arbiter of good taste, Mr. Brummell, I'm sure you will agree that it can hardly be appropriate to announce the betrothal at this time. After all, Lady Ariana is in mourning for her cousin."

Again, I felt as though Roger spoke as one newly elevated in life. He was engaged to Lady Ariana, but that could not be what was giving him his newfound superior air. Could it?

I focused my attention on Cecily Cranworth, perceiv-

ing I would get the most information out of her. "Perhaps
Miss Cranworth would favour me with the next dance."

Roger darted a glance toward the card room. Ever the
gamester, he longed to join the players. "Go ahead, Cecily. I'll find you later. Oh, and Mr. Brummell, we'll have
to get together someday very soon. I'll send word to you.
What is your direction?"

Little puts me off faster than presumption. The words
rude and *encroaching* crept to my tongue, but I held them
at bay. Besides, I had my own reasons for furthering our
acquaintance. For that reason, I gave him the information.
He flashed me a grin, then swaggered off.

I held out my arm for Miss Cranworth. "Would you
rather get something to eat than dance? I confess to being
rather thirsty," I said, glancing ruefully down at the newly
empty glass in my hand.

"Yes, please, Mr. Brummell."

I retraced the steps I had made with Lady Salisbury,
leading Miss Cranworth into the room where refreshments
were spread on long tables. Small, round tables with
chairs had been set out for couples to sit and enjoy a light
repast. With the aid of a liveried footman, I obtained
plates of food. Miss Cranworth and I then settled down
at one of the tables.

Adopting an air of tranquillity, I talked lightly of this
and that until I was certain Miss Cranworth was thor-
oughly comfortable.

"I am glad your brother brought you to London at last.
What changed his mind?" I asked, then popped a tiny
timballe of meat and pastry into my mouth.

"Connell's death," she said without the slightest tinge
of regret in her words.

"Lord Kendrick's death?" I asked, perplexed. "Oh, I am
sorry. I fail to see why that changed—"

"It changes everything," Miss Cranworth said fervently,
a flush rising to her cheeks.

I raised my right eyebrow.

She drank some champagne. "Ariana will have a husband. It is what I have always wanted: for Roger to marry Ariana."

"I am happy for you, then. I do confess to being surprised at your brother's engagement."

Miss Cranworth swallowed a bite of poppyseed cake before answering. "I think he was surprised himself it happened so fast." She shrugged. "It is too late now, though. When he said he would marry Ariana, it was in front of Lady Crecy, so he cannot go back on his word."

"Do you think he wishes to retract his proposal?"

"It does not matter. They will wed. Ariana will be my sister."

"And what of you?" I asked. "Doctor Wendell has asked me to write and let him know how you are going on in Town."

Miss Cranworth's lips tilted into a smile. "You need not go to the trouble. Curtis will be arriving in London at any time. It is all arranged." She rose.

I stood. "I did not know Doctor Wendell would come to London so soon."

"Oh, yes. Everything is going to turn out just as I planned, Mr. Brummell. You have been good, but you need not worry about me anymore."

With that mystifying remark, Miss Cranworth left me.

Lord Kendrick's death did not seem to have had an adverse effect on either of the siblings' lives. In fact, just the opposite was true. Miss Cranworth seemed to be supremely confident that she would wed Doctor Wendell. Had Roger's threat of marrying her off to Squire Oxberry passed? Matters had certainly turned to Miss Cranworth's advantage.

After Lord Kendrick's death.

I made my way back to the ballroom. Though I looked

for her, Miss Cranworth had disappeared. Her brother remained in the card room, though.

The rules and customs of Society dictated that I must dance with some of the ladies present. I could not simply arrive at a ball, conduct a few conversations, then leave without causing comment.

Thus I spent the next two hours dancing with various eligible misses. I partnered Lady Deidre, the Duke of Derehurst's daughter, and found her singularly unconcerned about Lord Kendrick's death. When I mentioned it, a tiny frown between her thin brows told me she had to think for a moment which one of her many admirers he had been.

I found Lady Penelope and wished her the best on her forthcoming marriage. Her fine grey eyes glowed with anticipation as she thanked me. I was happy for her.

But it was her mother whom I particularly wished to speak with before I took my leave of Lady Salisbury. I had to wait quite a while before I could extract Lady Crecy from where she held a group of older matrons enthralled in conversation. No doubt she was describing every step she had taken to secure Lord Wrayburn for her daughter.

Holding a glass of champagne high, I caught Lady Crecy's gaze and she came to me. "Oh, dear Mr. Brummell, this is the most wonderful night of my life."

"Take this then and drink to your daughter's future as a countess."

She tittered. "You know I should not, I have drunk so many glasses already."

"You deserve to celebrate tonight." I pressed the glass into her hand. "Tell me, how does your other charge go on?"

She accepted the glass and looked at me. "Lady Ariana?"

"Yes. I understand you kindly opened your home to her after her tragic loss."

"Yes. The poor girl had nowhere else to go. My maid, Marcelline—an excellent creature, I assure you—has been looking after her. Lady Ariana will not go about, of course, as she is in mourning, but the girl is happy enough to have Cecily and Roger visiting her."

"With Roger Cranworth's visits being the most welcome," I ventured.

Lady Crecy's grey curls bounced in excitement. "I should have known that you, Mr. Brummell, would not miss a thing! The two are engaged. That will all work out most satisfactorily. I cannot help but feel Lady Ariana could have looked higher for a husband, but under the circumstances, it is for the best."

"Curious, that. I never noticed any partiality on Mr. Cranworth's part toward Lady Ariana during our stay at Oatlands," I said in a contemplative tone. "You are very observant yourself, Lady Crecy, and may have been aware of something I was not. I am afraid my thoughts on the betrothal have not been . . . charitable in regard to Mr. Cranworth."

Just as I had hoped, Lady Crecy could not resist this lure. "Well," she confided, "I did not see anything at all between them until after Lady Ariana's cousin, uh, um, oh dear—"

"Died?"

"Exactly," the older woman agreed, the word *murdered* evidently absent from her vocabulary. "I must say, Mr. Brummell, that I have wondered if Mr. Cranworth believes that the title and the estates will now pass through Lady Ariana. That would make any son of their marriage a marquess."

"Roger Cranworth knows that for a certainty?"

Lady Crecy shook her head. "That is the problem. I do

not think he does. But his sort, you know, handsome, dashing, reckless—"

"In need of money."

"No doubt of it." Lady Crecy lowered her voice to a whisper, causing me to incline my head toward her. "I fear Mr. Cranworth is making the biggest gamble of his life, assuming that Lady Ariana will inherit. Presently, there is a band of solicitors going over the original papers creating the title to see how the inheritance passes."

"Surely, though, even if the papers did not specify male heirs only, a trustee would be set up. If Mr. Cranworth were hoping for Lord Kendrick's money and property, he would have to deal with them."

"That is precisely what that man from Bow Street said when he came to the house earlier."

"Mr. Lavender?" I exclaimed in a voice louder than I had intended.

"Yes, that was his name."

"Did he question Lady Ariana?"

"He did, but the girl is rather scatterbrained, if I do say so. She only talked about her engagement, no matter what Mr. Lavender said. I think she thought he was from Bond Street, instead of Bow Street, as she kept asking him about the shops."

I held back a smile. I could imagine the childlike Lady Ariana weaving rosy dreams of her wedding dress, and the bluff Scotsman trying in vain to sort out facts which would lead him to a murderer.

"Where are the Cranworths staying?"

"Curzon Street. They took rooms above a confectioner's. Hardly appropriate for a gentleman engaged to Lady Ariana, but what could he expect to find in the middle of the Season?" Lady Crecy said.

"Indeed."

Our conversation at an end, Lady Crecy was called

back to her group of friends. I bowed to her and secured permission to pay a visit to Lady Ariana.

I took my leave of the ball shortly thereafter. Ned and Ted carried me in my sedan-chair through the lamplit Mayfair streets. Inside the luxurious chair, I contemplated various possibilities.

First I imagined Lady Ariana absentmindedly taking one of Freddie's sharp jet hair ornaments. On the morning of the marquess's murder, Lord Kendrick and Lady Ariana would have been once again near the ornamental pool, arguing. The marquess repeated his threat to have his cousin clapped into a lunatic asylum. This time, Lady Ariana takes the length of jet and plunges it into Lord Kendrick's neck. Perhaps when she had shot that arrow into her cousin's back it had not been an accident after all.

Possible. The girl was unbalanced.

Then there were the Cranworths. Miss Cranworth hated Lord Kendrick. That had been made clear the night he forced his kisses upon her. They had been childhood friends at one time, secretly promised to one another. Even though Roger Cranworth refused to accept it, everything had changed when Connell had come into the title. Miss Cranworth could just as easily have found the hair ornaments in the drawing room. Perhaps she had seen Lord Kendrick go out for a morning stroll—or more likely, a late-night stroll—and followed him.

Hmmm. That just did not seem right. I did not feel Miss Cranworth could carry out such a deed unless . . . unless she had a partner. Someone who would know precisely where to stab the sharp jet into the victim's neck. Someone loyal, like Doctor Wendell, who so wanted to free the woman he loved from the possibility of marrying the contemptible marquess.

Then there was Roger Cranworth. Out of the suspects I considered him to be the one whose character would most run to drastic measures. He was reckless, a bully, and underneath his boyish good looks, he was a conniver of the first order. He was angry that the marquess would not marry his sister. Freddie had reported hearing the two men quarrel in the drawing room at Oatlands. There was the issue of a possible breach of promise suit. There was that cryptic remark Lord Kendrick made about how if Roger put up a fuss or went against him in any matter, the marquess would go to Squire Oxberry. Freddie had repeated the conversation to me. It followed then that the marquess felt he had some sort of hold over Roger. What that was, I did not know. Where had Roger been when Lord Kendrick had been murdered? And what of his reaction at the makeshift grave? "I never thought that smirk could be wiped from his face." That is what Roger had said.

Had he been the one to erase it forever?

Our arrival in Bruton Street put a stop to my deductions. I alighted from the conveyance and opened the front door.

A single candle on the hall table provided a dim light.

Ned and Ted walked past me to put the chair away into a large cupboard toward the rear of the hall.

Thus I was alone when I turned to close the door, and out of the shadows a crouched figure leapt in front of me.

❧ 22 ❧

"Lionel!" I admonished. "Do not jump out of the shrubbery at people like that."

"Sorry, sir," the boy said, cowering under my reproach. "I been waitin' for you. I expect I fells asleep."

His demeanor brought to mind another boy. Myself. I well remember the times I squirmed under my father's baleful gaze. I had never been able to please him, no matter what I did. Even though he has been dead since I was fifteen, I sometimes feel he survives by way of a nagging voice in my head, always critical. He did not live to see me rise in Society. I often wonder what he would think of me now.

I softened my voice. "You should not be out at this late hour, halfling." At that moment the watchman called, "Two of the clock and a clear night," almost as if to underline my point.

The boy grinned. "Now there's where you're wrong, sir. This time o' night is exactly when folks 'ave been takin' in lots of gin. Makes it easier to get whatever you want from them."

I motioned for him to enter the hall. "What did you find out?"

Lionel did not answer at once. Even though the light in the hall was low, the boy's awed gaze went over the black-and-white-tiled floor, the polished mahogany table on which a vase containing fresh flowers rested, the unlit crystal chandelier, the gleaming bannister which led upstairs.

"Lionel?" I prompted.

"Yes, sir." He turned back to me, eager to tell all. "Man you're lookin' for goes by the name of Neal. 'E don't have no rooms, leastways not that anybody knows about. Spends time in the country for some reason."

"He has business in the country upon occasion," I explained.

"But when 'e is in London, 'e sleeps on the floor of The Jolly Cow tavern in Little White Lion Street," the boy said, naming a road in the Seven Dials area. He lowered his voice. "Word is, Neal's an opium eater. Best have a care, iffen you're gonna have dealings with the likes of 'im."

Lionel was right about that, I thought grimly. I pulled coins out of my pocket, an amount exceeding the sum I had given the boy earlier. "Here now, you have earned this extra. I am proud of you. Even in this dim light I can see that you have come to no harm over this night's adventures."

Lionel's eyes gleamed at the coins. "Thank you, Mr. Brummell!"

"However, I shall not have you running back to Covent Garden alone at this time of night."

"I'll be bloody fine! Don't you worry about me none."

"Best not let Miss Lavender hear you use that word. Most gentlemen do not, you know. Now wait here while I find Ned and Ted. They will carry you in my sedan-chair back to the Haven of Hope."

The boy's mouth dropped open.

A few minutes later when I returned with the twins and they pulled the chair from its cupboard, Lionel was the very picture of astonishment. "Odsbodikins! I'm to ride in that grand thing?"

"Yes," I told him, smiling.

He entered the vehicle reverently, running his hands over the white satin seat and reaching down to touch the white fur that covered the floor. When he looked back at me, his eyes shone.

I gave instructions to Ned and Ted, commanding them to return without dallying about with Molly.

Before I closed the door, I studied Lionel. "You have been very brave tonight, prowling through the streets of Seven Dials for me. Why, now that I think of it, you remind me of a lion. Even the way you crouched in the shrubbery waiting for me makes me think you more a Lion than a Lionel. Do you care for the nickname?"

The boy's face split into a wide grin. "I likes it!"

I nodded. "Very well. I shall call you Lion, henceforth."

The door to the sedan-chair closed, and Ned and Ted went out carrying their charge.

I began climbing the stairs, only to see Robinson standing at the top, aghast at the scene he had witnessed. "Sir, you are not thinking of taking that urchin into our home, are you? We already have the feline and those two country yokels."

"Ah, Robinson, as much as I think I would enjoy his company, Lion belongs with Miss Lavender."

"Very good, sir."

From the inflection in his voice, he might as well have said, "Thank God in heaven, sir." I ascended the stairs and strode past him into my bedchamber. The first thing I noticed was that Chakkri stood looking out the window into the darkness. His tail lashed back and forth. At my entrance, he turned with a "reow" and jumped on the bed.

"Good evening, old boy. Or should I say good morning?"

"Good-bye forever is even better," Robinson muttered.

I swung around to face him. "Have you quite recovered from your earlier ailment?"

"Yes, sir," he said, a touch of guilt in his voice. "I shall just get your nightclothes out of the wardrobe."

Contrite, was he? Well, that was as it should be. Taking a tisane from his lady friend and then being unable to perform his duties. Bah!

The valet helped me ready myself for bed with exceptional care. His last act was to hand me a small glass of well-aged brandy. Wonderful stuff!

"Robinson," I said after taking a sip. "When we were at Oatlands, did you ever hear about a man called Neal? He is known to have a reddish birthmark on his cheek."

"Why, yes, sir," Robinson said, replacing the brandy decanter on a side table. "Quite a bit of gossip about him ran through the servants' hall."

I eyed him sharply. "Tell me everything."

"This Neal person worked for Doctor Wendell."

"Doctor Wendell!" I exclaimed. My theory of the loyal doctor helping Miss Cranworth kill Lord Kendrick suddenly looked stronger, much to my dismay.

"Indeed, sir. Doctor Wendell employed him as a sort of messenger between Weybridge and the London apothecaries. I expect there were some medicines and compounds Doctor Wendell could not get locally."

"Go on," I said, thinking what a convenient job for an opium eater to work for a doctor.

"It seems Doctor Wendell found out Neal was stealing from him, though. He fired him over six months ago. Talk at Oatlands was that no one could understand why Roger Cranworth then hired the thief as his man of all work."

"Roger Cranworth? Are you absolutely certain, Robinson?"

"Yes, sir. I saw Neal several times around Oatlands. You must have as well, though no one ever notices servants much." This last was said in a pious tone.

"What? Who is putting such ideas in your head? Is it that lady friend of yours?"

Robinson stood with a stubborn expression on his face.

"Never mind now. What else do you know about Neal?"

"Once, when I went to the kitchens, he was taking as much food as he could from the larder. Cook clucked her tongue, but Neal's a mean-looking fellow. I gained the impression she was afraid of him."

"As well she should be. Robinson, I have reason to believe Neal is the very one who held up your coach."

"He is the highwayman?" Robinson gasped. "You said you thought Lord Kendrick had been responsible."

"I am certain he was, but as we both know, he would hardly do the dirty work himself. Remember you told me it was no member of the nobility who held up your coach."

"That is correct, sir. Do you think Lord Kendrick and Mr. Cranworth were partners?"

"Undoubtedly."

"Will this help you find her Royal Highness's letter?"

"I believe it will. Leave me now, Robinson. I must think."

"Very well. Good night, sir."

I sat up in bed, my mind working furiously. Neal was the one Roger and Lord Kendrick had actually doing the thievery. Then, I imagined, Neal would bring the bounty back to his employers. Probably kept an item or two for himself to pay for his opium.

Chakkri moved across the bed to sit beside me. His dark blue eyes looked into mine.

"Let us think back now, Chakkri. The first night of the house party, which was the day Robinson was held up, I overheard that conversation between Cecily and Roger. At the end of it, Roger said he was going out for a walk. He might have prearranged a nightly meeting with Neal. The trio must have known many coaches would be coming to Oatlands for the house party and would be ripe for the plucking. Why had they not robbed anyone else?"

Chakkri placed a paw on my arm.

Absently, I stroked the top of the cat's head.

"Because once it was shown to him, Lord Kendrick realised the value of Freddie's letter to me, that is why. There was no reason to keep up the highwayman scheme with such a plum in hand. But I am getting ahead of myself.

"Going back to that first night, let us say Neal meets Roger outside the grounds of Oatlands. I can imagine Neal's conversation with Roger. He was disappointed there had been no jewellry in the coach he had robbed—mine—but there were some very fine clothes. And this book covered in blue velvet."

"Reow," said Chakkri, pushing his head into my hand. I had momentarily stopped petting him. A crime in his view.

"Roger takes the blue velvet scrapbook. He tells Neal to go back to London and sell the clothes, then return for further instructions.

"Evidently, Neal never returned to Weybridge. He probably kept some of the money from Mr. Kirkhead's rag shop and bought more opium for himself.

"As for Roger, once he glanced through the pages, he must have known the blue velvet book was mine. My name appeared on the first page, on the letters, at the bottom of poems authored by me, on the drawings. Why did he not come to Freddie or me after reading Freddie's letter, demanding money?"

Chakkri mumbled a reply through purrs.

"Of course! Roger must not understand French! Freddie's letter was written in French. So then what?" Excited, I got out of bed and began to pace.

Chakkri shook himself.

"Roger has the blue velvet book. Lord Kendrick and Roger Cranworth are at odds over the fact the marquess will not marry Cecily. They argue. Perhaps Roger threatens to reveal Lord Kendrick's participation in the highwayman scheme if the marquess continues to refuse to marry Cecily."

I thought hard. What exactly had Freddie reported overhearing during the argument between the two men in her drawing room? I snapped my fingers. "Lord Kendrick told Roger that if he dared make any accusations or went against him, he would go to Squire Oxberry. I had thought at the time the men were arguing over a breach of promise suit, but I was wrong. Lord Kendrick must have threatened to tell the Squire that *Roger* had been behind the robberies. That would neatly serve two purposes: make the marquess look the part of a hero, and absolve him from any suspicion. For who would believe Roger if he tried to incriminate Lord Kendrick once the marquess had pointed the finger at him?"

Chakkri sat on his hind legs at the edge of the bed watching me.

"That must be what happened, old boy. Roger must have been scared. But he had my blue velvet book. As a last-ditch effort, he must have told the marquess about it, ignorant of the book's true value, but hoping to keep the marquess in the game. Remember? Freddie said that Roger had asked Lord Kendrick to come up to his room, that he had something to show him."

"Reow!"

"Yes, it all makes sense. Lord Kendrick, being better educated, must have read Freddie's letter, understood it, and immediately hatched the plan to blackmail her. But he certainly did not tell Roger Cranworth. Why would he? He would not have wanted to share this golden egg dropped into his lap. I imagine he may have even slipped the letter into his pocket and thrown the book back to Roger saying it was worthless. That way, Lord Kendrick could keep his blackmail scheme to himself, and Roger still had no hold over him regarding the marquess's promise to marry Cecily.

"Now Lord Kendrick did not have to obey Freddie's command to leave Oatlands. He felt in control of her, and me. He began exercising that control immediately when he told Freddie he had the letter, and later when he boasted to me during the picnic."

I stopped pacing and looked at the cat. "But I cannot be certain that Lord Kendrick separated Freddie's letter from the blue velvet book. I have no evidence that he did. The letter might still be tucked away in the blue velvet book."

The question remained: Where was the letter?

My brain galloped along. Roger had been so smug at Lady Salisbury's party. He had asked me for my direction. He had said he would be calling on me. Most importantly, he had asked if Freddie had arrived in London! Could it be?

"I think so, Chakkri. Roger must have somehow—and I know not how—found out about the importance of the letter and its contents."

The cat lowered his head and licked a spot on his chest.

I felt a strong measure of frustration mixed with success. I might have deduced that Roger had the letter—perhaps it even now rested back inside the pages of the blue velvet book—but how long would it be before Freddie and I were put in immediate danger again? For who knew what Roger's demands would be? I would have to get the letter from Roger. But how?

If I barged into his lodgings and demanded it, there could be a nasty scene, probably resulting in fisticuffs. I could best him, I knew, but if he and I were subsequently both seen publicly sporting bruises, that would not do. Timing and discretion in this entire matter were paramount.

Wait a moment. Perhaps there was another avenue to explore first. Why not approach Neal—plenty of coins in hand—and see if he might be able to return the blue velvet book and letter to me and foil Roger's plans? Why not indeed.

I climbed into bed. One vital question still remained: Was Roger Cranworth angry enough at Lord Kendrick for ruining all his plans that he drove that sharp length of jet into the marquess's neck?

"I believe I have the killer, Chakkri."

"Reow!" said Chakkri, curling his tail into a *C*.

❦ 23 ❧

Sunday morning, while the rest of Mayfair felt compelled to put in an appearance at fashionable St. George's Church, I was on my way to that part of London most in need of transformation.

Seven Dials had got its name because seven streets met at the base of a Doric pillar which housed a clock with seven faces. The old column with the clock had been taken down about thirty years ago, but the name of the area remained.

I took a hackney coach to The Jolly Cow in Little White Lion Street. Alighting from the vehicle, I argued for several minutes with the coachman. He did not want to wait for me in this part of London. As is so often the case, money solved the problem.

Following Lionel's—or Lion, as I now called him—line of thinking, I judged that if the inhabitants of The Jolly Cow were up late drinking and revelling, they would not be awake early. Thus my chances of finding Neal before he rose and went about his criminal life would be good.

The theory proved accurate.

I had to pound on the door until the owner, a rotund, moon-faced man, let me inside. Do I need to tell you that coins changed hands before the proprietor was so accommodating?

On a straw pallet behind the bar, a wiry man dressed in dirty clothes snored. He laid on his side, the red birthmark on his cheek in plain sight.

I nudged him with my dog's head cane.

He came awake and was on his feet instantly, in the manner of one always on the alert for trouble. His redshot eyes looked me over from shining Hessian boots to the top of my head.

"Neal, I am George Brummell. I have business with you. Business that could be quite profitable."

The thief was a raw nerve. He blinked rapidly at my use of his name. "Do I know you?"

"Not exactly. You are familiar with some of my clothing, I believe, having sold it to Mr. Kirkhead in Monmouth Street." Sensing he was about to either bolt, or strike me, I waved a careless hand. "I am unconcerned about the loss. I have plenty more clothing."

Neal scratched the back of his left hand. "What's yer business then and how much money?"

I framed my answer carefully. After all, it would hardly do for Neal to get wind of just how valuable the blue velvet book and the letter were. I removed a silver shilling from my waistcoat pocket and held it between my gloved fingertips. "I merely want the answers to some questions first."

Neal nodded his head, the greasy, stringy strands of his hair barely moving. "As long as I gets the coin."

"You shall have it in your possession in moments."

"Ask away."

"You are employed by Roger Cranworth?"

Neal hesitated but a moment. "Not anymore. Gone all

respectable on me. Got hisself engaged to a *lady*. Took rooms in Curzon Street. Discharged me and said he'd hired a proper butler."

"When did this happen?"

"He found me late Friday night, might have been Saturday by that time of mornin'. He told me then."

"Did he pay you to be quiet about the Weybridge robberies?"

Neal snorted. "So what? You're payin' me to talk. I think I've already earned that coin."

I nodded politely. "Agreed." I handed it over to him. He grabbed it and held on to it for dear life. Or opium.

I reached into my pocket and produced the equivalent of five shillings, a crown-piece.

"A whole coachwheel?" Neal's expression grew crafty. I thought it prudent at that moment to release the mechanism on my dog's head cane. With a loud click in the quiet room, the sharp swordstick came into view. Neal looked from the blade back to me.

Holding the crown where he could see it at all times, I said, "Last Tuesday, you robbed a coach in Weybridge. There was a manservant carrying a small dog in the coach."

"Heh heh heh, I remember. Prig of a gent. Shoutin' at me while holdin' on to that dog. The dog bit him."

"What did you take from the manservant?"

"Couple cases with only clothes inside. I didn't think they were worth much. No offense iffen they were yours. Plain they were, not a bit of lace in sight."

Later he must have found the value of the clothes to be high, unless Mr. Kirkhead had cheated him, which I would not be surprised to learn. "Anything else? Think hard."

"The cases the clothes were packed in were mighty fine. Oh, and some blue book covered in fancy velvet with silver corners."

My heart leapt rather uncomfortably in my chest, but I remained outwardly calm. "What did you do with everything?"

"I met up with Roger as planned. He told me to sell the clothes and the cases. He kept the book."

"You are doing very well, Neal. Here, you have earned the extra coin." I handed him the crown. I could tell he wanted to run to the nearest place where he could purchase opium. From my pocket, I then removed the biggest lure: a gold guinea.

Neal licked his lips.

"I am a sentimental man, much to my regret," I bemoaned. "That blue velvet book contained poems and letters of value only to me. I want it back. I cannot just ask Roger Cranworth myself. These matters between gentlemen can become awkward, you understand. To your knowledge, does Roger still have the book?"

"I know he does. I seen it. I seen it myself."

Lying, I thought. He probably lies with the regularity of rainfall. We locked gazes. He must be assuming Roger still has the book and that he can steal it from Roger's rooms. That was fine with me. As I have said, I did not wish to try to break into Roger's lodgings myself. Yet.

I held the gold guinea up to the light. In the most casual voice I could muster I said, "If you would be so kind as to get the blue velvet book and bring it to me, this is yours."

"I will," he cried, unable to contain his excitement. Though whether it was the thought of the guinea that thrilled him or the opium the money in his hand would purchase, I did not know.

If he was going to get the book—and hopefully the letter—for me, the sooner the better. If he was bluffing, I needed to know that. Time was critical. On the other hand, if I demanded Neal go immediately, the thief might steal the book then see who would give him the most money for it: Roger or me.

"When will you have the book?" I asked.

Neal considered. With the money I had given him, I suddenly realised he could be in an opium fog for days. I felt like kicking myself, but, no, money had been necessary if I were to pry information out of him.

"I could have it for you by the end of the week," was the reply.

I made as if to leave. "I am afraid that will not do. I am a busy man. Tomorrow night would be the longest I would be willing to wait for it. If you do not think you can get it for me by then, I must hire someone else to do the job. I know where in Curzon Street Mr. Cranworth is residing. So you see it would be quite simple for me to offer my gold guinea to someone else."

Neal fidgeted like a five-year-old. "I'll get it for you by then. Not many parties and such on Sunday, but Roger will be out tomorrow night, I'd wager. He always is when he's in London. Miss Cranworth might be home—"

"Miss Cranworth is not to be harmed in any way, is that quite clear?" I demanded harshly.

"Fine, fine. No need to get all riled up. I'll get the book and bring it to you tomorrow by midnight. How's that? Where do you live?"

I struggled for calm, feeling myself closer than ever to retrieving Freddie's letter. Most especially, here was my chance to get it back before Roger Cranworth could begin blackmailing Freddie and me. Freddie was not in Town yet, though she had said she would arrive tomorrow. Once I had Freddie's letter, I could give Mr. Lavender certain details about the house party that I had previously withheld from him. Carefully edited, of course.

"Perhaps it would be best if you were not seen at my house." My gaze fell to a copy of the *Times* lying on the bar. I picked it up and scanned the front page. "There is

to be a Grand Masquerade tomorrow night at the King's
Theatre in Haymarket. Send word to me there once you
have the book. I shall be wearing a black domino and a
tall black hat with a red plume."

Neal started scratching again. "Seems a lot of trouble
just to conduct a bit of business."

"Meeting in a public place would be best for both our
safety," I pronounced in a tone that would tolerate no
argument.

Neal nodded. "Just be sure to have the yellowboy."

"I give you my word."

I walked to Hyde Park Sunday afternoon to make the
circuit of the Park. Since I had appeared at Lady Salisbury's ball last night, knowledge that I had once again
taken up Society's amusements would be known. I must
continue to frequent fashionable places to give an impression of normalcy.

After my trip to Seven Dials, I had felt dirty. I had
ordered hot water and a change of clothing. Because of
the late hour I had returned to Bruton Street last night and
the early hour I had departed the house this morning, a
nap had also been needed before I dressed to go out.

Hyde Park was crowded. As I greeted numerous acquaintances, some by just a doffing of my hat, the sun
shone brightly above. Later I planned to call on Lord and
Lady Perry to see the new baby. Then a visit to Lady
Crecy's was on my list. I was anxious to see Lady Ariana.

At that moment, a feminine voice hailed me. I turned
to my right to see Miss Lavender, her father grudgingly
following behind her, crossing the grass. Her stride was
most determined. Now what had her looking so peeved?

Lion! The boy had told her of his adventures. I had
neglected to ask him to remain silent.

"Mr. Brummell, even from a distance I knew it was

you. No one else dresses with such elegant perfection," she said, a martial light in her emerald eyes.

I made her a small bow. "Thank you! Ah, Mr. Lavender, keeping to your practice of not working on the Sabbath, I see." Except in regards to that deuced toothpick jumping up and down between his teeth.

"Aye, laddie. But I see you're hard at work."

I tilted my head. "Why, what can you mean? I am merely enjoying a spring stroll."

"Working twenty-four hours a day to stave off your boredom is how I see it. I reckon I should be glad you're not poking your nose in Bow Street work."

A sound suspiciously like a snort came from Miss Lavender. I noted she looked most fetching this afternoon in a light moss-green muslin dress. She said, "No, this time he's meddling in the Weybridge magistrate's work. He's trying to find the highwayman that's struck out that way."

"Is that so, Mr. Brummell?" the Bow Street man asked, his interest caught. "And just why would you trouble yourself with a country matter?"

Before I could reply, Miss Lavender was ahead of me. "It is so, and he's used an innocent young boy to help him!"

"My clothes, you know, I had to find out what had become of them," I explained in my best foolish dandy voice.

"Faith!" exclaimed Miss Lavender. "That's what you told me, and I believe you. 'Twas one thing when you came to me wanting to know the location of the rag-merchants. But then to bribe a boy of two and ten to go into Seven Dials to find a thief. How could you? Even though you said you were concerned for the Royal Duchess's safety, I still couldn't believe it when Lionel told me you'd paid him to find the ruffian."

Mr. Lavender seemed annoyed at my doing Squire Oxberry's job. I would wager the news that I had called on his daughter did not sit well with him either. At any rate, his eyes narrowed. "I'm having a hard time believing your stolen clothes were that important to you, Mr. Brummell. What was it that really caused you to expend your energy on such a matter?"

I hesitated. Mr. Lavender is not stupid. I would have to tell a version of the truth. "As Miss Lavender said, her Royal Highness, the Duchess of York, is a special friend of mine. She must be protected from danger. I felt Squire Oxberry not up to the task. Lionel ran the streets of Seven Dials for the past year. Miss Lavender told me so herself. I thought it safe enough for the boy to help me investigate the robberies."

Miss Lavender suddenly averted her gaze from me. "I am beginning to understand the way of things. In your mind even the most remote possibility of the Royal Duchess being set upon by thieves must weigh more in importance to you than a boy's safety."

"That is not true," I denied with some heat. "I cautioned Lion to be most careful, and he gave me his word that he would be. He grew up under the worst of circumstances, and is not a boy who fell off the farm cart last week. He can take care of himself. Did he tell you I have given him the nickname of Lion, by the way?"

"Yes," Miss Lavender said, her head still turned away from me. "He thinks you nothing short of a god. Foolish boy."

"I shall disabuse him of the notion. That is, unless you have already done so yourself, Miss Lavender?"

She refused to look at me. "Father, is that not Jack Townsend in conversation with the playwright Mr. Sheridan?" Miss Lavender said, referring to another investigator from Bow Street. "Let's walk over and greet him."

"In a minute," her father answered. "I'll be round to question you further about the house party at Oatlands,

Mr. Brummell. The Royal Duchess has charged me with the task of finding Lord Kendrick's murderer. I've got my suspicions."

I did not like the sound of that. "I have not the slightest doubt you are leaving no stone unturned," I told him.

"Justice is always my chief concern. I think I'll have one of the Runners keep an eye on your thief, Mr. Brummell. Neal, I believe Lionel told Lydia was his name. Not that I think you'd withhold any pertinent information in a murder investigation from Bow Street," Mr. Lavender said in a tone that said he thought just the opposite. He turned to his daughter. "We'll go talk to Townsend now."

I reached out and touched Miss Lavender on her arm above her gloves. The action startled her, and she turned to face me at last. "What is it?"

Mr. Lavender saw my hand on his daughter's arm. Every freckle on his face stood out. For an instant, I thought he would reach for his pistol.

"Please walk with me for a minute, Miss Lavender," I asked. "I wish to explain some things to you."

"Lydia, you'll come with me now," Mr. Lavender growled.

Nothing could have swayed the independent Miss Lavender's decision more. "I'll be with you shortly, Father. Go on ahead."

She turned her back to him. He walked away, but not before throwing a most disagreeable look over his shoulder at me.

I held out my arm for Miss Lavender to take so that we might walk a little, but she stubbornly refused to accept it. "What do you have to say to me?"

"Only that I apologize if I have offended you by engaging Lion's help. Please believe me when I say I am fond of the boy and would not see him hurt. It is only that her Royal Highness has shown me the utmost kindness over the years—"

Miss Lavender held up a hand. "I already understand, Mr. Brummell."

"Lydia, I—"

She bristled like an old dowager. "I haven't given you leave to call me by my first name!"

"Very well, Miss Lavender. Did you receive the flowers I brought you?"

"Yes. They are pretty. Thank you."

"Heigh-ho, what's this? Out searching the Park for your missing letter?" Sylvester Fairingdale crowed from his curricle.

Miss Lavender and I swung to face him.

Fairingdale knew about Freddie's letter! No, I decided. He knew about *a* stolen letter, but not the contents. If he knew the truth, all hell would have broken loose already. "Pay no attention to this dolt," I said to Miss Lavender.

"Aren't you going to introduce me to your charming companion, Brummell? I haven't seen you about Town, fair lady," the garishly clad fop said.

Miss Lavender looked none too pleased.

With great effort I restrained myself from lunging for the curricle to grab Fairingdale by his throat. "This is Miss Lavender, daughter of John Lavender from Bow Street. Miss Lavender, the fashion disaster you see in front of you is Sylvester Fairingdale."

Miss Lavender remained silent. The ninny eyed her with interest. "Don't believe a word Brummell ever says, Miss Lavender. Just look at how he's made London such a dull place with his dark coats. But, stay, are you helping Brummell find that stolen letter? He's frantic about it, you know."

I took a threatening step toward the curricle.

"Bid you good day," the coward called, applying the whip to his horse's back. "Hope to see *you* again, Miss Lavender."

"What an awful man," Miss Lavender declared. "Is he the sort of friend you have?"

"He is nothing short of my nemesis."

"What is this letter he said was stolen? You told me the highwayman took your clothes."

"Actually, I told you the highwayman took my belongings. Of course clothes were among them."

"You impossible man! Twisting words—"

"Mr. Brummell! Mr. Brummell!" Lady Crecy called, ordering her coachman to pull up to our side. Riding in an open carriage were Lady Crecy, her daughter, Lady Penelope, Lord Wrayburn and, looking pale but far from stricken with grief, Lady Ariana.

I performed the introductions. With the exception of Lady Ariana, Lady Crecy and the occupants of her carriage gave only the briefest of nods to Miss Lavender, recognizing that she was neither a member of the nobility nor the gentry. I felt her stiffen at my side.

"How are you, Lady Ariana?" I asked. "I am sorry I did not have time to offer my condolences on the death of your cousin before you left Oatlands."

Lady Ariana smiled her childlike smile. "Do not give it another thought, Mr. Brummell. Roger and I are so happy, you know. We are to be wed."

An awkward silence fell.

Lady Crecy was the first to rally. "Dear Mr. Brummell, have you heard the news about Lady Perry?"

"I understand she has had her baby," I replied.

"Oh, is that true?" Miss Lavender asked. "She is such a dear lady. I met her last year. Is the babe a boy or girl?"

Lady Crecy completely ignored Miss Lavender's question.

"I fear there is trouble, Mr. Brummell. Lady Perry has not had the baby. The last I heard, she was suffering mightily. A second physician has been called in to try to assist the birth, but it may be too late. Poor Lady Perry. Too young to die. Oh, I see the Duke of Derehurst and Lady Deidre. I must go. Good day, Mr. Brummell."

The carriage rumbled away.

I stood immobile.

❦ 24 ❦

"*Please excuse me,* Miss Lavender. I fear for Lady Perry and must go to Grosvenor Square at once. Shall I escort you across the way to your father?"

"No! If Lady Perry is having difficulty giving birth, I might be able to help."

My eyebrows must have risen all the way to my scalp.

"Not me personally. But a midwife I know who is very skilled."

"A midwife?" I repeated skeptically. "Miss Lavender, Lord Perry is an earl. I have no doubt he has the finest physicians in London overseeing his wife's care. Come, I shall escort you to your father."

"No! I'm going with you. Perhaps I can persuade someone at Lord Perry's house that a midwife is needed. I must. Even if her physicians save Lady Perry, no man can know what it's like for a woman to lose a baby."

I paused and studied the woman before me. She was ardent on the subject. Most expressly so. "Why do you think a midwife would be better able to help Lady Perry?"

"A good midwife practices cleanliness. Faith, the stories I've heard of women dying because some physician won't even wash his hands after—"

I interrupted her before she could tell me more than I wanted to know. "I do not need to hear details. But, cleanliness, you say?" Here was a doctrine I could embrace.

"Yes. But that is only one reason I believe midwives are better suited to the job." Miss Lavender's eyes implored me to trust her.

And I found that I did. I respect her opinions over some of those who hold the title of lady. Such as Lady Crecy, for example.

"Very well. But do not come with me. Instead, find the midwife and meet me in Grosvenor Square. You remember the Perrys' house?"

"I do, from last year."

"What is the woman's name?"

"Mrs. Hoffman."

"Good. I shall go ahead and convince Lord Perry to admit Mrs. Hoffman to Lady Perry's bedchamber. Did you and your father walk here? Do you need money for a hackney?"

"I have my own money, thank you." She turned and half ran over the grass to her father.

As it turned out, not much effort on my part was required to persuade Perry to permit the midwife to help.

When I arrived at his house, I learned he was above stairs with his wife. I was not surprised. Perry is not the sort of husband who would drink his way through a bottle of wine, closeted in his study, awaiting word of his heir's arrival. Or his death.

Some minutes passed before the earl appeared in the drawing room where I waited. His expression was one of acute wretchedness.

"Perry," I said, rising from my chair. "How is she?"

"Brummell, I—I do not know. These past twenty or more hours have been my worst nightmare. The physicians tell me the babe is turned the wrong way. They do not think . . . I may lose . . ." He broke off and ran his fingers through his dark hair.

I put my hand on his shoulder. "I know it is a source of strength for Lady Perry that you are at her side."

"But I can do nothing!" he cried passionately, walking away from me. "I thought I had hired the best medical people in London, but what if it is not enough? Look here, I must return to Bernadette. I only came down because my man told me you insisted on seeing me."

"I did and for good reason. Can we sit down?"

"No," he said distractedly. He pulled an intricately made watch, shaped like a mandolin, out of his pocket and consulted the time. "You must excuse me. I am not myself. I just want to be with Bernadette."

He hovered by the drawing room door. I walked over to him. "Listen to me, Perry. Do you remember Miss Lavender, the woman who runs the shelter for females in trouble? You met her last October. She came here to help with that Frenchwoman."

"Yes, yes, what about her?"

"I was just in the Park when Lady Crecy told me of Lady Perry's trouble. Miss Lavender was with me. She knows a midwife who could help."

He looked dumbfounded. "A midwife? Some woman, from God knows where, touching my Bernadette? Have you run mad?"

"Wait, Perry! What choice do you have? You just told me things look very bad. I think you should let this midwife assess the situation. I trust Miss Lavender's judgment. I know she would not bring someone here whom she did not truly believe could help. She cares deeply about the plight of women."

He thought this over. "Perhaps you are right. I do not know what else to do. They say in only another few hours . . ."

"It will not come to that, Perry. We must have hope. And Miss Lavender left immediately from the Park to find the midwife and bring her here. Her name is Mrs. Hoffman."

Perry heaved a sigh. "You are a good friend, Brummell. I shall leave word to have Mrs. Hoffman sent up when she arrives. Pray God it will not be too late."

With that, he hastened from the room.

I reached for a decanter of wine on a side table and poured myself a large measure. I drank that one, and yes, a few more, while waiting for Miss Lavender and the midwife.

At least an hour went by before Miss Lavender arrived with a thin woman in a neat brown dress. Miss Lavender introduced her. Mrs. Hoffman, not wanting to waste a moment, nodded to me and then ascended the stairs briskly, carrying a large bag.

Miss Lavender and I drifted to the drawing room to wait.

We talked of nothing of consequence, both of us too preoccupied with thoughts of Lady Perry. The house was hushed in expectation. At one point, we heard footsteps on the stairs, but a glance out the drawing room doors showed us it was one of the physicians stomping from the house in a huff.

After a while, Miss Lavender accepted a glass of wine from me. She recalled how kind Lady Perry had been to her on the occasion they had met, offering her tea and treating her almost as if she, Miss Lavender, were of the same station in life as that of an earl's wife.

I could not help but be impressed by the calm way Miss Lavender comported herself over the long hours. Every once in a while, when a silence fell between us, I noticed she clasped her hands and lowered her head in prayer.

It was during one of those quiet moments that I heard

a faint cry come from above stairs. Simultaneously, Miss Lavender and I stood up and hurried into the hall.

There it was again. Stronger this time. The unmistakable sound of a baby's cry.

"Oh, praise God," Miss Lavender whispered, tears running unchecked down her cheeks.

I felt a burning behind my own eyes. I had probably just swallowed some wine too quickly. "Here, take my handkerchief, Miss Lavender," I said, pulling one from my pocket.

"That's all right," she said with a sniffle. "I have one of my own in my reticule."

I stepped up to her and raised her face to mine. "Which is in the drawing room. Must you always be so independent? Here, allow me." I stroked the square of white linen gently across her cheeks, then held out the handkerchief for her to take.

She reached up to accept it. Her hand closed about the material with the two *B*'s stitched in one corner and encompassed the ends of my fingers. I looked down into her green eyes, the lashes wet with tears, and felt a strong desire to take Miss Lavender into my arms. I expect it was just the emotion of the moment that stirred these feelings in me. Do you not think so?

"Mr. Brummell, sir?" Lord Perry's man, Hearn, called from the top of the stairs.

Miss Lavender and I drew apart. "What is the news, Hearn?"

The valet descended the stairs to stand in front of us. "Lord and Lady Perry have a son. Mrs. Hoffman is tending to Lady Perry. Her ladyship is not completely out of danger, but her condition is vastly improved. Mrs. Hoffman is confident she can see both Lady Perry and the baby through."

Miss Lavender smiled, then blew her nose.

"Please offer Lord and Lady Perry my heartiest congratulations," I said.

Hearn nodded. "Yes, sir. Lord Perry desires me to say that he cannot leave his wife and son at the moment, but that he will send word to you tomorrow. He also asked that Miss Lavender leave the direction of her shelter with me. His lordship wishes to thank both of you."

Miss Lavender gave the number of the house in New Street where the Haven of Hope is located. We gathered our things and walked out into the night air. Both of us took deep breaths, then laughed the way one sometimes does after trouble has passed.

"I shall hail a hackney and see you home, Miss Lavender," I said, standing on the stone steps.

"All right," came the reply.

A few minutes later we were travelling along. "You realise what you have done for the Perrys this evening, do you not? I find my admiration for you increases at our every meeting, Miss Lavender."

She shrugged a shoulder. "If men who call themselves physicians would be open to new ideas, the lives of many other women and children could be saved."

"Well, I do not pretend to know what ladies discuss when they are without male company, but I should imagine that Lady Perry will extol the virtues of Mrs. Hoffman to her friends."

"That will be a start," Miss Lavender said.

"I do hope that you are no longer angry with me for enlisting Lion's help in finding the thief." I studied her profile. "Your skin is the most beautiful I think I have ever seen. More translucent than even my finest Sèvres porcelain. It almost glows from within. I should dislike being kept from beauty." This last I said in a light tone, though I meant every word. Freddie's face suddenly flashed in my mind. I experienced a nagging feeling of guilt, but I told myself I was a bachelor, a man about Town.

Miss Lavender, sitting opposite me, adjusted the brim of her hat. "If that bit of flummery is any example, I can well envision how you've charmed your way to the height of Society."

"You wrong me. Have I been forgiven?"

"Since Lionel came to no harm, I expect so. But you mustn't involve him in anything like that again."

"I thought the boy had hopes for employment with Bow Street. He will be exposed to all sorts of dangers if he becomes a constable."

"He is too young to be running about Seven Dials. Other, less dangerous commissions may be more appropriate for his age," Miss Lavender said with an air of finality. "So what is this about a stolen letter of yours, Mr. Brummell? Is it important?"

I ran my gloved thumb across the top of the dog's head cane Freddie had given me. "Nothing I cannot deal with. Here we are in Fetter Lane. Excuse me if I do not accompany you up the stairs to the private entrance of your home. I shall wait until you are safely inside before I leave." Miss Lavender and her father live in lodgings above Kint's Chop House. The rooms boast steps in the back of the building that lead directly to their door. A nice convenience, not having to go through the eating establishment every time they came or went.

Miss Lavender's lips twitched. "Of course. I'm sure you don't want to cross swords with my father at this hour. Good evening, Mr. Brummell."

I rose to assist her from the vehicle, but she was out before me. I waited until I saw her walk through her door before giving the coachman the order for Bruton Street.

Miss Lavender's mention of the letter renewed my anger at Sylvester Fairingdale. May his valet singe the fop's teased hair with the curling tongs.

Just how the devil had Fairingdale found out about the stolen letter? Roger would not have told him. The only people who knew about it were myself, Freddie, Ulga . . . and Robinson!

Alighting from the hackney in Bruton Street, I paid the driver and climbed the steps to my house. Robinson swung open the door immediately, obviously having been on the alert for my return. Trying to make up for his sedated state earlier, no doubt.

"Good evening, sir. Did you have a pleasant night?"

I handed him my hat and stick and began ascending the stairs. "Lord and Lady Perry have a son. Lady Perry had a terrible time of it, but all is well."

Robinson followed me. "I am glad to hear it, sir."

The moment I was through the door to my bedchamber I swung around to face him. "Who is the girl you have been walking out with?"

"I beg your pardon, sir?" Robinson asked, taken aback.

"You are not lacking in auditory capabilities. Do me the honour of answering the question."

Robinson raised his chin. "Her name is Fanny," he replied in a tone that doubly annoyed me because it was so much like my own when he questioned me about private matters.

Distracted, the valet strode to the tall wardrobe, clucking his tongue because the door to the wardrobe was slightly ajar. Robinson and I both like things to be neat and in their places.

But I was not to be put off my mission. "Robinson, did you tell your lady friend about the missing letter?"

Suddenly Robinson screamed and jumped away from the wardrobe. "There is a ghost, a monster in there!"

I stepped past him and opened the door to the wardrobe wider to see what had frightened him.

Two eyes glinted gold in the darkness. Chakkri lay on a stack of nightclothes, his tail curled.

"Reow," he said in a conversational tone.

"How did you get in there, you rogue?" I asked him, reaching in and gently extracting the cat. I stroked his fur, then placed him on the bed.

Meanwhile Robinson stood in high dudgeon, lips pursed, and arms crossed. "That animal has spread cat hairs all over your nightclothes, sir. I shall be forced to—"

"Oh, just shake them out and cease your complaints," I said impatiently. "I asked you a question regarding your lady friend."

"I do not see what my Fanny has to do with anything."

I raised my right eyebrow severely. "Did you tell her about the missing letter?"

"I may have mentioned it in passing. She is very easy to talk with, sympathetic to my every concern."

"Who is her employer?"

Robinson looked mulish.

"She works for Sylvester Fairingdale, does she not?" I demanded.

Robinson's mouth dropped open. "How did you know?"

"Because Fairingdale tweaked me regarding the letter this afternoon. Because Fairingdale wishes to take my place as the Arbiter of Fashion. Because Fairingdale most likely paid the woman to befriend you so he could spy on me," I said, beyond aggravation.

Robinson whimpered.

Chakkri remained blessedly silent. Well, other than just a slight coughing sound that a highly imaginative person might think sounded like the word *fool*. Naturally, I did not think so. Probably just some fur in his throat.

"Sir, I never told Fanny the letter was from her Royal Highness. I am sorry. Indeed, I am more sorry than I can say that I became involved with Fanny."

He did look remorseful. And hurt. "If you feel I have betrayed you, sir, I shall pack my things."

Oh, God. Here was Robinson's Royalty on the Way to the Guillotine expression.

"Perhaps I might find a position as valet to a banker or a mill owner," the valet mused sadly.

Chakkri rolled over on the bed onto his back. He stretched his fawn-coloured body to its full length and writhed as if one in the throes of ecstasy. Then he stood up and looked at me expectantly.

"There is no need for such dramatics, Robinson. Only keep your tongue between your teeth in the future," I said in a tired voice.

But this was a prime opportunity for Robinson to play his Martyr Act, and he was never one to miss an opportunity. "I should be punished for my disloyalty. I—I shall," he could barely get the words out. "I shall brush the cat for you, sir."

Chakkri jumped down from the bed and exited the room, hopping over the threshold as is his odd way.

"That will not be necessary, Robinson."

"Thank you, sir. Thank you very much indeed."

Long after the valet had departed for his own quarters, I sat drinking brandy by the empty fireplace. My thoughts centered on Roger Cranworth. If Neal did not bring me the blue velvet book, I would be forced to break into Roger Cranworth's rooms myself.

I would have a long wait until then, but in the meantime, I expected to be able to see Freddie and tell her that I hoped to have the letter that very night.

And that I knew who the Marquess of Kendrick's killer was.

Monday morning—well, two hours past noon, I should say—I procured a dozen yellow roses and set out for Grosvenor Square. I walked, leaving the quarrelling twins and my sedan-chair at home. The day was very fine, and I have often found that exercise increases my ability to think clearly.

Lady Perry was in no condition to receive company after her ordeal, even in her upstairs sitting room, but Perry came down to meet me. He was a different man than yesterday. Beaming, he entered the drawing room the image of the proud papa.

"Brummell, I wish you could see him, but Mrs. Hoffman has forbidden any visitors. He is the most handsome baby you have ever clapped eyes on. Has my nose."

I smiled. How on earth did Perry see his Roman nose on a mite of a baby? "What are you calling him?"

"Thomas."

"A good name. Here, these are for Lady Perry. How is she?"

"Thank you." He accepted the flowers and passed them

to a footman. "Weak, but there is no sign of childbed fever. Mrs. Hoffman is a marvel. I am forever grateful to you and to Miss Lavender."

"Miss Lavender is good."

"She is. If she were in Society, she would be married in a trice. I do not know what is wrong with the men of the middle classes."

"Miss Lavender is very independent. Perhaps she does not wish to wed." The new silk waistcoat I wore suddenly felt tight.

Perry laughed. "I thought all women wished to be wed. At any rate, earlier this morning I sent Miss Lavender a large draft on my bank to show my gratitude. She can use it as a dowry if she wishes."

A few minutes later when I took my leave of Perry, I reflected on the Bow Street man's daughter. Miss Lavender would be more likely to use the windfall for the benefit of the Haven of Hope than as a lure to entice a man to matrimony.

For some reason, the waistcoat did not feel constricting after all.

St. James's Palace, with its flanking octagonal turrets, was built in the time of Henry VIII. The red brick building can be approached by a gatehouse that stands at the southern end of St. James's Street. This was the entrance I chose to use after learning Freddie was in residence.

The guards permitted me to enter after checking a register. A series of white-wigged footmen led me through the Palace, where Prinny had married Princess Caroline eleven years ago. Not a happy union, you know, to put it mildly.

Freddie was the victim of another unhappy union. I felt my spirits lift a bit at the thought of seeing her, though I must say I feel a pinch uncomfortable meeting her at the

Palace. I prefer the informality of Oatlands.

We reached a very tall set of double doors. One footman went inside, while the other waited with me. A few minutes passed before I was motioned within.

"Leave us," Freddie commanded the footmen who bowed low.

The Royal Duchess looked tiny in the huge gold-and-white room. She sat on a long white sofa, Hero and Georgicus lying on either side of her. At least Georgicus was still in favour.

Ulga sat on a chair close by her mistress rather than her usual position in the corner of the room. Was this Freddie's way of keeping the wall between us? The Prussian maid did not appear any more happy to be in London than Freddie did. The lines on Ulga's face were pronounced. She looked tired, and her usual look of competence had been replaced by one of strain.

I bowed to Freddie. "I trust your journey to London was satisfactory." She did not offer me her hand to kiss. I settled for petting Georgicus and shaking Hero's paw.

Freddie's demeanor was reserved. "I am afraid I cannot deem anything satisfactory until the threat hanging over my head is removed. What news have you, George?"

"May I sit down?"

She indicated the matching sofa across from her. "I am unable to give you much time. My arrival in Town is no secret. Many will be calling on me today. Do you have the letter?"

I sat and looked at her, unhappy about the closed expression on her face. "Not yet, but I know who has it."

"Who?" She leaned forward eagerly.

"Roger Cranworth."

"What?" she cried.

"Roger Cranworth was Lord Kendrick's partner in the highwayman scheme. They employed a local ruffian named Neal to carry out the actual robberies."

"This is disgraceful. Poor Miss Cranworth."

"She may not even know of her brother's nefarious activities. If she does, she is powerless to stop him."

"How are we to get the letter from Roger?" Freddie asked. Then, before I could answer, she said, "He will be communicating with me, wanting something. Money, I assume."

"That thought has occurred to me. I have a plan to retrieve the letter."

"How?"

"There is no honour amongst thieves, you know. I am paying Neal to retrieve it. Tonight. Then all will be as it was before, Freddie."

"And if this Neal fails?"

I held her gaze. "I shall keep working at it until the letter is in my hands."

"What of Lord Kendrick's murder?"

"It seems logical that Roger Cranworth is responsible. The two men argued over the marquess marrying Roger's sister, remember. That and a disagreement over their criminal activities would be motive enough for murder."

"Dreadful, this is all quite dreadful. You will send word to me first thing in the morning, telling me if you have the letter." She rose, and I immediately came to my feet. "You cannot come here again, George. It would be remarked upon."

Was she forgetting all the times in the past I had called on her at the Palace? "As you wish, your Royal Highness."

"I shall be attending the Duchess of Northumberland's ball tomorrow evening at Syon House. Her Grace, Frances Julia, is a most kind woman. She cares about animals and children and is responsible for several charity schools."

"I received an invitation myself."

"All the world will be there. Her Grace rarely entertains on such a grand scale what with the Duke of Northumberland being so involved in military concerns."

"May I escort you?" I asked without much hope.

"Victor Tallarico has already offered, and I have accepted, but thank you."

Victor the Victorious.

"Until tomorrow. I hope you will do me the honour of saving me a dance," I said, then bowed and left the room.

With footmen to escort me, I made my way out of the Palace. I dearly missed the closeness between Freddie and me that seemed to have been extinguished like a bedside candle. Things might never be the same between us.

The knowledge twisted and turned inside me as I made my way through the streets of Mayfair.

Arriving home in Bruton Street, I was surprised to see Miss Lavender turning away from my door and walking down the steps, about to move in the other direction.

"Miss Lavender!" I hailed.

She glanced around and saw me, her lips tilting into a wide smile. The manner of her stride was almost a skip as she reached me. "Oh, Mr. Brummell, you'll never believe what's happened!"

"Lord Perry has given you a large draft on his bank as thanks for all you have done for his family."

Her mouth dropped open. Then she laughed. "You awful man. How did you know?"

Curious looks from passersby caused me to edge Miss Lavender to my door. "Here, come inside."

"I can only stay a few minutes," she told me, her green eyes shining underneath her chip straw bonnet. "I've so many ambitions for the shelter. With the money Lord Perry has given me, I can do so much."

We entered the hall. Robinson came hurrying from the kitchen. "Good afternoon, Miss Lavender. May I be of any service?" he asked in a humble tone.

Robinson *was* trying to make amends. He does not approve of Miss Lavender, thinking her a woman of too much learning, a bluestocking. Not to mention that here she was, an unattached female, at a bachelor's house. Most improper.

"Will you have a glass of wine to celebrate?" I asked the Scottish girl.

"No, thank you. As I said, I've not much time."

I dismissed Robinson, and he left us.

"I have my own celebration to arrange," Miss Lavender continued excitedly. "I thought tonight my assistant, Miss Ashton, and I might have a special dinner for the girls and discuss how best to use the money."

"That sounds very agreeable. They are bound to enjoy the treat. And Lion as well, I assume."

"Yes, Lionel too," Miss Lavender said. Her whole being radiated happiness. "Would you like to come?" she blurted.

"I am sorry. I have a prior engagement."

She looked at her shoes, then back to me. "Faith, what could I have been thinking? Of course you already have a Society entertainment to attend. I must have been thinking of Lionel, that's it. I didn't want him to be the only male at the table. He might feel awkward, you know."

Miss Lavender herself appeared ill at ease. So unlike her. "Actually it is not really a *Beau Monde* party, but rather the Grand Masquerade at the King's Theatre. Hardly an exclusive affair. Anyone can attend if they have a guinea to purchase a ticket."

"Really?" she asked. "I've never been to anything like that, a guinea being far too dear for my pocketbook. Fancy dress is it?"

"Yes."

"What are you going as? A king? Or maybe a sorcerer?"

I chuckled. "Nothing so elaborate. I have a black domino, a mask, and a tall black hat with a red plume that I usually wear to masquerades."

"Trust you to be elegantly plain."

I tilted my head. "What would you go as, Miss Lavender?"

"Me? Oh, I don't know, I've never considered. Girls without guineas to spare don't dream of such things," she said matter-of-factly.

"Allow me to point out that you do have a guinea to spare now. Perhaps one evening you shall go."

She gave a little half smile, then turned and walked to the door. "Enjoy yourself, Mr. Brummell."

"And you do the same, Miss Lavender."

She was through the door when I remembered something. "Oh, Miss Lavender . . ."

She turned. "Yes?"

From a stand near the door, I picked up my old lion's head walking stick. "Here. Please give this to Lion with my compliments."

Miss Lavender looked at the elegant cane. "How fine it is. Why would you give such a beautiful thing away? Have you grown bored with it?"

"The Duchess of York gifted me with the dog's head stick you may have seen me carry. I favour that one now."

Miss Lavender accepted the cane, eyes downcast. "The Duchess of York. I see. You're kind to give this one away. Lionel will be excited."

"He earned a reward for helping me."

When she left, I found myself staring at the closed door frowning. Had I hurt her feelings in some way? I gained the impression that I had. Hmmm.

Now this may come as a surprise to you, but I do not always comprehend the female mind. No, indeed, not always. Sometimes the ladies baffle me.

I did know the cause of Freddie's chilly behaviour and her fears, so I put my mind to that problem and rang for

Robinson. After I dined, I must ready myself for the important evening ahead. I could only hope that Neal would fulfill his part of our bargain, so I could end this matter of the letter which threatened to destroy my reputation. Then I could bring my suspicions regarding Roger Cranworth's involvement in Lord Kendrick's murder to Mr. Lavender.

❧ 26 ❧

As it turned out, Chakkri caused a delay in my departure for the King's Theatre.

The cat had slithered his lean body into one of the wardrobes again. This time, the result was a well-chewed ball of wet red feather, which had formerly been the plume in my fancy dress hat.

Robinson held the soggy mess between two fingers. "That animal has ruined your fine hat, sir. When will you decide to send him back to Siam?"

"When I decide to visit the country myself." I held the hat. The brim showed teeth marks and the side held a long scratch where perhaps the cat had held the hat down while he did his damage. I glanced over to where Chakkri lay on the bed, his tail curled, looking supremely unconcerned.

"What will you wear now, sir?" Robinson asked. "Do you wish me to hurry over to Fentum's and bring home something suitable?"

"No, thank you. I shall stop there on my way to the Masquerade. Only find my black domino and mask."

"Yes, sir," Robinson said, casting a look of reproach at the cat. "I already have it freshly pressed."

Chakkri rested his head on top of his front paws and closed his eyes.

While Robinson made sure there were no wayward creases in the black silk domino, I considered my predicament. Since I had told Neal specifically that I would be sporting such an accoutrement as a red plume in a tall black hat, I must obtain one.

Thus, a short time later, a hackney carried me to No. 78 Strand, where Fentum's Music and Masquerade Warehouse stands. A private door around the corner served as my entrance. The proprietor, a robust man with a white mustache that quite reminded me of Mr. Lavender's chosen facial adornment, produced a tall black hat and red plume for me. Pleased, I took a moment to scan the items he had displayed in a case while he prepared my bill. One of them was a long silver instrument, some two feet in length, with an oval *faux* ruby at one end.

"A silver wand the sorcerer did sway," the shop owner declared.

"A sorcerer?" I asked, remembering that Miss Lavender had thought I might appear at the Masquerade as a sorcerer.

"Yes, sir. You'll be able to conjure whatever spell you want with this," he said half seriously, pulling the wand from the case and handing it to me.

Or the heavy instrument might serve me well as a weapon. I had had to leave my dog's head cane with its deadly swordstick at home for the sake of my costume.

"I shall take this as well," I told him.

I donned the long black cape and fastened the new red plume into the tall black hat and placed it on my head. The garments completely covered my normal evening attire. With the black mask across my eyes, no one would know me unless I chose to reveal my identity.

No one, of course, except Neal.

I picked up the silver wand and left the shop. The night was fine, but patches of fog marred the view to the stars above. Paying the hackney driver, I paused outside the King's Theatre, deliberately delaying my entrance in case Neal had already been successful, had the blue velvet book, and had come to find me.

One could hope.

I bided my time and read a nearby placard: "No person will be admitted without a mask and either a domino, fancy, or character dress; nor any gentleman dressed in female habit. Ice creams, tea, coffee, lemonade, orange-ade, &c. will be abundantly supplied."

A couple, the man dressed as a shepherd accompanied by a giggling Bo-Peep, walked past me. The rules of behaviour at these entertainments state that one had to remain in character of the part one was playing all evening. Whispers often went around Town that high-born ladies would appear as flower girls or housemaids. I distracted myself imagining Sylvester Fairingdale forced to play the role of a farmer in peasant's clothing all evening. Likely he would be dressed better than ever before.

Finally I checked my pocket watch. After ten. Deciding I had lingered long enough, I followed a harlequin and two sailors inside the large theatre. The benches had been moved out of the pit, making the floor one large area, the scene of abandon. There is something, you know, about putting a mask over one's face and assuming another identity that makes people ignore the conventions of Society.

An orchestra played a bawdy song to the delight of pilgrims and priests. Bears danced, devils and Quakers cavorted together, and a red-haired goddess from ancient mythology struggled to free herself from the grip of a clown.

"Take your pulse, sir!" a man dressed as a doctor

yelled at me, grabbing my wrist. I raised the silver wand and, I give you my word, he disappeared.

My gaze swung back to the lady with the dark red hair, a notion growing in my mind. When the enraged female swung the torch with its paper flames she carried at the clown's head, I moved forward.

"Begone from this lady," I said in a theatrical voice, raising the length of silver high. The clown stumbled drunkenly away, leaving me looking into a pair of emerald-green eyes behind a purple mask. "Er, Miss Lavender?"

"Mr. Brummell, it is you, isn't it? I'd recognise that cool grey gaze anywhere," she cried, adjusting the folds of her purple pleated robe around her. But not before I had a delightful glimpse of her bare arms.

Too late, I questioned the wisdom of approaching her. The Bow Street man's daughter was the last woman I needed on my hands when I was expecting a thief to deliver stolen goods. Yet, what was I to do, leave her to that bully? She can take good care of herself, true, but this was different, I told myself. It had nothing whatsoever to do with that expanse of milk-white flesh on view.

I bowed in front of her, lifting my tall hat. "I am at your service. Only tell me, which of the goddesses are you here representing?"

"Aurora, for she announces the beginning of a new day."

"I see." And I also saw the sparkling dots on the white muslin that formed Miss Lavender's clinging gown.

"I'd no idea a Masquerade could be so depraved, else I never would have wasted my guinea," Miss Lavender said, overwrought.

I tore my eyes from her curves. The dress was tied at the waist, you understand, giving me the opportunity to study Miss Lavender's figure. I fully believe one should seize opportunities thrown one's way in life. Do you not agree?

Then, for the first time, I became aware that the Scottish girl was trembling. I reached out and adjusted the purple cape, which had slipped behind her exposed shoulder again. "You should not have come here alone."

"You're right about that. Will you escort me to Croft's Masquerade Warehouse in Fleet Street where I obtained this costume? I can change clothes there and go home."

I hesitated. Here was a coil. How could I leave the theatre before Neal sent word? I looked around wildly, searching for an excuse to remain a short time longer. I must be certain no harm would come to Miss Lavender. "Would you not care to view the shrouded corpse in its coffin on view? Or what about Jack Horner over in his corner?"

"No, I wish to leave. If you are indeed a conjurer, pray conjure a hackney for me," she replied. "I can't like what's going on here."

At that moment, the orchestra broke into Carlo Vernet's *La Folie du Jour,* and people began performing the daring new *valse* from Germany. Miss Lavender looked about as couples held each other and turned round and round, gliding about the room.

Without my permission, my mouth opened and I said, "Would you not like to try the new dance? Even the Prince has done so, just last year in Brighton."

"You want to dance with me?" Green eyes sparkled with sudden interest. "I shouldn't with someone with whom I wasn't acquainted, but since it's only you, Mr. Brummell, I'll feel quite safe." Miss Lavender held out her arms.

This artless remark had the most astonishing effect upon me.

I reached for the torch she carried and tossed it and my sorcerer's stick into the coffin with the corpse.

I then placed the palms of my hands against Miss Lavender's sides and pulled her close to me. Safe indeed! Her lips parted in surprise, yet she clung to me as I guided her into the mass of swaying couples. I held her even closer.

We carried on this way for some minutes.

You know, I find I quite like this new *valse*. And did someone say that red hair was not the fashion? Not I. On the contrary, I find that red hair is the most lovely of all the shades.

I must also report that so pleasant was this new dance that I had quite forgotten about Neal, the blue velvet book, and possibly even my own name, until a wigged footman with a highly painted face tapped me on the shoulder. I brought Miss Lavender and myself to a halt, noting the rise and fall of her chest. The dance had left her breathless.

"Your property has been recovered, sir. It awaits you outside the theatre," the footman told me. Then he, like the doctor earlier, disappeared into the crowd.

"What did he mean, Mr. Brummell?" Miss Lavender queried.

I looked back at her, still in the circle of my arms. I released my hold. "Nothing. He was playing his role as footman, I expect."

I must get away from her. Now. I must meet Neal.

Just then a cry of alarm sounded from the area of the entryway. People began swarming out of the theatre. "Murder!" shouted a voice.

With Miss Lavender's hand in mine, I hastened toward the exit and out into the cobblestone street. An odd picture it presented, with all manner of cupids, gypsies, Turks, even kings and queens standing outside the King's Theatre Royal, gaping at a spot on the dewy stone street. A thin fog hung over the area, but the lamps from a coach made the outline of the body on the pavement easy to see. Two constables guarded it.

Miss Lavender drew in her breath sharply, her hand clutching mine tightly.

Minus the slightest of doubts, I knew in an instant the deceased could only be Neal. I saw the grotesque way the body had fallen on the cobblestones on its stomach, the side of his face with the red birthmark a splash of colour against the pavement. A small hole, for one so deadly, tore the back of his coat.

Roger. It could only have been Roger who had committed such a cowardly act as shooting a man in the back. He had caught Neal in the act of pilfering the blue velvet book, perhaps topped my offer of a guinea as reward for the return of the book, pried the information as to where he was to meet me out of him, then shot the thief and sent that "footman" to tell me.

All these thoughts went through my head at lightning speed. As everyone stared and pointed at the body, the sounds of another carriage coming down the street, the link boy guiding the way and yelling "Bow Street!" reached us.

Too late I remembered Miss Lavender at my side. I suppressed a groan thinking of the depth of Mr. Lavender's disapproval of any sort of contact between myself and his daughter. Should I ease her away before any confrontation? I went to withdraw my hand from hers, but she tightened her grip. I moved my fingers back into place. Perhaps we would escape Mr. Lavender's notice.

She had another idea. When the Scotsman alighted from the vehicle, his daughter cried out, "Father!"

I am ashamed to admit that for the space of a second, I considered turning and making a mad dash down the street.

Instead, I remained where I was. Mr. Lavender had just begun examining the murdered man when he heard his daughter's voice. He located her amongst the crowd.

In her goddess attire. One shoulder exposed to public view. Her hand in mine.

Mr. Lavender's eyes popped from his head as if on wires. "Lydia!" Motioning to the two constables to remain with the body, he began making his way toward us.

At that juncture, in order to keep all the curious present from knowing my identity, I thought it prudent to meet the Bow Street man halfway, out of the earshot of onlookers. So I walked Miss Lavender beside the deadly scene into her father's care.

When she reached him, Miss Lavender flung her arms around her father, leaving him eyeing me warily over her head. A faint air of cherry-scented pipe smoke clung to him.

"Oh, Father, I should never have come here. It's only that when Mr. Brummell told me about the Grand Masquerade earlier today when I was at his house—" She broke off on a sob.

Mr. Lavender took a knife from his pocket and sliced me open from stem to stern. I saw it all happen in his eyes in that instant when he realised it was I there with his daughter, holding her hand—and that she had been to my house! Mentally I wondered who would take care of Chakkri after I was gone.

"Mr. Brummell, I asked you a question," the Scotsman growled in a low voice. "What are you doing with my daughter?"

Amazed to find myself still alive, I spoke. "It was the merest chance that we happened upon one another. Shall I see Miss Lavender safely back to Fetter Lane while you deal with this . . . unpleasantness?"

I noticed that Mr. Lavender's fists—balled at his sides—were quite large. "No," he said, popping a toothpick into his mouth and grinding his teeth against it. "Lydia, get in the carriage and wait for me there. I'll have a report on this killing and join you in a moment. Then you'll tell me how you came to be here in Mr. Brummell's company. And why you went to his house."

Miss Lavender obeyed him, which should tell you the depth of her distress at seeing the corpse.

"Well," I said in a bright tone I was far from feeling. "I shall just let you go about your business, Mr. Lavender. Though I must say it makes one cross the way a fellow cannot travel the London streets without being shot at." I looked pointedly at Neal's body.

And froze.

For I could see a glint of silver. In death, Neal grasped something in his hands. My blue velvet book with its silver corners. It was all I could do to remain motionless.

Mr. Lavender must have seen it at that exact moment. He pushed past me, promising that he would speak with me later. He bent down and turned the body over. Then the Bow Street man's fingers closed around the blue velvet book.

I give you my word it felt like his thick fingers closed around my neck.

❧ 27 ❧

Sleep eluded me that night. Reason told me that even if Roger had kept Freddie's letter in the blue velvet book before, when he killed Neal—and I did believe he was the murderer—he would have removed the letter from the book. He would not want to lose his valuable piece of blackmail material, after all. I need not worry that Freddie's letter was now in Mr. Lavender's hands.

Yet I could not be certain. If Roger were inventive, might he not have had a copy of the letter written out and left in the book? That way, yours truly could be arrested, and Roger's way would be clear to blackmail Freddie with no one to stop him.

But no, the scandal would be made public at that point. Roger would lose his hold over Freddie then. So what was Roger's plan? Why had he left the book at the scene of the crime?

Ah, of course. To implicate me in the death of a common thief. That made more sense. With me out of the way, busy defending myself to Bow Street, Roger's path to blackmailing Freddie would be clear.

I paced my bedchamber, trying to form a strategy that would allow me to remain a step ahead of Bow Street and Roger Cranworth. Who had killed twice.

Around seven in the morning, I rang for Robinson. The valet made not a murmur of protest about the early hour. I tell you, I do not know which is worse, his complaining or this eagerness to make amends.

By nine, I was seated in my book-room, clad in my Eton-blue coat over buff breeches. Chakkri, wise entity that he is, spent a restful night in the exact centre of my bed, dined this morning on André's special scrambled eggs with cheese sauce, and was presently ready for his extended morning nap. The cat scanned the lined shelves of books, but chose to hop up onto the small revolving bookcase that sits on the other side of my desk near a chair. He entwined his fawn-coloured body around the finial, curled his tail, and promptly fell asleep.

"Lucky devil," I muttered. Drawing a sheet of vellum from the desk drawer, I put pen to paper and began answering correspondence. My mind was only half on what I wrote, though. I was really waiting for Mr. Lavender. Once he comprehended the book was mine, he would be on my doorstep.

I did not write to Freddie. Better to wait until later in the day when I might know more. Then there was the chance she might take pity on me if she knew I was writing from gaol.

The knocker sounded a scant twenty minutes later. I continued my writing, not even glancing up when Robinson announced Mr. Lavender. "Send him in."

"Yes, sir."

I resumed writing, my demeanor unconcerned.

The Scotsman entered the room with my blue velvet book in hand.

I tried to bluff. "Good God, how ever did you find that? Sit down, Mr. Lavender. I shall take that book from you. Have you got my stolen clothing as well?"

Mr. Lavender let the book drop with a loud thud on top of the desk right under my nose. My hands itched with the desire to flip through the pages and see if, by some miracle, the letter was there.

The Scotsman never took his eyes off me as he lowered himself into the chair opposite the desk. "That is your book, then, Mr. Brummell?"

As if I could deny ownership when right on the first page my name was embossed in gold. I forced myself to casually go through the pages, *tsk*ing occasionally. "Of course it is mine. Dear me, that drawing Lady Perry gave me of Perry playing the pianoforte is missing."

"Stop your playacting, Mr. Brummell. You knew exactly where the book was. Neal had it." Mr. Lavender, minus his toothpick today, his face hard as granite, was all business.

I assumed my best foolish dandy expression, all the while continuing to examine the book. Freddie's letter was not there, dash it. "Er, yes, I knew the highwayman—Neal, I believe Lionel said his name was—had the book, unless he had sold it for the price of these silver corners."

Mr. Lavender glared at me in complete disbelief. "You can't think I'd believe you hadn't found that ugly customer, Neal, and talked with him, tried to buy your things back."

"Why? I avoid ugly customers, as you say, as a rule."

"That was Neal Snure's body on the street last night outside the King's Theatre."

I sighed. "That alters the case amazingly. I shall never find my clothes now. At least I have my book."

Mr. Lavender shot to his feet and used both hands to brace himself against the desk. "Had you spoken to Neal Snure about your clothes and this book?"

"Why should I? Once I knew your daughter had told you his name, I assumed you would handle the matter."

Mr. Lavender glared at me. "Last night when I found this book and saw your name in it, I had a bad feeling. In fact, Mr. Brummell, most times I hear your name or see your face I have a bad feeling."

"I say!" I protested. "That is a touch harsh."

"When the body was identified as that of Neal, that bad feeling grew into some mighty strong suspicions. You hunted him down, didn't you?"

I made a steeple of my fingers and smiled amiably. "Do you really think me so clever, then? I am flattered."

The Scotsman pointed a finger at me. "I won't address that remark. What I want to know, laddie, and you'll be telling me this instant, is *why*. Why is that book in front of you so important?"

"This book? What makes you think I care about it? Here, you can have it back if you need it as evidence. It holds only sentimental value for me, as you must know. No doubt you have been through it. Mind, I shall want it returned to me when you are done."

"Don't think you can trick me and wheedle your way around the subject," the Bow Street man countered, his voice rising. Then, in a normal but no less menacing tone, he said, "You wouldn't have raised one of your finely manicured hands to locate those clothes. It was that book you were after. Now the thief is dead."

"The lives of thieves are seldom long, are they?"

"I find it all curious. You're not *that* sentimental a man. Here's something else that's curious, Mr. Brummell. You leave London to attend a party at Oatlands. Your clothes and that book are stolen along the way, then—"

"We have already established that a highwayman had been plaguing the area."

Again the finger pointed at me. "Don't be interrupting," he said, burring his *r*. "Lord Kendrick is murdered at Oatlands for a reason I have yet to determine, though I have some ideas. While I am at Oatlands, the Royal

Duchess confesses to me that she has been upset for two days. When I question her as to why *two* days when the murder on her property had only occurred that morning, she faints. You come back to London and immediately hunt down the *highwayman* rather than poking your quizzing glass round trying to figure out who murdered Lord Kendrick. The thief ends up murdered outside the very place you're passing the evening."

"I thought you did not wish me involved in murder cases. I thought you would be singing Scottish songs of cheer that I have not investigated the murder. I fail to comprehend—"

"Then let me say it plain," Mr. Lavender volunteered. "Here are the facts. That book is stolen. Two people are murdered."

"One does not have anything to do with the other," I said.

Mr. Lavender's eyes flashed a warning. "Let me be the judge of that. I've been looking into the murder of the marquess. He wasn't well liked. His cousin was afraid of him, why, I don't know. He was a bully to her, but there's something more."

Should I tell him about Lord Kendrick's threats to have Lady Ariana put into a lunatic asylum? No, I could never do that to the girl as much as I wanted to divert Mr. Lavender's attention from myself. I cleared my throat. "I believe Lady Ariana to have had a difficult life."

The Scotsman's eyes narrowed. "She's got an odd kick in her gallop, that's the truth. If you know anything, you'd better not be holding back from me, laddie."

"Me? Hold something back from you? Why would I do that?"

He drew a deep breath. "Then we have Cecily Cranworth, the marquess's childhood love, angry because Lord Kendrick wouldn't wed her."

"Hmmm."

"Furthermore, neither you nor her Royal Highness, the Duchess of York, liked the marquess. Now what reason could the two of you have to dislike him? See, this is where things get interesting. You were observed in an angry confrontation with the marquess the day before he was murdered. You were overheard saying that the marquess's smirk would be something few people would miss. Why?"

I rose to my feet. Fairingdale had been talking again. Mr. Lavender was stumbling too close to the truth. His path must be redirected. "While I have previously eased the boredom of my days by sparring with you, Mr. Lavender, I see I cannot allow you to labour under any misconceptions in this case."

"Good." The Scotsman stood up straight.

"Regarding this riddle of Lord Kendrick's murder, if you find you need my help, why, I shall consider offering you my assistance. On the condition that you cease throwing out innuendos that I might have killed him. Or this Neal person."

"It's all somehow to do with that book, isn't it, and you're the owner of the book!"

"Actually, if you want to know the truth," I said in the manner of one careless of anything but his own pleasure, "it is all to do with your lovely daughter. I find that I shall use any excuse to call upon her. I am not above telling her that I desire the names and locations of the rag-merchants, when what I really desire is to gaze upon her—"

Quicker than thought, the Bow Street man was round the desk. He has the disadvantage of being a few inches shorter than me, but he was about to toast my ears and nothing could stop him. I did not even try. I leaned against the desk and took a moment to eradicate a piece of lint from my glossy Hessian boots.

"You'll leave my daughter out of this!" he barked.

I put my head to one side. "But you wanted to know about the book. I just told you. I cannot resist your daughter's dark red hair, so I called on her and asked for her help in getting my stolen possessions returned to me."

My ploy to distract the Bow Street man was working. "How did you get Lydia to put on that disgraceful gown last night? My own flesh and blood half naked in the middle of London!" he seethed.

"Oh, the fancy dress was her idea. I think she told me she rented it at a place in Fleet Street. Quite fetching."

"That's not what I meant!" he shouted. "And just what was Lydia doing at your house earlier yesterday? Answer me that."

I shrugged. "It was a private matter. Why not ask her yourself?"

"I did and she told me it was not my concern."

"There you are, then," I said reasonably.

"I will not have you flirting with my daughter!"

"Flirting?" My brows came together as I gave the appearance of one giving the subject deep consideration. "At the King's Theatre, we were merely dancing the new *valse*. Some, I expect, would call that flirting, I grant you."

Mr. Lavender's face mottled red. "The *valse*! That shameless dance from Germany! The one where couples are squeezing and hugging one another?"

"That is the very one!"

"*Do not,*" the Bow Street man roared, "do not *ever* lay your hands on my daughter again! She is a vulnerable lass. I'll not have her subjected to the attentions and flattery of an idle, useless ornament of Society, whose thoughts centre on tying his cravat, gaming away his money, and dallying with any female he finds attractive, including the Duchess of York!" he finished inexcusably.

Silence followed Freddie's name. I could hear the ticking of the long-case clock standing in the corner. With a

studied casualness, I extended my hand to the silver bell
that rested on the polished surface of my desk. I rang it
once. Robinson appeared immediately. Naturally, he had
been listening outside the double doors.

"Yes, sir?"

I had not taken my gaze from the Bow Street man and
did not do so now. "Robinson, Mr. Lavender is leaving."

The Scotsman gave me a look as black as midsummer
thunderclouds, then turned on his booted heel and followed Robinson out the door.

I waited until I heard the street door close before I
released my breath on a long sigh. I had succeeded in
leading him off the scent of Freddie and me, but it was
clear the Bow Street man knew of my attachment to Freddie. And because of my carelessness in not asking Lion
to keep quiet, Mr. Lavender knew of my connection to
Neal.

How long could I keep the matter of the missing letter
from him? Miss Lavender was aware of it, courtesy of
Sylvester Fairingdale. If her father did find out about it,
how long would it be before he made the connection between the letter, Neal, Roger, and Lord Kendrick's nefarious activities?

How long would I have my freedom before he arrested
me for murder?

I could not just sit here and do nothing. I rang the bell.

"Robinson," I said when he appeared. "At The Butler's
Tankard, has there been any talk of Cecily and Roger
Cranworth's new butler?" I remembered Neal had de-
scribed his replacement as starchy.

"Yes, sir. A Mr. Gilpin."

"Have you met him?"

Robinson's lip curled. "I have."

"Out with it, man," I said impatiently.

"Mr. Gilpin is nothing more than a jumped-up footman.
He puts on airs like he has presided over grand houses.

However, I have had it from Rumbelow, the underbutler at Vayne House, that Mr. Gilpin's employment as footman was terminated when he was found by the master of Dunn House in her ladyship's bed."

"Thank you, Robinson."

"Will there be anything else, sir? Some tea? Something to eat?"

I looked at Chakkri, still sleeping on the top of the swivel bookcase. Robinson's gaze followed mine. A gleam came into the valet's eyes.

"No, I do not require anything. And, Robinson, I would advise you not to spin that case around while the cat is asleep on top," I said sternly.

Robinson looked at me affronted. "As if I would harm the—the, ahem, the dear little soul." A bout of coughing followed this lie.

I clapped Robinson on the back before leaving the room.

Since fashionable Society converges upon Hyde Park at five in the afternoon to see their friends and be seen, I chose the hour to walk over to Curzon Street.

The way I view matters, Roger Cranworth had taken off the gloves of polite behaviour, so to speak, when he dropped Neal's dead body in front of the King's Theatre.

I climbed the stairs of the house and used my dog's head stick to knock on the door to Roger's rooms.

A thin young man, striving for an imperious expression, opened the door. His sly gaze ran over my finely cut jacket and breeches. "May I help you, sir?"

I assumed my most haughty damn-you stare. "I am here to see Mr. or Miss Cranworth."

"I am sorry, sir, both are from home. Will you leave your name so I can say who called?"

Using just my left hand, I extracted a silver card case

from my pocket and flipped open the lid. As I had antic-
ipated, Mr. Gilpin held out a gloved palm, ready to receive my card.

That is precisely when I put all the force of my right
fist into a direct hit to his jaw that knocked the young
butler out cold. I feel sure Lord Dunn would have cheered
me on.

Quickly, I shoved the unconscious man's body aside
with the tip of one of my Hessian boots and entered the
drawing room, closing the door behind me. The lodgings
were small but decorated in a costly manner. I rushed
through to what must have been Miss Cranworth's room
first, then dashed over to the other bedchamber, Roger's.
Throwing open the wardrobe door, the sight of clothing
piled none too neatly—Robinson would have been appalled—met my eye. I reached for three lengths of linen,
noticed they were overstarched—Neal was right about
Gilpin being starchy after all—and carried them to the
drawing room.

I found that not only am I nimble with tying my cravat,
but that my abilities extend to tying hands, feet, and a
length of cloth around my victim's mouth.

That done, I repeated what was now becoming a routine
performance: searching for Freddie's letter.

After not quite an hour, the results were the same as
my other attempts. Fruitless.

Glancing at a clock that I noted with a start looked like
a Sèvres, I saw the hour was after six. The Cranworths
would be returning soon.

I hesitated, standing in the middle of the drawing room.
Even though the situation grew more desperate every day,
I could not wait for Roger Cranworth to return and force
a confrontation. I would not put it above him to use his
sister as a shield.

No, the only thing for it was to challenge Roger tonight
at Syon House. With his newfound position in Society as

Lady Ariana's fiancé, he was sure to attend. If nothing else, Lady Crecy would bring him along. The ball would be crowded. Syon House has extensive grounds in which one could meet an enemy, and if memory served, small, closetlike chambers off the Long Gallery. I could steer Roger Cranworth into one of those and have a private conversation with him.

I could not have known then what the disastrous results of a meeting with Roger Cranworth in one of those very chambers would be.

❧ 28 ❧

Syon House stands surrounded by its own parkland just outside London. A square building of white Dunstable stone, the exterior might strike some as severe, even forbidding, with its four high corner towers.

However, Syon House is one of my very favourite buildings. The interior is a monument to the work of Robert Adam, the brilliant neoclassical designer.

I have only visited once before, oh, it must have been two years ago, with Freddie. But tonight when I entered the Great Hall to join the receiving line, I was struck again by the staggering magnificence of the Hall. With the exception of the black squares in the black and white marble floor, the Hall is entirely white. The floor is a striking piece of art, with a Greek Key pattern running through the black and white squares broken by circles of a marigold design. The soaring ceiling echoes the floor in true Adam style. Roman statues flank the walls, with Apollo at the northern end. I think it is the very cool, pure, classical perfection of the room that appeals to me and humbles me with its beauty.

With the Hall crowded with guests, tonight colour was everywhere in the form of the ladies' gowns. At one end of the Hall, musicians played a light tune. Dancing would take place later. Through a set of open double doors, I could see the courtyard strung with coloured lamps, and tiny candles peppered the walkways.

I greeted the Duke of Northumberland with a low bow of respect. He has been a military man since the age of seventeen when he set out to form a company of his own recruits and serve in the Seven Years War.

"Good evening, Brummell," his Grace said.

I bowed. "Your Grace, I am honoured to be invited to spend an evening at Syon House."

He smiled fondly on his Duchess. "Every once in a great while I must leave war matters long enough to host an entertainment."

Greeting the Duchess of Northumberland, I could see how his Grace could be persuaded to leave business for a while to pass time in her company. Julia, as Freddie calls her, is a sweet-faced lady with light brown hair and brown eyes.

We exchanged pleasantries, and soon I made my way to the right, up the few steps that lead from the hall into the Ante-Room. The contrast between the Hall and the Ante-Room is startling. The floor is a highly polished scagliola in reds, blues and yellows. The room is a vivid blue with gold accents everywhere, making it a luxurious space.

Making it less attractive at the moment was Sylvester Fairingdale appearing at my elbow. The fop twisted his lips in a sarcastic manner and leaned toward me in the pose of a confidant.

"Looking for your ladylove, Brummell?"

I eyed his bright orange coat worn over a blue satin waistcoat on which orange trees had been embroidered. Ghastly! "I see the Duchess of Northumberland's well-known kindness extends to inviting even the most worthless of fribbles. Do you owe money to the green-grocer?"

"What?"

"That is the only reason I could think of for your advertising his goods on your clothing. And does your propensity for oranges extend to orange girls?" I queried, referring to those females who sold oranges at the theatres.

"You're drunk, Brummell," Fairingdale scoffed.

"Or drugged, perhaps? You have a housemaid named Fanny, I believe?"

Fairingdale's left eye twitched. "I know nothing about any drugs or herbs the girl uses."

"Nor, I daresay, does Lord Wrayburn, whose house in which you both reside. I think it best if you sent Fanny back from whence she came. Robinson will not see her again, you know. That was a cruel trick you played."

Fairingdale raised his chin. "You talk nonsense."

"Do I? I think not. Continue on your present course of hiring servants to drug others and you will have an opportunity to hear the babblings of your fellow inmates at Newgate."

"I think you'll be in that prison before me for the death of Lord Kendrick," he hissed furiously. "Either that, or the Duke of York will have you transported to the Colonies once he catches on to you and—"

I took a step closer to him. "Do not dare say her name," I commanded in a low, enraged voice. I took a breath, trusting my face not to betray my emotion to the guests nearby. "I warn you, Fairingdale, you go too far when you bring the lady's name to your lips. I do not give a snap of my fingers what else you say to me, or about me, but I shall not stand for your sullying her Royal Highness's name. Chalk Farm at dawn? Pistols? Swords? Am I making myself clear?"

The fop turned and minced away without a word, but

I think my point had been taken. I walked further into the room, forcing my muscles to relax, forcing a smile to my lips, acknowledging friends.

To the right of me a hidden door that leads to the kitchens and service rooms belowstairs stood open. I was surprised to see Ulga standing a few feet from the door.

"What are you doing up here, Ulga?" I asked the Prussian maid. When I reached her side, I saw the deep lines of fatigue and tension carved into her cheeks.

"I am vorried about her Royal Highness. She did not vant to come here tonight. She has been under so much strain lately." This last was uttered with a sharp glance at yours truly.

"Where is she?" I asked, looking about for Freddie.

Ulga shook her head. "I do not know. Ve arrived almost an hour ago in the company of Victor Tallarico."

"Er, yes, she told me he was escorting her." I accepted a glass of wine from a footman coming from the servants' area into the Ante-Room. I drank it down and hoped for another. "Are you just going to stand here all evening, Ulga, and not join the other ladies' maids?"

"Yes," came the stubborn reply.

"As you will," I said and moved away, looking for Roger Cranworth or Freddie. Now that I was in Syon House once more, I remembered exactly where the two turret rooms, as they are called, are located. I could have an undisturbed chat with Roger in one of those chambers.

Proceeding into the dining room, I saw long tables had been set out with an array of delicacies. At the present time, I only wanted another glass of wine. An obliging footman provided me with one. I scanned the room for Roger and saw Lady Penelope and Lord Wrayburn.

Although I like the couple, I wished I did not have to waste time speaking with them now when I wanted to confront Roger Cranworth. Still, one has one's social duty.

After informing me the date had been set for her wedding, Lady Penelope said, "I do hope that Lady Ariana has improved in health by then."

"Has she been ill?" I asked. "I saw her in the Park and she appeared in good health."

Lord Wrayburn shot his fiancée a warning look, but she went on, showing the first sign of becoming as gossipy as her mama, Lady Crecy. "Well, it is not so much a physical disorder as a matter of the heart."

"I am sorry to hear it," I replied in a way that told her I wanted to know more.

Again, Lord Wrayburn looked askance at Lady Penelope and again she was undeterred. "I fear that unlike the kindness with which I am treated by my own fiancé, Lady Ariana's betrothed has caused her to feel uncertain about their future."

"How unfortunate, especially for one with Lady Ariana's delicate constitution."

"Exactly so," Lady Penelope concurred. "Mr. Cranworth's behaviour is unkind indeed."

"Perhaps I shall have a talk with him," I said, giving myself the excuse to leave them. "Have you seen Mr. Cranworth?"

"He passed by us not long ago," Lord Wrayburn said.

Behind her fan, Lady Penelope whispered, "He looked like he had consumed too much wine. His face was flushed and he bumped into a lady."

I thanked them and bowed.

So, Roger had been drinking. That might work to my advantage. I carried my own glass and made my way through the Red Drawing Room. Here I was startled to see Cecily Cranworth seated on a crimson sofa with Doctor Wendell.

Strolling up to the couple, I could see Cecily flushed with happiness. The doctor rose. "Well met, Mr. Brummell. I wouldn't expect that you'd think to see me in such glorified surroundings, but Miss Cecily Cranworth has agreed to be my wife, and I came here with her party."

I congratulated them both heartily, then said, "It is good to see you in London, Doctor. And where is your brother, Miss Cranworth?"

Her big brown eyes clouded. "I saw him a few minutes ago. I fear he is quite drunk, for his gait was unsteady." She indicated the Long Gallery. "He went in that direction. I hope he goes outside and breathes some fresh air."

I excused myself, bowed and turned my steps in the direction of the Long Gallery. The Gallery is lined on one wall with books, two fireplaces and settees and chairs. The other side features eleven windows which look out onto the grass leading to the river Thames.

The area was crowded with finely dressed members of Society noisily conversing with their friends. I had the devil of a time making my way, as at every turn I was greeted by one acquaintance or another.

Then, about halfway down the long room, I spied Victor Tallarico ensconced on a settee with a beautiful blonde-haired girl I knew to be Lady Amy.

"Where is the Royal Duchess, Tallarico?" I demanded.

The Italian reluctantly looked up from his paramour. "Good evening to you, Mr. Brummell."

Lady Amy chuckled. I bowed to her. "I beg your pardon for disturbing you, Lady Amy—by the way, that pink gown is most becoming—but I must see—"

A sudden silence in the room caused me to swing around. Tallarico and Lady Amy rose to their feet only to bow low. I saw the cause of the commotion and executed a bow as well.

The Prince of Wales—dressed almost as elegantly as yours truly—entered the room smiling, the Duke and Duchess of Northumberland followed just behind him, the rest of his loyal public bowing, curtseying and waiting for him to speak. He gave a friendly wave to everyone and started to open his mouth.

That was when I heard a female voice scream. The sound came from the direction of the end of the Gallery.

A collective gasp brought everyone out of their bowing and scraping. The Duke of Northumberland quickly strode in the direction of one of the turret rooms. Prinny followed more slowly. I escaped his notice as I made my way to the duke's side.

His Grace swung open the door to a small jewel-box of a room, all pink and blue. Suspended from the domed ceiling is a mechanical singing bird in a cage. The bottom of the cage is a blue clock with a white face.

But it was another white face that drew attention.

Roger Cranworth lay sprawled on the floor directly under the clock. His unseeing eyes stared upward as if he were checking the time.

Freddie stood over him, her hand covering her mouth in horror.

❧ 29 ❧

The Duke of Northumberland took command. He ordered that a doctor be summoned, only to find he already had one in his house. Doctor Wendell hurried to Roger Cranworth's body. The doctor felt for a pulse, but looked at us grimly and shook his head. It was too late. Roger Cranworth was dead.

And Freddie was the one alone with him when he died.

I managed to slip into the small room and stand beside her. "Freddie," I whispered. I squeezed her ice-cold hand for a moment. "What happened?" Overcome with shock, she could not speak. Her wide gaze fixed on the corpse and did not waver. The Duke of Northumberland, Freddie and I watched silently as Doctor Wendell examined the body.

Prinny stood outside the room as if he was on guard himself—he always imagines himself a great military man—though I suspect he did not want to be in the room with a dead body. He did allow Victor Tallarico to enter.

Just when Doctor Wendell said, "It appears Mr. Cranworth is the victim of some sort of poison. I suggest that glass on the floor be examined for traces of the drug," Cecily Cranworth's face appeared at the door next to the Prince, and she heard the words.

Seeing her brother on the floor, she began calling his name and crying hysterically. Doctor Wendell abandoned the dead man and hurried to Cecily's side, keeping her outside the small room and attempting to comfort her.

Victor Tallarico said, "*Dio mio,* was he murdered or did he take poison to do away with himself?"

"That is a matter for Bow Street," the Duke of Northumberland replied. He then ordered everyone from the turret room. We filed out, and he shut the door on the dead body. He then issued orders for a messenger to ride to Bow Street. In the meantime, he posted two footmen outside the turret room door.

Guests milled about, stunned. The duke saw to the gathering. Everyone would no doubt be most annoyed at this interruption of their fun by the death of a lowly member of the country gentry, but the party was over. Perhaps they could spend the remainder of the evening gossiping about why her Royal Highness, the Duchess of York, had been the one at the corpse's side.

Julia, the Duchess of Northumberland, led the Prince, Cecily Cranworth, Doctor Wendell, Freddie, and me into the Red Drawing Room. Victor Tallarico slipped in at the last moment. "I escorted the Royal Duchess here, Mr. Brummell," he told me, then went to sit by Freddie.

The Duchess of Northumberland closed the doors to the room to keep out the curious while we waited for Bow Street.

There followed an agonising time while Cecily Cranworth could not be consoled. She seemed equally upset over Lady Ariana, who would have to be told her fiancé was dead. Doctor Wendell asked that Lady Crecy be located and brought to the drawing room. That lady arrived and took Cecily into her arms. Doctor Wendell was finally able to give Cecily a drop of laudanum in a cup of tea.

My mind reeled. What the deuce had happened? Who could have poisoned Roger Cranworth? I did not believe for a second that he had committed suicide. Was there yet another person involved in the highwayman scheme and the subsequent plan to blackmail Freddie and me? Or had Roger been killed for another reason? Why was Freddie alone with Roger in the turret room?

He must have approached her regarding the letter. If only I could speak to Freddie privately. But I could not.

I looked at her. Clad in an ivory silk gown with silk roses trimming the high waist, Freddie's skin was much whiter than her dress. She darted a look at me, but quickly looked away. Victor Tallarico did not have any luck either. His attempts to converse with Freddie were met with a little shake of her head. It was as if she had turned inward and would not be drawn out. The Duchess of Northumberland sat in a chair next to her and offered tea from a tray brought in by a footman.

"Thank you, Julia," Freddie said in a quiet voice. "If someone could send word to my maid, Ulga, that I am all right."

The footman cleared his throat and looked at his mistress.

"Yes?"

"Her Royal Highness's maid is just outside the door, Your Grace. She is quite distressed and wishes to be of service."

Freddie addressed the young man. "Tell Ulga to remain in the servants' area until it is time to leave."

The footman bowed and walked backward—as one does in the presence of royalty—from the room.

Prinny said, "What happened back there, Frederica? Who was that man in the room with you? I daresay he is unknown to me."

Freddie's small hand trembled on her teacup. "Mr.

Cranworth was a country neighbour of mine."

"Didn't come up to Town much, or I'd know about it," the Prince said. "What were you doing alone with him?"

"He asked to speak with me privately," Freddie replied. "I am not certain what he wanted. He—he collapsed before he could tell me."

In an effort to divert the Prince, I said, "As Miss Cecily Cranworth was saying to me earlier, her brother had recently become engaged to Lady Ariana, Lord Kendrick's cousin. Lady Ariana is staying with Lady Crecy here in London. Perhaps his betrothed is the reason Mr. Cranworth is in Town."

"Lord Kendrick? The marquess who was murdered at Oatlands?" the Prince asked in no small measure of surprise.

"The very same," I replied.

The Prince looked at Freddie. "Where, exactly, is my brother?"

"I believe him to be in Geneva, sir," Freddie answered. "However, I wrote to him after the ordeal with Lord Kendrick. He may return to London now, I cannot say."

That is just what we all needed: the Duke of York to return and make things worse.

As it turned out, the person who made things worse was none other than Mr. John Lavender. He arrived with four constables and was led directly to the turret room. Before he entered the room, he looked over at Freddie and me with a dark expression that did not bode well.

Everyone rose to gather once more outside the turret room. At last I had my chance to speak to Freddie.

"Freddie," I whispered in her ear. "What happened?"

She spoke without looking at me. "You did not recover my letter last night as you had promised, did you, George?"

"No," I said in a dismal voice.

"Instead I heard from Roger Cranworth. He wrote me

that he would seek me out at Syon House tonight. He said he had something that belonged to me."

"So you met him in that room?"

"Yes. He sought me out earlier and told me when and where—" Her voice broke. "I—I agreed, and—and he said he had the letter. Then before he could say anything more, he—he grasped his chest in pain and fell down." Tears formed in Freddie's eyes.

The Duchess of Northumberland could not hear us, but she saw Freddie's distress and came to take her hand.

I walked toward the turret room like one about to come upon a scene of horror and unable to turn back. At the door, the scene played out. Mr. Lavender crouched down and examined the corpse. I saw each movement in vivid clarity. The moment when he reached inside Roger Cranworth's pocket. The next moment when he withdrew what I knew with a certainty was Freddie's letter from inside Roger's coat. A second sheet of paper accompanied the lethal letter. A translation from the original French, I thought, so that Roger, unversed in the language, could read the letter aloud to Freddie if necessary while making his demands.

Mr. Lavender scanned the lines. Twice. Then, without a word, he folded the papers and put them in his pocket. He rose slowly to his feet, turned and saw me standing in the doorway.

There was an emotion in the Scotsman's eyes I had never seen before when he looked at me. Disappointment.

He quietly gave his men orders for the removal of the body.

I had to step out of the way as the constables carried the body of Roger Cranworth from the room and toward a hidden door in the Gallery that led outside.

Cecily Cranworth's sobs served as a distraction for everyone. While the attention was on her and Freddie, I stepped into the turret room just as the constables stepped out and before Mr. Lavender could exit the room.

The Bow Street man said, "The nobility are not known for their high morals. But I didn't want to believe it of you, laddie."

"Do not believe it," I said, my voice strong but low. I compelled him to believe me. "That letter was written in a moment of high distress. Her Royal Highness has never broken her marriage vows."

He measured my sincerity, then said ominously, "Perhaps not, but if it were thought that she had, both of you would be ruined."

"I know what you are thinking—"

"Brummell?" the Prince called.

I swung around. "Yes, sir, I shall be right there."

Mr. Lavender made as if to move past me.

"Wait," I said. "I deliberately misled you earlier. I *have* been investigating Lord Kendrick's death. I *do* have information for you. Give me another day."

"You're asking me for time? Time where you could find a way to protect the Royal Duchess?"

"Do you really think she is capable of killing anyone?"

"In the world you live in, Mr. Brummell, reputation is everything. If Cranworth were blackmailing you, both you and the Royal Duchess had motive to kill him." The Scotsman shook his head. "Each and every one of us is capable of killing if the provocation is great enough."

"She did not do anything wrong, I give you my word as a gentleman," I insisted.

"Are *you* confessing, then?"

"Look here, give me a day, just one day. Do not show the letter to anyone in the meantime. I am asking you on the strength of our . . . well, our friendship."

He studied me intently. "Ach!" was the gruff reply I received before he stepped past me and exited Syon House.

"Zeus!" the Prince exclaimed when I joined him. "I've

a mind to continue the party at Carlton House," he said, indicating a large group of people waiting for him. "Come with us, Brummell."

"Sir, I beg that you will excuse me. I am acquainted with the deceased's fiancée and wish to offer my condolences."

He waved a royal hand. "Very well, then. All I can say is that I will be glad when Frederick returns and sees to his wife. Gads, she shouldn't be allowed to have a corpse at Oatlands. Now here she is with a dead fellow in the middle of a party. Looks damned odd."

"Yes, sir," I agreed in order to placate him. "You know the way her Royal Highness likes to help those less fortunate. In this case, she was too late."

"Eh?" Prinny said, already anticipating how to amuse himself at his residence at Carlton House.

I bowed low. "I shall call on you later in the week, sir."

"Do," he said absently, walking away.

I hastened to where the Duchess of Northumberland, Lady Crecy and Doctor Wendell hovered over Cecily Cranworth.

Lady Crecy said, "Oh, Mr. Brummell. What are we to do? Miss Cranworth cannot stay by herself, so I have offered her my house."

"That is most kind of you, my lady," I said. "Er, where is the Royal Duchess?"

"Signor Tallarico escorted her back to St. James's Palace. What a shock it must have been for our dear little Royal Duchess to have someone expire right in front of her."

"Yes." Mayhaps she would accept Tallarico's comfort.

"And now," Lady Crecy was saying, "we must go home and tell Lady Ariana. Oh dear, oh dear."

My mind raced ahead. "Lady Crecy, allow me to come with you. Perhaps I could be of some assistance."

Lady Crecy pressed my arm. "How good of you, Mr.

Brummell. One needs a gentleman present in circumstances such as these. Lord Wrayburn has already taken Penelope home in his carriage and is sure to have departed for Wrayburn House before we arrive home. While I am convinced Doctor Wendell is a fine man, well, as I said, a *gentleman* is needed."

Riding in Lady Crecy's luxurious Town coach a few minutes later, I had time to think. Lady Crecy sat next to me, with Cecily Cranworth and Doctor Wendell opposite.

I had been so sure that Roger Cranworth had killed Lord Kendrick. Now Roger was dead. I still believed he had killed Neal. But who had given Roger poison? I refused to even consider that Freddie, desperate over the letter, had had anything to do with Roger's death. That meant that the poison that killed Roger had been given to him prior to when he met her in the turret room. But how much earlier? My knowledge of poisons is somewhat limited, you understand, never having had occasion to use one myself.

Could Roger have been given the drug before the ball at Syon House? Or had someone slipped him a poisoned drink at the party?

Who wanted both Lord Kendrick *and* Roger dead?

I looked at Cecily Cranworth. She would have motive to kill Lord Kendrick, but not her brother. Despite Roger's care-for-nobody ways, Miss Cranworth still loved him. More importantly, she knew her friend Lady Ariana loved him. Cecily would do nothing to hurt Lady Ariana.

What about Doctor Wendell? He would have knowledge of poisons. He had been at the Oatlands house party, angry at Lord Kendrick's brutish treatment of Cecily Cranworth. But as for Roger . . . When I arrived at Syon House, Cecily and Doctor Wendell had told me of their engagement. Roger, thinking himself soon to be rich by blackmailing Freddie, apparently had given the couple his blessing. Doctor Wendell would have no reason to kill

Roger. He would not want Cecily hurt—as she appeared now—by her brother's death.

Inside Lady Crecy's grand house, we gathered in the drawing room. A footman was sent to Lady Ariana's room to bring the lady down. Some minutes went by before the pale, wispy girl slipped into the room.

Cecily Cranworth promptly burst into fresh tears.

Doctor Wendell sat close to Cecily on the sofa murmuring words of sympathy.

Lady Crecy stood wringing her hands.

I said, "Lady Ariana, come and sit in this chair. I fear we have bad news to share with you."

The girl obeyed. Lady Crecy seated herself and watched anxiously as I pulled a chair close to Lady Ariana.

"Why is Cecily crying?" Lady Ariana said in her child-like voice.

I took a deep breath. "Because something very sad has happened."

Vacant eyes looked at me. "Sad?"

"Yes. Lady Ariana, I am afraid that Roger Cranworth partook of some wine or other drink which made him quite ill this evening."

The girl looked at me with a benign expression.

"Lady Ariana, I am so very sorry to tell you this because I know how much you love Roger, but the illness was a fatal one. He could not be saved."

"Dead?" she said uncertainly.

"Yes." I tried to take her hand, but she pulled it back. She clasped her hands in her lap.

"No, you are mistaken. It is Connell who is dead," she said, thinking of her cousin, Lord Kendrick. "And he deserved to die."

Lady Crecy gasped and reached in her reticule for her salts.

On the sofa, Cecily Cranworth allowed Doctor Wendell to put his arm around her as she sniffled.

I tried again. "You are confused, Lady Ariana."

She shook her head. "No, I am not. Connell deserved to die. He killed Uncle, you know," she said, referring to the old Marquess of Kendrick. "He gave him something to drink that caused an attack of Uncle's heart. Connell did it so he could be marquess. After Maynard died, Uncle was the only one standing in the way."

Good God! I knew Lord Kendrick was a dissolute criminal, but a murderer besides? Yet I remembered thinking it very convenient that a second son without prospects, dependent upon his father for a miserly allowance, should suddenly find himself the possessor of a title and wealth.

"Lady Ariana, listen to me carefully," I said gently. "Please look at me. I am unaware of what Lord Kendrick did or who killed him. I am speaking now of your betrothed, Roger Cranworth."

She smiled, a faraway look in her eyes. "Yes, Roger and I are to be married. He was reluctant at first, but then I gave him the ticket to good fortune, and he said he would marry me."

A chill ran through me.

"Ticket to good fortune?" I looked at Lady Crecy. She shook her head, implying she knew nothing of any money.

Lady Ariana went on. "Connell had given it to me to hide in my room. It was a secret. A folded piece of paper. Connell told me not to look at it or he would send me away to a lunatic asylum. He said that I must be careful not to say anything about it because it was his ticket to good fortune."

The letter. She was talking about Freddie's letter. It had been in Lady Ariana's room at Oatlands, as I had suspected. I had just been too late to reclaim it.

"I did what Connell said. I did not want to be sent away." Lady Ariana looked at me for approval.

"You did just as you ought," I said.

"That is what Roger said. After Connell died, I told Roger I loved him. I asked him to take care of me." She frowned. "At first, he said no. He said he could not afford a wife, but then I told him about the ticket to good fortune and what Connell had said. After I gave Roger the folded paper, he said that as long as I did not tell anyone about the paper, we would be married."

The dastard, using someone fragile like Lady Ariana to launch a blackmail scheme. He probably never would have married her, finding some excuse to break the engagement.

Lady Ariana went on: "But since Roger has been in London, he hardly ever comes to see me. He still wants to marry me, does he not? I begin to wonder. It is wrong for a gentleman to go back on his word, you know." She turned to me. "I have been very angry thinking he would not wed me after he promised."

"Lady Ariana, I know that Roger loved you very much," I lied. "He did want to marry you and would have, I am certain, had he lived."

"But he is alive. It is Connell that is dead."

"No!" Cecily Cranworth screamed. "Roger is dead, Ariana. They are both dead!"

Cecily began crying again. Lady Ariana's face was a perfect blank. Try as we might, neither Lady Crecy, Doctor Wendell, nor I could get her to say another word. I think that Cecily's words had finally penetrated, and the girl had retreated somewhere in her mind.

Doctor Wendell left Cecily in Lady Crecy's care and motioned for me to join him in the hall. I took my leave of the ladies and followed the doctor.

"Mr. Brummell, it is of no use. Sadly I have seen cases

like Lady Ariana before. She needs rest and the care of
people who love her. I think she should return to the country."

I nodded. "I expect you have the right of it."

"Clearly the girl is not in her right mind, babbling on
about that ticket to good fortune."

"Will she be all right? Is she, in any way, dangerous?"

"There's no way to really know. What I'll propose is
that Cecily and I wed immediately. Lady Ariana can live
with us. Cecily will not want it any other way."

I held out my hand to Doctor Wendell. "You are good.
Write to me and let me know how matters progress."

Though the hour was very late and I risked encounter-
ing a footpad, I walked the few streets home. I had to try
to clear my mind of its jumbled thoughts and focus on
who wanted *both* Lord Kendrick and Roger Cranworth
dead. Although the idea that the killings were not related
did occur to me, I dismissed it. Instinct told me the same
person had committed the crimes.

Could it be Lady Ariana? The girl was out of her
senses, that was plain to see. Doctor Wendell could not
say with any certainty whether she was dangerous. Could
she have been so frightened that Lord Kendrick would put
her in that lunatic asylum that she killed him? Then, later,
when Roger showed signs of abandoning her after he had
promised to marry her, could she have killed again? She
said she had been angry at the thought he would not fulfill
his promise to marry her.

I entered Bruton Street with what must have been a
mighty frown on my face.

Robinson was all concern. "Sir, what is wrong?"

"Roger Cranworth was murdered tonight," I said wearily, climbing the stairs.

"Heavens! His death does not have anything to do with
the Royal Duchess's missing letter, does it, sir?" he asked
as we crossed into my bedchamber.

"I fear it has everything to do with that blasted letter," I snapped, causing Chakkri, asleep on the bed, to raise his head and point his ears forward.

I immediately regretted my tone. Robinson became even more solicitous of my needs, real and imagined. When he asked if I wanted him to go down to the kitchens and warm some milk to help me sleep, I lost my temper. "When have I ever, in the time you have known me, drunk warm milk? Take yourself off. I can prepare myself for bed. I do not require, nor do I want, your help."

Robinson's face fell. In a quiet voice he said, "I am sorry, sir. Before I leave, if you will permit me to say one thing."

"Go ahead," I told him, pouring myself a large measure of brandy.

"I am sorry that I was taken in by that girl, Fanny. I should have known better, since she was employed by that odious Sylvester Fairingdale. I am afraid, sir, that I was duped by a pretty face. She seemed respectable and caring, though she did try to get me to reveal the secret ingredients of the blackening I use on your boots. I never dreamed the tisane she gave me would cause such ill effects. She explained that all the herbs and such were of the first quality as she obtained them from the very same apothecary that her Royal Highness, the Duchess of York, uses to mix potions whenever she is in London. I was a fool to believe Fanny. Please forgive me."

I had been standing with my back to him. At these words, I turned around to tell him to forget the matter. But he had left the room soundlessly.

I picked up my brandy and looked at the cat. "Well, I shall tell him in the morning. I should not have been sharp with him."

Chakkri let out a low "reow."

The brandy slid down my throat and I closed my eyes, feeling the warmth invade my body.

Then my eyes snapped open. "Good God!"

I placed the brandy on a side table with a sharp click. "I am the fool, Chakkri, not Robinson. The answer has been right in front of me the whole time! I just did not want to consider it. I did not want to believe it. I did not want it to be so."

"Reow!" shrieked Chakkri. Then he laid down and curled his tail into a *C*.

❧ 30 ❧

I remained awake most of the night, trying to decide
what to do. Before dawn I had an idea, but it was not in
the least pleasing.

Without waking Robinson, I dressed and traversed the
streets between my house and Curzon Street. There was
something inside Roger's rooms I wanted. No one answered my knock. Mr. Gilpin must have fled upon hearing
of his employer's death.

I have never broken into anyone's residence before, so
I hope I will be excused for taking quite half an hour to
defeat the lock.

I had what I wanted and hastened back to Bruton Street
just as the sun came up. The fickle English weather had
turned chilly. Under the coverlet, I fell into an uneasy
sleep and woke a few hours later, feeling as if my mind
was still grappling with what I had deduced the entire time
I slept.

Freshly bathed, groomed and attired in a true blue coat
made of Bath superfine atop light-coloured breeches, I
was about to place my gold-framed miniature of Freddie

in my pocket. I paused and looked down at her face. Then I opened a drawer and laid the miniature inside.

A few moments later, I stepped down to my book-room.

I had explained to Robinson that he need not feel guilty any longer regarding Fairingdale's plot to discover my secrets. The valet had accepted my words and had gone so far as to criticise the length and style of my hair. Recall that he had not been happy when Diggie had fashioned it in the new way.

Freddie's compliment of the style had prompted me to tell her I would keep it for her. Today I gave in to Robinson's objections and allowed him free reign with his scissors.

Seating myself at my desk, I prepared to write three letters. The first was to a King. I chose my words with the greatest of care, hoping to appeal to his appreciation for loyalty.

The second letter proved even more of a challenge. For I was not writing it in my own hand, but in that of Roger Cranworth. On my predawn mission, I had obtained a sample of Roger's handwriting and even managed to find blank sheets of his stationery. The message was short, but I am no more a forger than a lock-picker, so the task was time-consuming. When I was satisfied with my handi-work, I took the failures over to the cold fireplace and burned them.

Then I drew a sheet of paper out and wrote Mr. Lavender a brief note. I reiterated my petition that the Bow Street man keep Freddie's letter confidential and allow me the day to uncover the murderer before taking further action.

"Robinson, deliver this personally to Mr. Lavender." I gave directions to the Bow Street man's residence, as well as the names of taverns he would likely frequent for a midday meal. As a last resort, he was to deliver the note to Miss Lavender at the Haven of Hope. On no account was he to go to Bow Street. I did not want to take the smallest chance of someone I knew seeing my valet there.

As it was, Robinson assumed his Martyr Expression when faced with travelling to areas of London he pretended did not exist. "Where will you be, sir?"

"St. James's Palace, then perhaps the depths of the Serpentine River. No, I believe I shall visit the British Museum."

When Robinson left the house in high dudgeon a few minutes later, I reflected that he was back to his old self.

Removing a large sum of money from a locked drawer in my desk, I could only hope that my plans to reveal the killer would succeed so that Robinson would still have a master to serve.

I entered St. James's Palace, noting two burly men I recognised as being from Bow Street outside the gates. Did Mr. Lavender think Freddie would attempt to flee London?

Ushered once again into the large gold and white drawing room where her Royal Highness receives guests, I bowed low.

Freddie sat staring at nothing, dressed regally in a peacock colour gown with a high upstanding collar split open in front. Hero and Georgicus woofed a greeting. Ulga was twisting her hands together near a window.

"Why have you come, George?" Freddie asked in a faint voice.

"To say good-bye."

"What do you mean? Where are you going?" she said, rising from the sofa.

"Surely you know the answer to that. I am going to Bow Street to see Mr. Lavender. I shall confess to the murders of the Marquess of Kendrick and Roger Cranworth on the condition that Mr. Lavender give me your letter."

She flew across the room to me. "Have you run mad?"

"What else am I to do?"

"I do not know. Something, surely!"

"Freddie, Mr. Lavender has your letter. He is a man who will stop at nothing to see justice done. There will be no choice in his mind but to turn the letter over to the Bow Street magistrate. And you know what that means. Quicker than a pickpocket in Seven Dials, your letter will be in the hands of your husband or Prinny. The scandal will overtake London faster than the fire of 1666. Your name will be ruined. They will blame me for the deaths, speculating that first Lord Kendrick, then Roger, was blackmailing us."

"George! I shall not allow you to do this. You are not thinking rationally! If you confess to these murders, they will hang you!"

"What alternative do you suggest?" I said, watching her carefully. "Do you know who actually committed the murders?"

"How I wish I did!"

"There is nothing else I can do to protect you, Freddie, other than turn myself over to Bow Street. I shall give them the excuse that I had an argument with Lord Kendrick over the way he treated his cousin, with whom I had formed an attachment. I killed him in a moment of passion. Then, Roger Cranworth found out and I had to kill him too."

She grasped my arms and gave me a little shake, tears running down her cheeks. "That is nonsense! No, you will not do it. I shall send for Mr. Lavender. After all, I hired him at the start. I will tell him that he is to return the letter to me."

"He will never do that, and you know it, Freddie. You told me yourself you hired him because of his integrity.

Two lives have been taken. Mr. Lavender will hold someone accountable no matter what the cost to you or me."

Her throat clogged with tears, Freddie pleaded with me. "My dearest George, I know I have not been myself since the day I found out you had kept the letter. I have been cold to you, I know. I placed all the blame on you when, in truth, I am just as responsible, for I was the one who wrote the letter! I have been angry with myself and extended that anger to you. Can you forgive me?"

"There is nothing to forgive, Freddie. I have missed our friendship, true, missed it more than I can say. You must know what you mean to me," I said, stroking her cheek with my fingertip.

She grasped my hand and held it tight. "You never really lost my friendship. Never. I have been overcome with anxiety throughout this entire ordeal. Now you must stop this talk of confessions and stay with me today, for I have missed you and want your company."

"No, Freddie. I cannot."

"George!"

"Come now, I have lived a life that has far exceeded my expectations. Look outside, at how beautiful the day is. I shall walk over to the British Museum and gaze upon the beautiful objects there once more before going to Bow Street. You know how I appreciate beauty," I said.

She tried to chuckle, but only began to weep.

At that moment, the sound of footsteps and a loud masculine voice could be heard from outside the door. I dropped Freddie's hand and turned in time to see his Royal Highness, the Duke of York, filling the doorway.

Ulga rose and dropped into a deep curtsey. I bowed low. Freddie was all formality. "Sir, I did not expect you."

The tall, cold man that is the Royal Duke, second in line for the Crown, gazed down at his wife in a mockery of surprise. "Well, it is your birthday, Frederica. I couldn't miss your special day."

"While I dislike contradicting you, sir, my birthday was last Wednesday."

"Was it? Well, well. Came back to England for nothing, then. Good afternoon, Brummell. Haven't seen you in a while."

"No, indeed," I said, barely able to keep my composure. "And I was just on the point of leaving."

"Don't let me stop you," the Royal Duke said.

Freddie looked panicked.

Once I was past her husband I turned back and looked at her. I held a finger over my lips, then exited the room without a word.

❧ 31 ❧

The British Museum in Bloomsbury—an area of
London I once deemed a foreign country—held a fair-
sized crowd of people that afternoon. I strolled through
the first floor, gazing at old books and manuscripts, made
my way through the section on natural history, and finally
climbed the stairs to the second floor, which housed Roman antiquities.

I glanced at my pocket watch, noting it was almost
three, when finally I saw her. Oddly enough, I felt not a
flicker of unease in the presence of this murderess.

"I knew you would come," I told her.

"There vas nothing else I could do after vhat you said
to her Royal Highness today. The strain has been un-
bearable, but your saying you vould confess to the murders was vhat broke me. Vould you really have gone to
Bow Street and confessed?"

"I would have gone to Bow Street, yes, Ulga."

"You love her too. Vhy did you scare her like that,
telling her you vould sacrifice yourself for her?"

"Because I could think of no other way to make you

come and tell me that you had killed Lord Kendrick and Roger Cranworth. Besides, I was not absolutely certain, and I have been known to be wrong before."

"You vere not mistaken. I killed both of them. They had to die. They threatened my mistress. Do you realise how long I have known her Royal Highness?"

I offered my arm, and we began to walk toward a display of Roman coins. "Tell me."

"Since the day her mother gave birth to her. I vas her Majesty's personal maidservant. Only vhen the princess vas to ved the Royal Duke from England did I become her maid."

"Over fourteen years ago, then."

She nodded. "Before I left Prussia, the old King made me promise to alvays take care of his daughter, to see that no harm came to her."

"And you did your duty well for a long time. Then Lord Kendrick got hold of that letter. I am sorry I kept it, Ulga."

"You should be!" she exclaimed, then lowered her voice. "I have been happy that her Royal Highness has had you for companionship. She is married to a man who does not love her. But sometimes I feared that she vould give in to the feelings she has for you and act imprudently."

"That has never been the case. The one kiss you saw was the only time, and it was not supposed to happen. But why, Ulga, why did you feel you had to *kill* Lord Kendrick?"

"He vas an evil man! I heard in the neighbourhood that he had killed his own father. Once that man had her letter to you, I knew he vould never leave my little Duchess alone. I vas vorried that night and could not sleep. I looked out my vindow and saw him staggering near the dogs' cemetery. He had been up all night drinking. Celebrating my mistress's sorrow and planning how to use her." Ulga's eyes glittered. "I dressed, I don't know vhat I thought I vould do. I vent outside and tried to talk to him, but he laughed at me. He said he had no use of another maid that night and that I vas too old anyway, as if I had offered myself to him."

"He had forced himself on Cook's niece."

She nodded. "An evil man, I tell you. I hated him so much in that moment. I thrust my hands into the pocket of my dress and discovered the hair ornaments that Signor Tallarico had given the Royal Duchess. She had left them in the drawing room. I had picked them up and meant to put them away, but forgot."

The Prussian maid was growing more agitated. I guided her over to a display of Herculanean armour. "I wager it happened very fast."

"I hardly remember doing it. My hand grasped the sharp length of jet. I struck out at him. He made a terrible sound in his throat, then fell to the ground."

I offered her my handkerchief. She efficiently dried her eyes. "The sun vas coming up. I tried to dig a grave. I had the thought in my mind that no one vould find him. I vent inside and put the other hair ornament back in the drawing room."

"But then Phanor died and Old Dawe went out to the dogs' cemetery."

"Yes. I never meant to give Mr. Dawe such a shock."

"No." I drew a deep breath. God help me but I felt sorry for Ulga.

"I thought it vould all be over. But, the Royal Duchess hired Mr. Lavender, and you could not find the letter. Instead, that other evil man, Roger Cranworth, sends my mistress a message telling her he has something that belonged to her. He vas going to take up vhere the marquess left off!" Ulga's face was the picture of outrage.

"So down in the servants' hall at Syon House, you prepared a special drink for him. You waited outside the passageway for him to come by, looking for Freddie. When he passed you, you stepped forward and offered him a glass of wine."

She cried silent tears. "Yes. I told him I vould take a message to the Royal Duchess about vhere to meet him. He said he had already sent a footman. But he took the glass and drank the contents in front of me. Stupid man. Only I turned out to be the stupid one. I thought he vould die immediately, but the poison did not vork right avay." Ulga's face twisted with horror. "My poor little lady, having that man die in front of her. I failed to protect her, Mr. Brummell. Even after everything I did, the vhispers had started. I have not kept my promise to the old King. How can I keep my lady from ruin now?"

"Listen to me, Ulga," I said urgently. "This is what we are going to do. You must return to Prussia. I have money and will book you passage on the next ship. I have already written a letter for you to carry to Freddie's brother, the new King of Prussia. I have told him what you have done, and that you acted in extraordinary circumstances to protect his sister. He will have to decide your fate. I have begged for his leniency."

"But vhat vill you tell that Mr. Lavender?"

"I have written another letter. I copied Roger Cranworth's handwriting. When Roger's body was found, Victor Tallarico raised the question of suicide, giving me the idea. In the letter I wrote in Roger's handwriting, Roger confesses to killing Lord Kendrick, then taking poison himself. He says he intends to enjoy one last evening of revelry then the poison will act and he will die. Everyone will assume he misjudged the timing of the drug. Roger Cranworth is guilty of another murder, his accomplice, Neal, so I do not feel it wrong of me to make him take the blame for Lord Kendrick's death."

Ulga thought hard. "Vhat about the letter the Royal Duchess vrote you?"

"I obtained it after I left the Palace," I lied, wanting to get her out of England without delay. I would have it soon enough.

Ulga breathed a sigh of intense relief. "So my Royal Duchess vill not have the scandal."

"No."

"Except from vhat I have done."

"No, because you will go to Prussia and allow the King to decide your fate there. That is our best chance of keeping what you have done from being made public here in England. Now, I have brought paper and pen so you can write Freddie a letter. Tell her you have been dreadfully homesick and must return to Prussia. Tell her you could not bear to part with her in person. Afterwards, I shall escort you straight to the docks." I opened my coat to extract the needed items. My fingers were shaking, though, for despite my sympathy for Ulga, she was guilty of murder. I hoped I was doing the right thing by sending her back to Prussia, where she would have to accept responsibility for her actions.

The paper and pen finally in hand, I looked up.

Ulga was no longer at my side.

Instead, she stood by one of the tall, open windows by a statue of Caesar.

Her eyes met mine. In a flash I knew her intentions.

"No!" I yelled, bumping a museum guard in my haste to get to Ulga, and bolting across the room.

Too late. Pretending to slip, Ulga let her body fall from the open window to the stone pavement below.

People screamed. I ran through the horrified museum-goers, down the stairs and outside, where a crowd had already gathered around the older woman's body. I pushed through to where she lay, a miniature of Freddie as a young girl clasped in one fist, my handkerchief in the other.

Slowly, with great regret, I removed the items from her hands.

The constables came in due course, along with a wagon to remove Ulga's body. The museum guard told the constables how I had dashed across the room and tried to save the woman. When I identified Ulga as maid to the Royal Duchess, one of the constables said that, in that case, Mr. Lavender must be notified.

That would make my task of getting the letter easier, but how I wished it had not turned out this way.

Standing at the back private entrance to Mr. Lavender's lodgings above Kint's Chop House, I used my dog's head stick to knock on the door. As I suspected and, indeed, hoped for, no one answered. Miss Lavender would be at her shelter at this time of day. I had thought Mr. Lavender would be somewhere going about Bow Street work. Now I knew he was most likely at the British Museum asking questions. He would seek me out soon enough.

You may be wondering why I was so sure that Mr. Lavender would have Freddie's letter at his house. Well, my reasoning went like this: By now, the Scotsman had most likely discerned that Freddie's letter had been the cause of two deaths. A wise man would not carry such a deadly piece of paper on his person. That left him with two choices, either Bow Street or his residence. Because of the depth of scandal that letter could cause, I was banking on the latter.

For someone who worked against criminals, Mr. Lavender had a remarkably flimsy lock on his door. Either that, or I was getting better at breaking into people's rooms. Unfortunately I was not that good and ended up cracking off a bit of wood and a tiny piece of metal. Mr. Lavender would have to have the lock replaced.

I entered silently and scanned the room. Prior visits to

the premises told me there was a small parlor, kitchen, and probably two bedchambers.

I moved in the direction of the nearest bedchamber. All of a sudden Miss Lavender appeared in front of me, clad only in her shift, a pistol in her hand.

I could not have been more surprised if Prinny announced his intention of becoming a monk. "Good God, Miss Lavender! Are you going to shoot me?"

She tossed her dark red hair which hung down her back. "Should I? You've broken in here like a criminal."

"I beg your pardon. I did knock first."

She put the gun down on a table and rubbed her temples. "That's your excuse? Oh, don't bother to lie. I've had a terrible headache. Father came home in a rare temper last night, waving a letter and ranting about you. He gave me a severe set-down over my appearance at the Grand Masquerade and demanded that I never see you again."

"Ah, as to that letter—"

She crossed her arms in front of her, seeming to realise for the first time the state of her undress. "Father didn't let me see it, but I read it after he left for Bow Street this morning."

"Of course you did."

"Are you her Royal Highness's lover?"

"You are an impertinent girl."

"A girl waiting for an answer."

"No, I am not. Nor have I ever been," I added, anticipating her next question. "And that is all the explanation I shall give."

She considered this. "Father doesn't really believe that you or the Royal Duchess had anything to do with those killings."

"I am gratified to hear it."

"Why have you gone to the extreme measure of breaking into a Bow Street investigator's house? To steal the Royal Duchess's letter?"

"I prefer to think of it as retrieving stolen, personal property. In point of fact, I have another letter which will explain all. I plan on giving it to your father at the first opportunity."

Miss Lavender glanced at the clock. "That should be any minute now. Father told me he'd be home between five and half past."

"I do not think so—" I broke off, the sound of footsteps coming up the outside stairs reaching my ears. My gaze flew to Miss Lavender's.

She said, "Is the Royal Duchess's letter necessary to a criminal investigation?"

"No," I stated flatly.

She bit her lip. "I've been asleep all afternoon. I never heard an intruder. Her letter is in the left-hand drawer of the desk. Meet me at the Opera House tonight."

With that, she hurried back to the bedroom.

I darted over to the desk and opened the drawer.

There was Freddie's letter.

I grabbed it and dashed to the other entrance of the lodgings, the one that led to the stairway of Kint's Chop House. Just as I heard a Scottish curse coming from the back door, I opened the front door and raced down the steps to the eating establishment. I had never been inside there. I looked to see only dark wooden tables and a long, empty bar. At the opposite end of the chop house, miracle of miracles, a small fire burned.

I swept across the room, tossed the letter onto the fire and stood back watching the vellum become ash.

"I'll thrash you for this, Mr. Brummell," a voice with a Scottish burr came from behind me.

I turned with the hint of a smile on my face. "Why, Mr. Lavender, what a surprise. I was just going to step above stairs and ask you to join me for a drink. I have a letter I think you will find solves all your problems."

❦ 32 ❧

Two hours later in Bruton Street, I wearily sat down at my desk to write a message for Freddie. I wondered how much to tell her.

I thought back over the confrontation with Mr. Lavender. If you could have observed my meeting with the Scotsman, you might have compared it to two jugglers at a county fair. The Bow Street man studied the suicide letter from Roger Cranworth, a dubious expression on his face. I sensed he was not in the least bit convinced that all had transpired as I would have him believe. Nevertheless, he had no evidence to the contrary now that Freddie's letter was ashes. Ulga's death had been ruled an accident. The museum guard had told of my trying to prevent the Prussian woman's fall. There was no more for Mr. Lavender to do than read me a lecture on muddling Bow Street affairs.

But what to tell Freddie? Ulga had acted out of love and loyalty. I believe she was a good person, but something inside her mind was not altogether right. That something had been provoked when Freddie had been threatened with ruin.

After long consideration, I decided I would never tell Freddie that Ulga had been the killer. Like everyone else, she would believe Roger Cranworth's "suicide" note. I put pen to paper and in a few short lines explained Mr. Lavender's discovery of a suicide note on Roger Cranworth's body. The mystery of the murder at Oatlands was solved. I went on to say that Freddie's lost item had been found and destroyed. I consoled her on the loss of Ulga, saying that I had been with the maid when the terrible accident had occurred. I closed by assuring Freddie that I knew she would return to Oatlands shortly, but that I hoped I might soon be invited to join her for a weekend.

I just had time to change into evening clothes and travel by sedan-chair to the Royal Italian Opera House.

Ned and Ted were not speaking to one another, their competition over Molly having overtaken common sense. I had to endure their miming instructions to one another.

Inside, I knocked on the door to Lady Salisbury's box, finding the marchioness there alone.

"My lady," I said, bowing low. "I hoped to see you here."

"Hmpf," barked the gruff-voiced marchioness. "You wanted to hear the opera and hoped my box would be empty."

"You wrong me!" I sat down, scanning the crowd for Miss Lavender. There she was, seated below amongst the lower orders, striking in a strawberry-coloured gown. She sat transfixed by the music. Onstage, the singer worked herself into a fury of emotion, poured out in song.

"You will be happy to know Lord Kendrick's killer has been revealed," I said to the marchioness. I knew I could count on Lady Salisbury to tell her friends what I was about to pass on to her. That way, the story I wanted told would be heard. I proceeded to whisper all about Roger and Lord Kendrick's highwayman scheme, how they had fallen out, and how Roger had killed the marquess, then how he had killed himself in a fit of remorse.

Lady Salisbury listened while keeping her gaze on the stage. "Roger Cranworth hardly seemed the type to take his own life," she said when I was done.

"Yes, well, we never know what goes on in the minds of others, do we?" I replied casually, my gaze on Miss Lavender.

At that moment the Scottish girl turned her head and made a sweep of the theatre. Her gaze met mine. With a little motion she indicated I should meet her in the hall.

I looked back at Lady Salisbury, only to find her watching me closely. "You're right, George, we never do know."

"May I get you some champagne, my lady?"

"You may." She nodded.

The idea that she had seen the exchange between Miss Lavender and me crossed my mind, but I dismissed it as fanciful.

Outside in the hall, few people milled about. I obtained Lady Salisbury's champagne, then lingered, waiting for Miss Lavender to come upstairs.

All at once she was at my side. We moved toward the velvet draperies of an empty box which would afford us some privacy. "You are looking beautiful this evening, Miss Lavender," I said. "No sign of any headache."

"Thank you. I do feel better and am enjoying the music."

I softened my voice. "I trust everything went well with your father this afternoon."

She smiled. "He had to believe that I slept through your burglary. The alternative was too horrendous for him to consider. And since you provided him with evidence that helped him close a murder case and collect his fee from the Royal Duchess, he must be content."

"Yes, well, I, er, must thank you for helping me with

that letter. I am in your debt. I say, are you listening to me, Miss Lavender? You seem distracted."

Suddenly, without any provocation on my part, the Scottish girl reached up, placed a hand on the back of my neck and tugged me toward her. She pressed her lips to mine, leaning her body into me. I held Lady Salisbury's champagne to one side.

Now, when a beautiful woman wants to kiss a man, a gentleman should give in and let her have her way. Some might call it wrong, but I am against that way of thinking.

I decided all this in the two seconds following my first taste of Miss Lavender's mouth.

After I recovered from being stunned into inaction, I wrapped my free arm about her slim waist and pulled her close to me, returning the pressure of her mouth with energy.

Then, just as abruptly as she had begun the kiss, Miss Lavender ended it. Just as surprised as I was when it started, I now stood looking down at her.

Her breathing was a bit strained. "That should give Sylvester Fairingdale something to think about and squelch the nasty gossip about you and the Royal Duchess."

"Eh, what?" I said, more than a little baffled.

I followed her gaze and saw my nemesis gaping at the scene of my kissing Miss Lavender! The expression on Fairingdale's face was priceless. I daresay Miss Lavender's ploy had worked.

I turned to congratulate her, only to see the swirl of her long skirts as she hurried down the steps to rejoin the lower orders listening to the music.

I downed Lady Salisbury's champagne.

Though I entered the house in Bruton Street quietly enough, Robinson came hurrying from his rooms. "Sir, where have you been? I thought you said you were going to the opera and would be home after a visit to White's. Here it is going on five in the morning. You have not been gambling all night, have you?"

"Robinson, I thought by now you would have learned not to ask me where I have been when I choose to stay out all night."

And, no, I shall not tell you either.

Following me up the stairs, I could hear the valet clucking his disapproval.

To mollify him, while undressing I told him the whole sordid story—minus the exact contents of Freddie's letter—about Lord Kendrick and Roger Cranworth and finally, about the true nature of Ulga's demise.

"I cannot believe I never thought of Ulga when considering who might have murdered Lord Kendrick," I reflected while Robinson went to turn back the bedclothes.

"No one ever notices servants," Robinson opined. Evidently some of Fanny's ideas had stayed with him.

Hampering his abilities to prepare the bed for me was Chakkri. The cat slept in the centre of the bed, but with his head on one of my pillows!

I stepped forward to nudge him to the side. Awakened from his slumber, the feline rose and stretched, searing me with a look of disdain. "Come, Chakkri, no need to be offended. Lie down here. Let me see you curl your tail into a *C* for Chakkri."

But the cat jumped from the bed, paused only to shake his hind leg in a gesture of disgust, then hopped onto the chair to sleep.

"Now that was too bad of you, Chakkri," I said and climbed into bed. "Have you seen him curl his tail into the letter *C*, Robinson? He is quite clever."

The valet's lips pursed. Then he said, "Yes, I have, sir, but it looked more like a *U* to me. For *Unspeakable,* or perhaps *Unconscionable,* or *Unsavoury,* or—"

"That will be all, Robinson."